Sasquatch Saves the Day

An Ele Carmichael Novel

M. Sparks Clark

Loophole Books

Copyright © 2023 by Melissa Dawn Hancock

All rights reserved.

No part of this publication may be reproduced, distributed, or transmitted in any form or by any means, including photocopying, recording, or other electronic or mechanical methods, without the prior written permission of the publisher, except as permitted by U.S. copyright law. For permission requests, contact Loophole Books, P.O. Box 1, Guthrie, OK 73044.

The story, all names, characters, and incidents portrayed in this production are fictitious. No identification with actual persons (living or deceased), places, buildings, and products is intended or should be inferred.

Book Cover by Shawn Hancock

First edition, 2023

To Delia <3 Our laughter-filled "road trips" made me want to send Ele and Nona on adventures as fun as ours. May our next big adventure be to Ireland! Love you, friend!

To Holly, without whose constant moral support, knowledge, and encouragement, these books might not even exist. I will be forever grateful you wanted to get together to "talk books," my bestselling author friend! Love you!

CHAPTER 1

"Bat. Shit. Crazy." I said in a tone that implied this was non-negotiable. "That's all there is to it. That woman was bat shit crazy!" Vance and Nona were laughing, and I could tell Bert was about to tell me to give her the benefit of the doubt. It was the next-to-last night of the International Sasquatch Protection Society's Annual Conference and Nona, Vance, Bert, and I (unofficially known as 5S—Society in Secret Service to Sasquatch Security—& officially as ISPS Chapter #111) were enjoying a nice dinner out in downtown Niagara Falls, Ontario. This year's event was being held on Canada's side of the twin cities of Niagara Falls and earlier in the afternoon, we made an ill-fated decision to attend a side workshop entitled, "Phenomena Surrounding Sasquatch Activity".

PSA #31 Word to the wise: If you ever find yourself at something like say.... a crazy-ass bigfoot convention, steer clear of

workshops with words like phenomena in the title. Unless, of course, you want to find out just how deep the rabbit hole goes.

It sounded a smidge "out-there" but also potentially interesting—and hell, if you would have told me six months ago that I would not only believe in bigfoot but consider myself friends to a few of the creatures, I would have laughed heartily in your face and told you that *you* were bat-shit crazy. And yet, here I am in life—sharing my property with a couple of bigfoot who are about to welcome new babies to their family, interacting with them with fair regularity, and somewhat delusionally imagining myself as "Auntie Ele" to the baby bigfoot whose arrival we are all eagerly anticipating—and trying to figure out how to entice the owner of the thousand-acre woods adjoining my land to sell to me so I can start a secret bigfoot preserve. I used to be normal. I was just a novelist, living in NYC writing best-selling thrillers in coffee shops around the big apple until my cheating bastard ex inspired my EX-odus from New York City to the backwoods of Oklahoma.

"Aww... come on, Ele. I thought she had some interesting theories." Bert was, as usual, seeing the best in people, giving everyone the benefit of the doubt.

"Oh yeah, like how bigfoot are the gods of extraterrestrials and the white witch is their alien keeper that they report to when the floating balls of light send out their distress signals?" I looked at Bert with a raised eyebrow and he paused for a moment, digesting what I had just pointed out.

"Well, hell. When you put it like that, I guess even I have to admit it. She did sound a bit bat-shit crazy!" Vance laughed at Bert's admission and he and Nona lifted their mocktails.

"I'll toast to that," Vance said with a broad smile. Vance was standing in solidarity with Nona, who was pregnant with his child and abstaining from alcohol. Not me, baby. I lifted my fully alcoholic dirty martini and Bert lifted his beer.

"It takes all kinds!" said Bert. "Thank you ladies for joining us this year at the convention. And for joining our efforts to protect and preserve." Bert toasted, and we all clinked glasses and took sips of our prospective drinks. Then the waiter brought out our steaks.

"Thanks for asking us," Nona said, smiling at Bert and reaching over to squeeze Vance's hand. Nona and Vance were newlyweds. It's crazy how fast life can change. I once heard someone say that, "For the most part, life stands still, but change—change happens all at once." You can go through years of things staying relatively the same. Nona and Vance had been pining for one another for twenty years, Nona having mentally blocked the possibility of a relationship, and Vance not realizing that this lovely lady before him was the one who got away twenty years ago. It was incredible, really. It only took my being kidnapped and the two of them coupling up in a search party to try and save me for the truth to unfold and for them to finally, *finally* get together. In that short time, they had conceived a child despite the fact that they are old as fuck. (Just for clarification: Old As Fuck=Nona in her mid-forties and Vance in his early fifties. So, maybe not old as actual fuck, but pretty damned old to be having a baby. Truth be told, we were all ecstatic about the proposition of a tiny human among us.)

"You know, though, the conference has been surprisingly informative. It's been so much fun." I marveled aloud. Having not known what to expect, I found myself pleasantly surprised. "I've learned a lot, and I think it's incredible that our first encounter with the wack-a-doodle wasn't until the end of the second day of a three-day conference, considering the conference is about sasquatch." I pointed out. Everyone nodded in agreement as we ate. None of us were under the illusion that any of this shit was normal, it simply was. Most of the people I had met at the conference had been like us, regular old humans just having had the fortunate–or unfortunate (depending on how you looked at it)–bigfoot experience. Tomorrow I had a meeting scheduled with a woman from British Columbia who had started a secret bigfoot preserve–just like I was hoping to do–so I was super stoked about that. And by tomorrow evening we would all be on planes again, Bert and Vance heading back to Oklahoma, and Nona and I to New York City where I would drag her ass around to all my old haunts (aka: every cool coffee shop in the city). While this may sound hellish to some—since Nona owns a super cool destination coffee shop in OklaChito, Oklahoma—she is not only totally down for this, but as excited as I am. We are coffee-loving soul sisters.

I'm so excited to introduce her to Sookie Evanovich, my brilliant longtime agent and one of my very best friends. While I'm here, I'm scheduled to do the author photo shoot for the back cover of my soon-to-be-released novel, *Bigfoot Watching Woman Watching Bigfoot*, which I will do incognito, of course, since the book is being released under a pen name. Because I had given the publishing house so many best-sellers, they were putting some money behind the book release despite the fact that we agreed my identity would remain secret for a year and if the book got traction on its own, we would never reveal me as its author. I didn't have the greatest interest in becoming "you know, that crazy lady who writes bigfoot books." Nona said I was being paranoid. She read it and loved it.

I was also taking Nona to meet Evie, my other best friend in the city. Evie was with me when I caught Doug cheating and she lovingly picked up the pieces of me in the moments and weeks following the discovery. She helped me move out and has been kindly storing all of my possessions ever since. Evie was the friend who helped dress me and keep me as stylish as she was able over the past two decades. I dreaded her assessment of my current beauty statement (or lack thereof) and suspected we would be doing some shopping while we were in the city, at Evie's insistence. In addition to all of that excitement, we were going to go see Nona's superstar son's pop band, Suddenly Sparrow, perform at Madison Square Garden. This was going to be the ultimate NYC girls trip, followed by an epic road trip home to Oklahoma driving a U-Haul filled with all of my earthly possessions that I left behind.

I moved to Oklahoma via air with only three suitcases about six months ago after impulsively buying a fully furnished, luxury cabin in the Kiamichi Mountains, sight unseen, in order to escape my cheating bastard ex, only to discover that the land I had purchased already belonged to a family of bigfoot who were, quite frankly, not too fucking thrilled to have me there. But I digress. Ultimately, it all worked out and now I'm officially what others would consider bat-shit crazy, so perhaps I shouldn't judge. Maybe I simply have not yet met the white witch and the floating balls of light. Geez-fucking-Louise. I really hope that is not the case. The four of us were walking down the sidewalk back to our hotel and I could see my breath in the crisp fall air.

"I wonder how JoJo is?" I pondered aloud.

"Has anyone talked to Ahmet since we've been here?" Bert asked, and we all shook our heads 'no.' Ahmet was the fifth member of 5S—Society in Secret Service to Sasquatch Security (Vance and Bert came up with this name as teenagers, in case you were marveling at the "creativity" of five middle-aged weirdos naming their bigfoot club). Dr. Ahmet Pamuk was our newest member and, until recently, had been a hermit for nearly a decade, so needless to say, he had declined the offer to go to the International Sasquatch Protection Society's Annual Conference. Go figure. I wouldn't have missed it for the world. I mean, who the hell knew, right?

Ahmet officially used JoJo, the pregnant bigfoot who lived on our properties (his adjoined mine to the north) and whom he was keeping a doctor's eye on since our recent discovery that she was carrying more than one baby in there, as an excuse not to come to the convention with us. JoJo had tried to go into labor way too early, but thankfully Ahmet's knowledge had helped stop the early labor and he said he wanted to stick close in case she needed him. Vance and Bert had suckered Ahmet into doctoring bigfoot for them a few years back when the vet, who had helped them since they were kids, passed away. It's not like the bigfoot in the area need a lot of outside doctoring, but occasionally, they require assistance, and Vance and Bert were always the ones to get it for them. Ahmet was an emergency room doctor during 9/11 and had retired early to be a hermit in the Kiamichi Mountains of Oklahoma. Bert sold him his cabin, so when they were in desperate need of a doctor for a bigfoot with an infected foot, they begged him for help. Ahmet already believed he had caught glimpses of the creatures on his daily hikes through his property, so was relatively unaffected by the news that bigfoot was real and needed his help. Bert told Ele that when they asked Ahmet for help, he'd simply grabbed his doctor's bag and followed them and because of him, the creature lived and didn't even lose his foot.

Ahmet and I had become fairly close over the past few months as we investigated the Sasquatch Serial Killer. (And helped the FBI to catch the killer—not to brag, but yeah, we were pretty fucking awesome.) I'm sure that Nona, Bert, and Vance all think our relationship is romantic, but honestly, it is a completely platonic friendship and both of us are happy that way. Finding out that the man I loved and trusted for nearly two decades had cheated on me, and not just the once, had completely obliterated my desire to partner up with anyone new anytime soon, or maybe anytime ever. Regardless, it was nice to have a funny, intelligent friend to talk to, and Ahmet was both of those things. We just seemed to get each other, which, of course, is unbelievably nice–not to mention he is a willing dog sitter for my teenage puppy I call Bif (short for B.F. which is short for Bigfoot). Ahmet is watching him so I can relax and enjoy myself at the conference and on our epic Girls NYC/Road Trip. Bif may like Ahmet better than me anyway, so all is well.

We could hear the falls as we neared our hotel and the twinkle of the streetlights was pure magic. I watched other tourists strolling happily along like my friends and I were. Listening to tinkling laughter and the cadence of friendly conversation, I realized I missed civilization. Not that Oklachito, Oklahoma, wasn't hopping in its own way. And certainly living in the woods had its charms, but I had truly enjoyed the last few nights in Niagara Falls eating out at upscale restaurants and I was beside myself with excitement that Nona and I would have a few days in New York City together. No place on earth has quite the same energy, and I was ready to fill my lungs with it. But for this moment, I looked at the friends I was walking with, Nona and Vance to my left and Bert to my right, and thanked my lucky stars for this odd new start I had made mid-life.

When we made it to our hotel, we climbed onto the elevator and prepared to part ways. We were all on different floors because the hotel was so full we had taken whatever rooms we could get. Vance and Nona were together on the second floor. I was on the third, and Bert was on the fifth. The elevator stopped on the second floor. "Meet you all in the lobby at 7:30 for breakfast?" Nona asked, double-checking that we were sticking with our usual plan.

"I'll be there with bells on," Bert said, and we all smiled.

"I'm gonna hold you to that—the bells, I mean," Vance's smiling face announced through the crack in the closing elevator door. Again we traveled upward again. I looked over at Bert and realized that he suddenly looked very sad.

"What's wrong, Bert?" He looked up at me, a glint of surprise in his eyes.

"Nothing. Nothing." He waved his hand and put on his customary bright face. The elevator stopped at my floor and the door opened.

"Okay." I pushed the door open button to hold the door. "Well, if you ever want to talk about something, you know I'm here, right? It might surprise you to know that I'm very good at listening, despite my smart-ass demeanor." Bert looked genuinely touched at my offer.

"Thanks, Ele." He said sincerely. "I might take you up on it one of these days." I didn't release the door, in case 'one of these days' was today. Realizing what I was doing, he continued. "But not today. I'm good. Thanks for asking, though."

"Alright, Bert. Call me if you change your mind. But hey," I looked him in the eyes. "If I can offer an unsolicited opinion?" There was the slightest nod of his head. "I may be completely off on this, but you seem lonely. I just want to say, I know I didn't know Libby, but from everything you and Nona have told me about her–I think she was the kind of woman who would want to see you keep living your life to the fullest. Sorry if I'm overstepping. See you in the morning." I stepped off the elevator, looked back at him, smiled, and waved. The last thing I saw as the elevator door closed was a slow sad nod, then the return of his crooked smile and the waggle of his fingers in a little wave. As I walked to my room, I wondered if my instincts had been right about Bert. He must get lonely. And this year's conference was very different for him, as it was usually just him and Vance who came. They probably usually shared a room, but with Nona here and the two of them just hitched, Vance and Nona had shared the room instead. Vance and Nona surprised us all by eloping the weekend following the bigfoot festival and I had never seen a happier couple.

Bert seemed to still be mourning his wife, even though Libby passed away close to five years ago. Some people never remarry and I wondered if Bert was one of those guys. Forever faithful to his one and only. It was a lovely notion in theory, but there was one thing I felt sure about–Libby would want more for Bert. From everything I'd heard about her generous spirit, I couldn't help believing that if she couldn't live on with him, then she would want him to grab life by the horns and live it fully for the both of them. I wondered if Bert's sad look had anything to do with this or if I was just projecting. My arrangement had been worlds apart from Bert and Libby's marriage. Doug and I had never married but were as committed to one another as if we were, or at least I was. I know I often felt adrift now that I was on my own, like I might just float away like an escaped helium balloon with no one there to anchor me down, and I supposed the same was likely true for Bert. I tried not to dwell on it, and making friends and getting a puppy had helped enormously, but sometimes, I still felt like a deserted island.

CHAPTER 2

Mildred Spencer was not at all what I had been expecting. She was a sixty-something fiery red-head (though her brilliant red hair was clearly to the credit of a bottle) and she was completely enthralled that I wanted to start a refuge as well. The four of us were having lunch with her as I was trying to warm Vance and Bert up to the idea.

"Bert's trying to convince the owner of the thousand acres adjoining mine to sell to me. He lives on the west coast and isn't doing a thing with the land, anyway. So, I don't actually own the land I would need for the sanctuary yet. I have a small bit of land, but not nearly enough for such a huge undertaking as a sanctuary." Mildred turned her brilliant smile to Bert.

"Well, I bet he can make it happen," she said with assurance. Mildred had only just met Bert, but she must be a quick study, because she was right. If anyone could make it happen, it would be Bert. Winning Vance and Bert to the sasquatch sanctuary idea was my first battle. Bert agreed to try and convince the owner to sell to me because we'd recently had a scare that the property had been sold to a bigfoot hunting business, but I could tell that somehow he and Vance had likened my idea for a bigfoot refuge to the forcible removal of Native American tribes to reservations back when the white man was claiming everything here for their own. (Not that I'm trying to compare bigfoot to Native Americans, but their plights certainly bore some similarities.) I'd tried to explain to Bert and Vance that I simply wanted there to be a place prepared and waiting for any bigfoot that was looking for a new home. I wasn't wanting there to be some kind of forced migration. Mildred got it and I could tell that she was starting to get through to them.

"There are so many sasquatches becoming displaced here in Canada from the parceling off of land that has been their home for generations, or from giant logging corporations coming in and clear-cutting. I've managed to spread the word that there is a place for them if they need somewhere to go and I have new arrivals weekly."

"How do they find out about you?" Vance was intrigued.

"Through other bigfoot. Through friends of bigfoot like you all, and all the other people here at the convention. A lot of these people who are here bought small tracks–say 5 to 20 acres–of land, only to discover it was already inhabited. The stubborn ones, the ones the sasquatch can't scare away, often end up here. Often, these people are willing to share their land with bigfoot but the creatures are struggling to have enough game. After all, when people move in, the wildlife tends to move further into the woods when possible. Our sasquatch friends then end up desperate, sometimes breaking into people's garages and stealing dog food or stuff out of the freezer." She was right. I had heard so many similar stories. "My refuge is well stocked with deer and small game as well as fish in the ponds and streams and when it gets a bit depleted (which has only happened once before), I restock. I put the word out that any sasquatch needing a home is welcome. I have one rule—'Live in Harmony'." Mildred shrugged, "So far, so good."

"How exactly do they find you? I mean, literally, how do they know how to get to your place?" Bert's interest was rising as well.

"It operates a bit like the underground railroad did during times of slavery. We are adding new 'stations' daily. When a sasquatch hears about us and indicates they want to come, we have a chain of stops they can go to in order to get to me. Help is still a little sparse to my north, but I made a few contacts this week that I think are going to be helping in the future. I'm taking in all I can, but there is a need for more places for them to go. As far as I know, there is nothing intentional in the U.S. and since you're so centrally located, it could be perfect."

"If I get to buy the property next to mine like I'm hoping to." I directed this to Bert with a smile. "But, as already established, I've got the best realtor in the world, so if there's a way, he can do it." Bert smiled ever so slightly and asked what I had been wondering as well.

"Why aren't you offering a seminar to tell people about what you're doing? Make more connections?" Bert asked.

"Honestly," Mildred looked around before she said the next bit. I couldn't help noticing an odd-looking man wearing sunglasses who was sitting in the corner, or notice that Mildred was looking at him as well. She lowered her voice, and we all leaned in to hear. "Because I don't trust our governments not to interfere. I'm sure someone is keeping an eye on the official events of our annual conventions. The general public might think we're crazy, but law enforcement knows these creatures exist. Quite frankly, I just want the government to leave me alone, so everything I do is word of mouth. I considered making my refuge 'official'." Mildred burst out laughing at the shocked expressions on all our faces. "Not as an official sasquatch refuge, mind you, but there is a small owl that is endangered in our area that I could have applied to be a refuge for and received the tax breaks, but then I would have researchers and preservationists wanting to visit all the time and I just wanted privacy for my guests, so I opted to go it alone. I am in the rare position that I can afford to do it this way, so I do. I know my intentions, and I'm able to communicate them with the people and creatures who need to know I exist. That's all I care about."

"I'm impressed." Bert was smiling full force now. "It sounds like you've thought of everything."

"Well, not everything. I get surprised regularly with things I didn't think of. But we muddle our way through." Mildred turned her attention to Nona, who had mostly remained silent.

"When are you due?" We were all a little shocked. It was a presumptuous question, especially considering that Nona wasn't showing that much, and by her age, how on earth would the woman be sure there was a baby and that Nona wasn't just carrying that middle-aged bulge so many women get. Mildred smiled, again intuiting our misgivings about her comment.

"You've touched your abdomen a half dozen times since we started lunch," Mildred explained. "And I had my youngest in my forties, so I'm pretty perceptive. My daughter lives on the refuge with me and helps with all those unexpected details. She grew up around sasquatch and has some pretty strong opinions about their preservation."

"Oh, wow! She sounds wonderful." Nona smiled at Mildred. "I'm due April 25th." Nona hesitated. "How was it? Giving birth in your forties? I had my only other child in my early twenties, so needless to say, I'm a little nervous."

"It was the best thing I ever did. My first OB-GYN really encouraged me to abort, so I switched to a supportive one and they helped me through the pregnancy. I ended up on bed rest for the last few months, but Melody is one of the best things that has ever happened to me, and I feel so lucky to have her in my life." I looked at Nona and Vance and they were both misty-eyed. Mildred pulled a small notepad from her purse and scrawled her name, phone number, and email address on it, then ripped it from the pad and handed it to Nona. "Call me if you ever want to talk. It's been a while, but sometimes it seems like yesterday. I'm happy to offer a listening ear or any advice if I have it."

"Thank you." Nona took the paper, and I could tell she was genuinely touched. Mildred was scratching on another piece of paper from her pad and she tore it out.

"And as for you and your little venture," she handed me the piece of paper with the same information. "Keep me posted and call anytime with questions or if you just want to talk. I'm happy to help in any way I can and I'm excited that I'm not the only one crazy enough to think of this." She laughed and looked at her watch. "I better scoot though. I don't want to miss a moment of Dr. Sorenson." Bert came to life and looked at his phone.

"Me neither. Want to walk together?" And the two of them were off. Nona was going to go lay down until the 3:00 session and I was going to take a crash course on DNA collecting. This session was being taught by a researcher who wanted to go public with the existence of the creatures and the idea that we should approach the whole thing from a scientific angle, gathering as much proof as possible so the scientific community would get on board. I wasn't sure I wanted everyone to believe, but I thought the class could be enlightening. And Vance was going to a Q & A that he had been looking forward to, so the three of us parted ways. My head was swimming with everything Mildred had shared. Was I really truly considering opening a sasquatch sanctuary?

Yep. It looked like I was.

Nona and I were waiting at our gate. Bert and Vance's flight left about thirty minutes ago, and I watched as one of our flight attendants scurried around the little booth to get ready for boarding. My heart leapt in anticipation. I broke into a very questionable rendition of "New York, New York" quietly as we waited. I am not a singer. Nona giggled.

"You are really excited, aren't you?" She seemed surprised and I guess it was a little strange to be so excited to visit a place I had lived for so many years and had only been away from for a little over six months.

"I am," I smiled and kept singing.

"I am too!" Nona said. "It's been years since I've been to New York City." Nona joined me on the final line of the song, "If I can make it there, I'll make it anywhere…" and people were looking at us like we were off our rockers but then the flight attendant started her spiel and we all turned our attention to her, awaiting our turns to board the plane. This week was going to be great fun.

My ears were still not right after our quick flight from Niagara Falls, straight up and straight back down again. We had stashed our bags in our hotel room and were now sitting with Nona's son, who was as wonderful as Nona had said he was, which, from my experience, is a bit unusual. Everyone is smitten with their own kids and, quite frankly, they never live up to the hype. Ha! Said like a true childless spinster, but I wasn't bitter. I was completely at peace with the decisions I had made in life. It was simply a fact that people over-inflated how great their children were.

"Okay—now, *what* were you attending in Niagara Falls?" Javier asked. He was every bit as loveable as his mother, but he was clearly confused as to what the hell Nona was doing at an International Sasquatch Protection Society Conference. Imagine that! Nona laughed.

"Oh, hon. A lot has happened since you last came to visit," she smiled broadly, clearly ecstatic to be with her son.

"More than this?" He lovingly touched his mother's abdomen and then surprised us both by bending over and talking to Nona's stomach. "Hey kid! It's me. Your big brother. I have been waiting a very long time for you." I watched as Nona's eyes immediately filled with tears. "Aww... mom. It's okay. It is okay? Right? Everything is okay with the baby?" He suddenly looked worried that she hadn't told him something.

"Everything is perfect, Javi." She pulled him into another embrace. She had hugged him about forty times in the ten minutes we had been with him. "I'm just so thankful that you are happy about this. I know it's weird. I know I'm old. You could be reacting so differently. I'm just so relieved that you seem to be as happy about the baby as I am." Javier's face softened as he pulled back from his mother. He placed a hand on each shoulder and looked her straight in the face.

"Mom, I could not be happier. I'm not kidding when I say I've been waiting a long time. I've wanted a little brother or sister for as long as I can remember. But–I understand why you never had one until now." There was a somberness to this statement that made me realize the depth with which he mourned his mother's abuse. I couldn't imagine how it had been for him when the truth finally came out that his father had been beating his mother all those years. Nona said he had never been around when it happened. Her ex had been very strategic and never became violent when their son was home and oddly, unlike many abusive partners, the abuse did not extend to his son. Javier had grown up literally believing his mother was just extremely accident-prone. It wasn't until the last time when Nona had nearly died that the truth came out. Javier had faced his father and the only thing that kept him from leaving Austin with his mother was that Geraldo also managed his band, Suddenly Sparrow, which was quickly rising to the top of the charts. Javi had insisted his father go to counseling and Geraldo agreed because he was terrified of losing his only son. At least it was something. Nona's face clouded for a moment.

"On that note, will your dad be there tomorrow night?"

"Oh!" Javier looked sad. "No. No. He doesn't travel with us anymore." It was awkward for just a flash and then he smiled and asked, "So–how is Vance?" Nona's face filled with compassion for her son, but shifted into a self-conscious smile at the mention of Vance.

"He's great. He's so excited about the baby. I really can't believe I'm so lucky."

"Well, you deserve it, mom. So, how did you manage to get away from Coffee O'Clock for so long?"

"Oh, I can't believe I forgot to tell you. I hired someone! Chloe Clark is a wonder, and she has picked up on everything so quickly that she could cover me this week. Can you believe it? Now, I'll be able to come to see you more." And unlike many young twenty-somethings might react, Javier seemed genuinely thrilled that he would be seeing more of his mother.

"Oh, mom! That's great." He said with a smile. Remembering I was in the room, Javier turned his attention to me. "Elena, it's so nice to finally meet you. My mom hasn't been able to stop talking about you since you moved to town. She needed a best friend there. I'm so happy she found you." My chest bloomed with a sudden warmth. I was so pleased to know that Nona must truly feel the same way about me as I did about her. I mean, I thought I knew that. But it's always nice to hear it from someone else. I smiled at the two of them and thought Nona looked a little like she was blushing. It seems she has as hard of a time as I do letting down that independent woman shell. Independent women support independent women. That's how we manage so well.

"It's so nice to meet you too, Javier. Your mother has saved my life. I probably wouldn't have stayed in Oklahoma if it hadn't been for her and her coffee shop. You know that's our plan for the week, don't you? I'm taking her to all my old coffee haunts around NYC." Javier started laughing.

"That's your dream vacation, mom!" He nudged her.

"I know!" Nona laughed. "I get to go to coffee shops all around the city and see you in person and in concert. It's all my favorite things in one go."

"Speaking of which, I left tickets for you all at Will Call. I'm so excited for you to see the new set. It's Gucci." Nona and I looked at one another.

"Gucci?" she asked with amusement in her eyes.

PSA #32: If you happen to be young—which, of course, why would you be? This is a book about the middle-aged's adventures with bigfoot. BUT. If you *do happen* to be young, might I recommend that you resist the urge to use words like "Gucci"? You will regret it later. I promise you. "Totally tubular" are actual words that came out of these lips in the 80s and I still close my eyes and shudder at the memory.

"Cool. Alright?" Javier chuckled. "It means cool, mom. You're gonna love it." Javier had the same sparkle in his eye as his mom. "Now, are you ladies ready to go eat or what?" He looked at the time on his phone. "We better get going if we're gonna make the reservation," he said as he called his driver and we followed him down to the car.

CHAPTER 3

Nona and I were living our best lives, eating and drinking our way through the Big Apple. Dinner last night at a new hip five-star restaurant that was next to impossible to get into was actually phenomenal and merited all the hype and Javi was adorable–he was hilarious, thoughtful, and incredibly kind. In short, he was exactly the son I would have thought Nona would raise and none of the things I expected from a mega-popstar.

"This is unbelievable. I'm in heaven right now," Nona said sincerely as we sat down, which made me laugh out loud. Mostly because I totally understood. We were starting our morning at my favorite coffee shop in the city.

"I wrote most of Moody Blues in this courtyard," (Rainey K. Moody's book three) I looked around marveling at how little it had changed.

PSA #33: Never underestimate the magical powers of a great coffee shop.

"Oh my God! Oh my God!" Nona was shouting. She leapt out of her seat and pointed at the passing bus. On the side was a massive full-sized book cover with the title proudly emblazoned *Bigfoot Watching Woman Watching Bigfoot.* "It's your book! Ele, it's your book!" A couple of people were now looking at us.

"Yes, Nona. Sookie has clearly convinced the publishing house to invest in promotions. Now I would prefer no one to realize I'm the author!" She put her hand over her mouth and smiled.

"But, Ele! This is going to work. Look how cute that cover is! You are doing it." Apparently, for the first time, Nona was realizing our hairbrained plan might just work. "You are REBRANDING BIGFOOT! This is amazing." She sat back down and smiled. Taking a satisfied sip of her coffee, she sighed, looked around and picked up where she was before the bus passed. "Well, I love it here! I understand how you could write a whole series of books here. It is absolutely dreamy. I would love my outdoor space to look like this."

Running to the coffee shop—what, to most, would be an ordinary experience of necessity, was to Nona and me a beautiful experience to behold–one might even say an event. We were at one of my very favorite spots to hang out, drink coffee, and write near Chelsea Market, which was one of my favorite places in the city. I was tickled pink that Nona loved it as much as I did. This particular coffee shop operated in the lobby of The High Life Hotel and on a beautiful fall day like today, we could order our drinks from the coffee truck in the courtyard and sit in the sunshine's worshipful presence. It was just cool enough that the warmth of our lattes brought our body temperatures to the perfect place–the balance of the sunshine and coffee combined with the crisp chill in the air was divine. It was sweater weather at its finest, but not too cold to enjoy sitting outside. And the coffee was to die for.

"I actually considered buying my coffee from this roaster when I was setting up shop, but opted instead to go with a local Oklahoma roaster." Nona mused as she took a sip, breathed in deeply, and sighed. Because Nona was pregnant, she had cut her coffee consumption to one cup in the morning, but my how she savored that one cup. During our short time in NYC, she was allowing herself an extra cup in the afternoon in order to try more places. The doctor instructed her to make twelve ounces a day her max, which was a genuine sacrifice for Nona, who usually drank coffee like most people drink water.

"Well, this coffee is amazing, but they've got nothing on you, Nona." I encouraged her, and I was sincere. I wouldn't say it otherwise. Nona had put together an incredible coffee shop. I'd spent my whole adult life writing in coffee shops all over NYC and around the world and considered myself a bit of an expert and I would put Nona's little "Coffee O'Clock" shop up against the best.

"Thank you," Nona said sincerely. "Coming from you, that is a real compliment."

"Ele!" I heard my name being called and looked up. "Ele!" I leapt from my seat to run and hug Sookie. Sookie Evanovich had been my agent from the beginning and while you are not supposed to make your agent your best friend (Sookie tried desperately to maintain a professional distance from me for the first five years), I eventually broke her down. And now, twenty years later, she is one of my oldest and dearest friends. We rocked back and forth, hugging each other, and then I turned to introduce two of my favorite humans to one another.

"Sookie, this is Nona." I was beaming. "And Nona—Sookie." Nona rose from her seat and before I knew it, the two of them were hugging as well. I ran to the truck to get Sookie her standard Chai Latte, and we all sat down while the barista worked on Sookie's drink.

"Okay, so what the hell?" Sookie didn't mince words. She just jumped right in. "You guys were just at a bigfoot conference in Canada?" she asked, eyes closed, shaking her head incredulously. "Have you seen them, too?" She addressed this question in disbelief to Nona, who started nodding and laughing as well.

"You sound like my son. Yesterday he was asking Ele and me the same thing. Yes, I have seen them. And yes, we are aware it sounds like we are absolutely insane, but the conference was actually quite normal in almost every way."

"She's not lying. I would say there was an 87-ish% normality rate of the people at the conference. I thought we would see a bunch more wack jobs." The barista called my name, and I hopped up to get Sookie's drink.

"Thanks, doll!" she said, smiling at me as I sat her drink in front of her. It was so unbelievably nice to be home with two of my favorite humans. "Okay, then. Show me a picture." Sookie held out her hand for my phone. I was confused for a moment.

"Of what?"

"Of *bigfoot*, of course," Sookie sighed aloud. "Surely you have pictures?!"

"Well," suddenly I wondered why I had never even thought of pulling out my phone and snapping a shot when I was with them. And I realized almost as quickly that they must send some kind of inhibiting message to the humans who come into contact with them not to.

"Why not? That's the first thing I would do. You know, this really makes you guys seem like crazy conspiracy theorists." Sookie sounded skeptical now and so I tried to explain.

"I think they must send the people who they let see them some kind of telepathic message not to photograph them." I said sincerely.

"Oh, *okay*. Now I understand. Now you sound *totally* normal. It was bigfoot's *telepathic message* that stopped you."

"Shut up! If you ever meet them, you will understand." Sookie nodded and I think she was humoring me, but I watched as she switched mental gears.

"So, what are your plans for tonight?" Sookie asked and I could tell she had something in mind. "Because—" Sookie said this with building anticipation in her voice. "Suddenly Sparrow is in town and is sold out, but I think I can get us tickets if you all want to go with me." She said, gushing with excitement. I laughed aloud. Sookie was odd in that even though she was technically middle-aged, she was constantly current on all pop culture. Music, movies, books—if it was a *"thing,"* Sookie knew about it and was likely a fan (or at the very least, had an opinion). "*What?*" My laughter and the look on Nona's face confused Sookie.

"Well, if you can't get us in. Nona for sure can." I said, and it was Sookie's turn to look confused.

"That's my son's band," Nona explained, but Sookie maintained a clueless expression. "Javier Hernandez is my son." Nona elaborated, wearing a proud momma smile.

"NO!" Sookie slapped Nona on the arm. "You. Are. SHITTING. Me!" Nona burst out laughing.

"Nope. Totally true. Still got the faint white stretch marks to prove it. If you want to go with us, I can ask him to leave us a third ticket. And I'll get you in after the show backstage with us." Nona said kindly as Sookie swooned.

"Umm–Yes, please," was all she could say. And then she turned to me and slapped me on the arm. "WHY DIDN'T YOU TELL ME THIS?" She asked, as if I had betrayed her trust in some unforgivable way. I couldn't help but burst out laughing again.

"I don't know. It didn't occur to me. I didn't know you were such a fan." Sookie shrugged.

"How could you? You ran off to no man's land without looking back. How could you possibly keep current on my constantly evolving musical tastes?" This was all said with a sigh of resignation. I shrugged back. I couldn't deny the truth in it. Nona was already texting Javier, and she looked up at us with a smile.

"Done," Nona said with satisfaction. "Javi's adding a ticket to ours at Will Call. I'm so happy you like my son's band. I mean, *I* think they're good." Nona said modestly, as if this were debatable. Sookie laughed aloud.

"Good? They're fucking brilliant! I mean, they do currently have three songs on the charts," she reminded Nona. Suddenly, I realized the buzzing sound I kept hearing was coming from my purse. I couldn't imagine who could be calling me. I pulled the phone from the bottom of my bag just in time to see "Ahmet" disappear from the screen as the call went to voicemail.

"It's Ahmet," I said, ignoring Sookie's raised eyebrow. "God, I hope Bif is okay. I haven't checked in for a couple of days." I excused myself from the table and hastily dialed Ahmet's number. Sookie went back to fan-girling out on Nona about Javier. Ahmet answered on the first ring.

"Is everything alright? Biffy?"

"Oh, yeah. Sorry, Ele. I didn't mean to scare you. I probably should have just texted. Bif is fine." Ahmet chuckled. "He's great actually but he must be able to hear your voice through the phone because he just lit up like a firecracker and is currently licking my hand and trying to get to the phone in his love for you."

"Aww... hi buddy! Hello, my big Biffy boy! I miss you!" I was talking in that unique voice reserved by animal lovers for their beloved pets or mothers for their babies.

"Oh, brother! He's all over me now." I could hear a scuffle. "He is on my lap and licking the phone. You're too big for this boy!" Ahmet laughed as he was clearly struggling to get my teenaged pup, who was much too big to be a lap dog off of his lap. "Go play. Here, fetch!" Again I heard another scuffle. Ahmet must have thrown a toy for Bif to fetch.

"Did I catch you at a bad time?" Ahmet's voice was warm and playful. I could hear the rustling of their game of fetch and could perfectly see a picture in my mind's eye of my lanky, black and white border collie smiling up at him expectantly, waiting for him to throw the toy again.

"No, it's not a bad time. Nona, Sookie, and I were just having coffee."

"Oh... where?" It surprised me to hear a hint of longing in his voice. As my entire relationship with Ahmet had existed in the backwoods of Oklahoma, I sometimes forgot he had once lived here and loved this city as much as I did.

"Chelsea," I said, and Ahmet let out a little sigh.

"The High Life Hotel?" He asked eagerly. "Are you outside in the courtyard with the coffee truck?"

"How did you know?"

"It's my favorite and I could tell you were outside by the traffic sounds and the birds."

"Okay! Well, I'm getting you a bag of coffee beans while I'm here and I can see that our next girl's trip should include at least one boy," I teased.

"Nah. I don't know if I'll ever go back." Ahmet had left the big city to escape the dreams or "visitations" of those lost in 9/11. Their spirits came to him as instant replays of the last moments of their life, often with an added message for loved ones that Ahmet inevitably felt responsible to deliver. For years after the tragedy, he would dutifully deliver these messages to the loved ones of those who came to him in his dreams until he was about to go mad.

"Well," I paused for a moment. "If you ever decide to, there's a girl's trip waiting to happen." Ahmet laughed. "So, why did you call?" That was what I liked about talking to Ahmet. It was so easy to just get lost in the comfortable banter—in the ease of his friendship.

"Oh, I just thought you might want an update on JoJo. She's been worried sick about you, by the way. Bob has been checking your house for her because I had to put her back on full bed rest. We didn't think to tell them you were going on a trip and I guess since Bob rescued you, they feel a responsibility for you and couldn't figure out where you had gone off to."

"Oh, no! It didn't even occur to me to tell them I would be out of town." I mean, really. Who would think of that? It's not like it's commonplace to have bigfoot for neighbors who apparently behave more like a concerned elderly couple in a neighborhood watch would. I would have to apologize to them. "Are JoJo and the babies in danger?" Ahmet had put JoJo on bed rest once before to help stop her from going into labor with her twins, but had relented to modified bed rest the past few weeks because JoJo was not handling staying off her feet very well. Neither of us were sure what exactly pregnant bigfoot were busy doing all day, as neither of us were bigfoot experts, but clearly, she felt she had more to do than lie around all day.

"It's getting close, Ele!" Ahmet said excitedly. "She has started dilating."

"Wait. What? Do we need to come back now?" Ele did not want to miss the birth of the twins. After all, she was pretty certain it was a once-in-a-lifetime kind of experience.

"No. I think we need those baby bigfoot to stay inside for another couple of weeks to be safe. But you are coming home to the excitement of JoJo's impending delivery. On a side note, Bob told Vance that they had relatives coming."

"Wait, Vance went with you?" I didn't think Vance had been home long enough. "And did you just say that Bob and JoJo have relatives coming?" Had I misunderstood something?

"Yeah. I thought it would be easier to have Vance with me, and when I picked him and Bert up at the airport last night, he agreed to join me this morning. I've met with them once on my own while you guys were away, but Vance is just so much more adept at communicating with them than I am." I was walking along the edge of the courtyard under the trees where there weren't any tables. Sookie and Nona were laughing like old friends. Happiness bubbled up inside me. My two worlds were colliding in the most lovely way. Maybe Sookie would visit me in Oklahoma after all. I'd wanted her to come to the Bigfoot Festival, but she was busy with a major book release of another high-profile client, or at least that was the excuse she gave me and with all the serial-killer insanity that went down, I guess it was just as well. But I still felt a fierce determination to get her to come and visit. Sookie is New York City–through and through. Even the idea of her in the backwoods of Oklahoma incites a giggle from deep inside me. So great is the ludicrousness of the thought. "So, are the relatives coming because of the babies? Like to visit?" I asked Ahmet. My understanding of bigfoot social dynamics was negligent at best. I was confused and by the silence coming from the other end of the line, I could tell that Ahmet was trying to figure out what I meant.

"Oh, no. I wish it were something like that. No, Bob told Vance that his relatives keep getting shot at where they are. The area in which they've lived for years had been sectioned off and several of the new landowners would love to mount one of their heads on the wall."

"Oh, God!" It was my turn to gasp. I couldn't help thinking, 'and so it begins.' Ahmet must have read my mind.

"So... it looks like your Sasquatch Sanctuary idea may be coming in the nick of time. Vance and Bert told me about the lady you met with who has a preserve in Canada. That sounds fascinating."

"Oh, Ahmet! Mildred was wonderful. I can't wait to tell you all about it." As I turned to look back at Sookie and Nona, I noticed a man in the corner of the garden wearing sunglasses and smoking a cigarette. He looked familiar and in an instant, I knew why. I had seen him before. He was at the restaurant when we had met with Mildred about the preserve. I remembered clearly because when we had asked Mildred why she wasn't offering a session at the conference since what she was doing was clearly so important; she had specifically mentioned not wanting to lay everything out for the government spies that were most certainly at the conference undercover. The idea had amused me and I had glanced around and saw this very man who looked like a mix between a stereotypical 1970s private investigator and a balding ferret with a cigarette. I can't help it, my subconscious writer's brain is always taking notes.

"Ele?—Are you there?" Ahmet asked, thinking the call had dropped.

"Yes. I'm here. I'm sorry." She glanced over to where Sookie and Nona were engaged in a lively conversation. "There was a man I thought I recognized." A man *I did recognize*, I thought to myself with certainty.

"Everything okay?" Ahmet sounded concerned.

"Yeah, everything's fine. I guess I better get back to the girls, though. Thanks for the update. Keep me posted if there are any changes with JoJo and thanks again for keeping Bif for me." I could hear an excited whimper at the mention of his name. "I can't tell you how much I appreciate not having to worry about him—knowing that he is likely happier with you than he would be if I were home."

"Well, that's just not true. But you're welcome. We are having a fine time. Aren't we, boy?" I could just see Ahmet rubbing Bif's head and Bif smiling adoringly up at him. It made me smile.

"Okay, so I'm picking you up a bag of coffee before we leave today. Any other New York delicacies I can bring you back?" There was a pause and for a second and I thought we had got disconnected when Ahmet said in a slow, intensely serious voice.

"I would kill for one of Joe's Bagels." I laughed out loud.

"Done! Just text me if you think of anything else. Bringing you back a little taste of NYC goodness is the least I can do." I walked back to the table smiling and when I got within earshot, I heard the two of them in a serious discussion about my bigfoot sanctuary idea. They smiled up at me.

"So, Nona was just telling me—" she smiled and took a long pause for dramatic effect, "—that you've lost your fucking mind."

"Hey! I didn't put it like that!" Nona laughed and gave me a look, saying she was sorry, but I just laughed.

"I knew you would be excited for me, Sookie. Did she also tell you about the bigfoot babies that are about to be born?" I lowered my voice. "Nona, do you recognize—" I glanced over to the smoking ferret, but he was gone. "Shit."

"She didn't have to, remember? I'm your agent for your thinly veiled memoir-cum-novels." Sookie said dryly. I was confused for a minute, distracted by the disappearing man, and then I realized Sookie was answering my question about the bigfoot babies. She was clearly getting a kick out of the whole bizarre mess.

"Speaking of which," said Nona. "We just saw the bus ad! That was amazing!"

"You did?" Sookie asked excitedly. "I haven't seen it yet." I was still thinking about the smoking ferret who had suddenly disappeared, and Nona had picked up that something was wrong.

"What's going on, Ele?" she asked softly and Sookie looked at the two of us in confusion.

"Well," I sighed. "This is going to sound absolutely insane, but there was a man over there just a moment ago that was also at the cafe when we were meeting with Mildred about the preserve. I wanted you to look and see if you recognized him too, but he left when I turned my back."

"Are you sure?" Nona asked.

"I'm positive. He looked like a balding smoking ferret dressed as a 1970s private investigator."

Sookie laughed out loud. "Images of an animated Rockford Files with a ferret playing Jim Rockford are dancing in my brain now and I can see how you might not be able to forget that," she said but discerning how much it had concerned me, Sookie put her hand on mine. "It's probably just a coincidence. Niagara Falls isn't across the globe, you know. And this is one of the most popular destination coffee shops in the world."

"That's true," I said doubtfully. Nona caught my eye and I could tell she had her doubts as well.

"So," Sookie said, trying to change the subject. "About that thinly veiled memoir-turned-novel–"

"Oh, yeah! How did you do it, anyway?" I didn't want to waste this precious time with Sookie worrying about unlikely conspiracy theories, so I simply switched gears as well. "How did you get the publisher to roll with bigfoot adventure stories? And just FYI—it was Nona's desire to 're-brand bigfoot' that led me into writing the silly stories at all." Sookie pointed at Nona as if to say, 'I'll talk to you in a moment.'

"First of all, I'm an effing genius, Ele. You know this. Second, we got lucky. Bigfoot is trending. Third, NONA! Ele is a serious novelist, one of my best. Stop filling her head with this nonsense." Nona looked sufficiently chastised, but I could tell she wasn't one bit sorry that it was happening. Nona was a softie for the creatures. If my reputation had to go down the toilet to assist in their plight, well, then so be it. "You just better pray they hit! Otherwise, in a year, serious novelist Elena Carmichael will be known as the crazy lady who writes bigfoot books."

"God, don't I know it. The thought has made me a praying woman, Sookie." She laughed at this and took a big swig of her chai latte. "Seriously though, Sookie. You must come visit me after the babies are born." I persisted and Nona gave Sookie a look, hesitated, and then spoke.

"Ele may have an elaborate fantasy going on in that brain of hers of being Auntie Ele to the bigfoot babies." She looked at me apologetically. "I'm sorry, Ele. But you know it's true." I nodded in confirmation.

"Of course I know it's true. And none of you guys will let me live it down! But I admit, I'm a lost cause. I understand that this is highly unlikely, but I just can't help imagining what it will be like to have little twin bigfoot babies on my property. I wish they wore clothes so I could go shopping for them." Sookie loved animals. When I lived here, we had zoo passes and made the Central Park Zoo one of our most traveled walking paths together. The Gorilla Escape was Sookie's favorite path. And although bigfoot weren't exactly primates, I could see Sookie was getting as suckered in by the idea of a couple of baby bigfoot as I was.

"Maybe I'll come. We'll see." Sookie looked at her watch. "Why didn't Evie join us?" Sookie asked. Sookie and Evie had become friends through me and although they were not quite as close to each other as I was with each of them, I knew they grabbed drinks together regularly.

"She was tied up this morning. We are meeting her at 2:00 for our afternoon coffee."

"So what does she think about all of this bigfoot stuff?"

"Oh! I haven't told her. I need to keep it a secret. People really do have to believe that this is a novel and not my real life." I was suddenly horrified. "You haven't actually been telling people it is a thinly veiled memoir turned novel, have you?" Sookie laughed at my mortification.

"Of course not! I wanted them to publish it, not drop you all together and have you committed." Something told me she was only partially kidding. I sighed with relief.

"Okay, good."

"I just didn't know how much you were telling people–close friends, I mean."

"Evie is dear to me, but there was just no reason to disclose this to her. The more I keep it on the down-low, the better. I couldn't help but tell you since you're so intimately involved in my writing career, being my agent and all. That, and I know what an animal rights activist you are, so I hoped if you believed that bigfoot were real, you would see why it's important to combat this trend of painting them like vicious beasts. It would be one thing if they were vicious beasts, but all of those I have met have simply wanted to be left alone to live their lives in peace." Sookie nodded with understanding and then glanced at her watch again. "But you know Evie is not an animal person."

Sookie nodded, both of them remembering an unfortunate incident at Central Park with Evie and an overexcited labrador.

"Oh man, gotta run. Duty calls." She chugged the rest of her Chai Latte. "But I CAN NOT WAIT for tonight! You want to meet there?"

"Sure. Meet us at Will Call at–what? 7:00?" I looked to Nona for confirmation, and she nodded.

"That seems good." Sookie blew kisses and was already on the run to her next thing.

"Wanna check out Chelsea Market?" I looked at my watch. "We have four hours until we meet Evie for coffee at Stumpville. That's another one of my favorite old coffee stomping grounds." I waggled my eyebrows at her, and Nona rolled her eyes. "Grounds. See what I did there?" She groaned and did not dignify my pun with a further response.

"Yes, I would love to go to Chelsea Market. Oh my God, you were right. I LOVE Sookie! You told me I would, but I was nervous about meeting her." Nona paused, clearly reflecting on the meeting. "I think that went fine." It hadn't even occurred to me that Nona would be nervous about meeting my friends.

"It went more than fine. Sookie loved you back! It went perfectly. I think you will really like Evie too. She is a bit more serious than Sookie, but she's one of the kindest people you'll ever meet. She literally took me in to live with her the moment I caught Doug in the affair and she took care of me like a mother hen."

"She sounds wonderful. I can't wait to meet her."

CHAPTER 4

The four of us made our way to the special VIP section Javier put us in. He'd sent us through an exclusive entrance on 31st street between 7th and 8th. When he said "WILL CALL" he really meant "VIP WILL CALL". We were following the very business-like woman who had covered us in VIP lanyards, little swag bags with band merch, kisses on each cheek, and directions to follow her. She informed us we had the four very best seats in the house. When Evie heard our plans, she was so visibly envious that Nona had immediately called Javi and asked if it was possible to get just one more spot, and apparently when you are the lead singer and guitarist in the band, anything is possible.

"Javier is so excited that you guys are here. He wanted me to apologize for not bringing you backstage before the show, but he said they want to give you all their best performance, so it is better for them if you wait until after." We all nodded. My breathing grew heavy at the briskness of our walk and I could tell it was affecting Nona as well, as the two of us were now used to driving almost everywhere we went. I was going to have to follow Ahmet's example and start hiking daily through our woods for exercise. Of course, Sookie and Evie seemed perfectly fine. Half sprinting down the city streets was a daily activity for them. Speed walking the back corridors of Madison

Square Gardens was nothing to them. Finally, the woman slowed down, stopping at a door marked VIP ENTRANCE.

It was the last song of the third encore of the night and the four of us were jumping up and down to the poppy beat of one of Suddenly Sparrow's biggest hits. The night had been perfect. I didn't know their music, but it really didn't matter. We danced and sang and jumped around like we were a couple of decades younger than we were and I saw the lady who delivered us to our seats slip through the VIP door to the side and smile as she watched us, just then the song hit its last beat and Javier said, "Thank you, New York City! You are always in our hearts! Good night!" The band all came to the front of the stage together and bowed and they bent over and signed a few autographs and then made their way offstage. Meanwhile, they whisked us backstage and as we went through a door, we ran right into them as they came off of stage. Sookie gave a little yelp of excitement and Evie and I snickered at her, but Nona's heart and full attention belonged to her son. She wrapped him in a big embrace and then pulled back and put a hand on each sweaty cheek and said to him, words dripping with love and affection, "That was amazing! Javi, you keep getting better and better." Javier looked sheepish and shy for a moment.

"Thanks, mom." Just then, Nona turned to the other band members and wrapped them each in embraces, pouring compliments on each of them as well. Clearly, Nona was mama to them all. We followed the band to a room that was filled with refreshments of all the legal kinds. I always wondered if big stars like this had platters of cocaine waiting for them, but maybe they were keeping it clean because of our visit, or maybe Suddenly Sparrow didn't roll that way. Nona introduced Javier and the band to the three of us and I thought Sookie might pass out there for a moment, but she regained her cool. These young people all seemed so nice. They were all buzzing with adrenaline from the show and no one but the drummer seemed too put off by four middle-aged women invading their space and maybe I was just reading the drummer wrong. His aloofness could just be introversion. That happens to me sometimes. People think just because I'm quietly observing that I'm judging or pissed off or something. Because of this, I long ago trained my face into a pleasant resting face instead of my natural resting bitch face, which, can I point out, is an expression that is just plain mean? We can't help how our face looks at rest! Just then, their road manager came in.

"Great show, guys! I mean it. PHENOMENAL! Nona!" He turned to her and gave her the kiss on each cheek and Nona was cordial, but certainly not her usual warm self.

"Guys, I'm sorry to interrupt, but you have some contest winners to come meet and a few interviews."

"Manny, I told you mom was going to be here tonight. You were supposed to keep the night open."

"I know... I know, Javi." He shrugged his shoulders and held both hands palms up, helplessly. "But, you know, the life of a star. It's the price you pay!".

"It's okay, Javi." Nona put an arm around her son's shoulder. "I think we are all just about spent anyway, but call me tomorrow? We can get together before Ele and I head out." Javier nodded. He was clearly pissed and I couldn't help but wonder how much power he had over his own life. Sometimes, celebrity equals imprisonment to others' expectations rather than freedom.

"Love you, mom. Thanks for coming." He turned to the three of us and, like a true gentleman, bid us farewell and even remembered our names. The kid impressed me yet again. "Elena, Evie, Sookie–" Javi held out his hand to Sookie, who I thought for a moment was going to faint, but then she pulled herself together and shook his hand.

"Thank you for having us." Just then, she pulled a card from her pocket. "If you ever decide to write your life story, I'm your agent." I laughed. Leave it to Sookie to make this a business meeting in the midst of her fan-girling. He turned to Evie and shook her hand as well, and then gave me a quick hug as he had his mother.

"Well, I'm sorry ladies to be leaving you so soon, but it was an absolute pleasure to meet you." He turned to us and flashed us a seriously heart-melting smile and then he and the band headed out the door following Manny. The four of us looked at each other.

"Well, what now, ladies?" Sookie asked with a grin. "Were you serious, Nona? Are you through for the night, or could you go for some cheesecake?"

"Um…I could always go for some cheesecake," Nona smiled at our little sisterhood.

PSA #34: When the possibility of cheesecake is on the table–THE ANSWER IS ALWAYS YES!

"Venito's?" I asked wistfully, already knowing the answer as Sookie looked at her watch.

"We could just make it, but they close at eleven and we would be rushed. How about Sonny's?" Sonny's spouted claims of being the world's most fabulous cheesecake (Sookie agrees) but I prefer a little bakery over on East 11th. To me, Venito's wins the world's best cheesecake hands-down. "Sonny's is open until 1 am and we can walk there in less than 5 minutes." Sookie said pointedly. I knew all of this, of course, but Sookie likes to make a case.

"Sonny's it is!" I said joyously, still high on the music. "Nona, you are about to have the second-best cheesecake in New York City!" Sookie playfully slapped my arm.

"Don't listen to her, Nona. It's the best!" Evie laughed at this. She didn't even like cheesecake–the weirdo. She always ordered one of their black and white cookies, which, in fairness, were also delicious. My heart was full to bursting at seeing my dear friends again and watching them embrace Nona. We were no longer three peas in a pod, but four, and it was delightful. Some of us are born with family, some of us procreate, and some of us just find our family along the way. It was like looking for the shiny rocks. No one knows why it is, but some rocks just stand out and you like them enough to bend over and pick them up and put them in your pocket. It didn't happen often for me, but once I had put a rock in my pocket, I was devoted. This was a weird analogy I was creating, all lost in my thoughts. Thinking of my friends as shiny rocks in my pocket. I shook my head to rejoin reality and picked up my speed to keep up with the three of them who were just stepping out onto the street to make our way to Sonny's for the second-best cheesecake on the planet.

Evie and I sprawled on the floor of her mini-storage in the basement of her apartment. We had just emptied Evie's storage of all of my belongings that she had kindly been storing for me since my move to

Oklahoma. I came straight over right after my photo shoot for Bigfoot Watching Woman Watching Bigfoot. I loved that the photo we were going with for the back cover mirrored the front cover. It was me looking through binoculars, my hair put up in such a way that no one would ever know it was me. Nona was spending our last day in the city with her son and it was perfect because it was giving Evie and me some much needed one-on-one time, even if we were working.

"How are you doing?" I felt bad because I knew Evie was going through a lot right now with her mother's dementia escalating to the point of it no longer being safe for her to live alone. Evie was kindly moving back into the apartment in Little Italy that she had grown up in. It was a pretty sweet apartment, but moving back to her childhood home only to watch her mother decline with dementia had to be a bleak prospect.

"I don't know. One day I feel fine and ready to tackle the future of helping mom cope with her memory loss and the next I just want to crawl under my covers and stay there forever. This is NOT how I would choose to spend this season of my life. And I feel like an asshole, but sometimes I just want to run away."

"God, Evie. I'm so sorry. Is your brother planning on helping at all?"

"You know Jason. His intentions are good, but his follow-through leaves something to be desired. But don't you worry, mom lets me know daily how much he is doing for her," bitterness tinged her laugh ever so slightly. "I will never understand how some women favor men so irrationally. My father was chauvinistic. God rest his soul. You know I loved him." I did. Evie had been a daddy's girl through and through, and I'd enjoyed dinners with her family on occasion over the years.

"But mom ran herself ragged to accommodate him, never once calling him out on the way he spoke to her or the unrealistic demands he placed on her. And she does the same thing with my brother. He is a saint and yet she can barely say thank you to me for dropping my life and home and freaking moving in with her so she doesn't have to move into a nursing home! It is unbelievably infuriating." Evie heaved an enormous sigh, laid the rest of the way down on the near-empty storage room floor, threw her arms out to each side, and stared at the ceiling. I lined myself up next to her, laying my head over her arm so that it was in the crook under my neck and threw my ankle over my raised knee and stared up at the ceiling with her. I too heaved a deep sigh on her behalf.

"Well, first of all, I will say it even if she won't. You are a freaking saint and she is lucky to have you as a daughter. Two: are you still seeing Jan?" Jan was a therapist the two of us had used off and on over the years while we were trying to evolve into the powerful independent women we longed to be.

"Yes."

"What does she say?"

"She keeps telling me not to do anything that I do not feel comfortable with and to own the decisions I do make."

"Is that helpful?' Evie laughed.

"Depends on the day." Evie sat up. It was about 1:45 in the afternoon. My U-Haul was loaded. All that was left in Evie's basement storage room were a few of her things that I offered to drop by her mom's, but she refused. She told me she had another month on her lease and she intended to use it. "I am starving. Want to get a sandwich?" Evie asked as she sat up, untangling herself from me.

"God, yes! I still need to pick up some bagels from Joe's to take back for Ahmet. Do you mind if we get sandwiches there?" Evie and I had eaten there hundreds of times over the years. Joe's was one of about three sandwich shops that we most often frequented, so I was pretty sure she wouldn't mind.

"Joe's is perfect. Ahmet, huh? So, what's the dealio with him?" I played it off like I had no idea what she was referring to.

"No dealio, just a friend. He's taking care of my puppy for me—oh, Evie! You have got to visit me and meet Biffy. You will love him." Evie raised an eyebrow skeptically. Evie was the polar opposite of Sookie when it came to an affinity with furry creatures, but it wasn't entirely her fault. She had been raised in an NYC apartment and never had a pet of any kind of her own and the only real exposure to a dog in her life was her neighbor's dog that would bite her every time no one was looking. The little beast was a sadistic bastard too because somehow it knew just how hard to bite without breaking the skin, so no one would ever believe Evie. Since her mother enjoyed her relationship with Rita Fazoli, and since there was no actual evidence (a.k.a.-broken skin), she'd always just told Evie to toughen up. This did not a dog lover make. We headed out onto the street. It was only about a fifteen-minute walk to Joe's, so we fell into step with one another.

"Do not think I didn't notice what you just did there. I asked about Ahmet, not Biffy. Really though, Ele. Is there something there?" Evie and I had been through a lot together. We'd been friends since before I met Doug. We'd shared our dating woes. I had been there for her through her one whirlwind marriage and divorce and more first dates than either of us cared to remember. She'd been there for me through the same dating games before I settled with Doug and then carried me through my un-settling with Doug, and well, Evie is the best. I linked my elbow through hers and leaned towards her so she could hear me over the busy street sounds.

"What is there–is friendship. He's just a good friend, but thank you for caring."

"Alright. Alright. I just hate to see you go off men for good."

"Me? You're one to talk."

"Well, I happen to be seeing someone. Someone very interesting, in fact." Evie said with a sly smile. I stopped and spun her towards me.

"WHAT? Why am I just now hearing about this? Who? When? How?" She spun me back into motion, linking arms yet again and picking up our pace, we were almost to Joe's.

"Let's get our sandwiches and I will tell you everything."

We dove into our sandwiches (lox and cream cheese on bagel), because—extreme hunger. After three or four bites, I couldn't stand it any longer. "Okay, spill it! Where did you meet him?" Evie was grinning from ear to ear. I always want to hear the scoop if my friends are dating someone, but this was especially exciting because Evie had nearly sworn off men entirely after her divorce from a very brief but volatile marriage. It had been over seven years ago and she had done very little dating in the time since and not because men weren't asking. Evie is ethereal. She almost looks like what I would imagine a fairy with exquisite taste to look like. That's an odd description, I know, but she has fine pixie-like features, a naturally thin build and bright blue eyes that literally sparkle when she gets excited so that you can almost imagine wings fluttering on her back and lifting her off the ground. This is where the fairy comparison ends, however, because she does not in any way dress like she belongs at a medieval festival or a cosplay event. Evie is always so put together with perfection and taste. She could be dropped into the middle of Paris Fashion Week at any moment and look perfectly suited to be there. Even today, when we had been working to clean out her basement storage and load all my stuff in the truck, she was wearing a designer tracksuit that could almost pass for dress clothes (and which I would likely wear in that capacity) and Chanel tennis shoes, which while a little over the top, are adorable. She took time to chew and swallow the large bite she had just taken when I asked the question and then she smiled a quiet, shy smile, leaned in conspiratorially, and spoke.

"He is one of my mom's new specialists." The significance of this was not lost on me. I'm pretty sure Evie has watched every hospital drama ever made with rapt attention. And streaming old episodes of McDreamy has most likely been her replacement for dating actual men since her divorce. I raise an eyebrow.

"A doctor, huh?" I smiled at her and she beamed back.

"So, how long has this been going on? Tell me everything."

Evie abandoned her sandwich and spent the next twenty minutes telling me every beautiful detail of her new romance. By the time she had finished, I was pretty sure that Evie was in love. He had been through an ugly divorce as well about five years ago and had thrown himself into his work, just as Evie had. He sounded perfect for her and I was so happy for my friend.

"Ahmet's a doctor too." This was where I had to tread carefully because in my mind he was still working as a doctor–only to bigfoot–but I had made a conscious decision not to tell Evie about the whole bigfoot thing for two specific reasons. One: she would never, ever come to see me if she knew and I would really love for her to visit me sometime.

And two: Evie is extremely practical and critical at the idea of anything paranormal and she is not even a little bit melty about animals. So I knew that not only would the idea be incredibly off putting to her, it would be a real struggle for her not to try and rationalize it all away and if I were to insist that I actually had interacted, at length, with bigfoot, she would have a hard time not questioning if I was still sane. It seemed that with Evie, it was best to delete this little tidbit of my life.

"Really? You didn't tell me that." She paused and smiled. "And interesting that you follow my story of John by telling me about Ahmet." Ah, shit. She was right. That was interesting. I found myself saying the words that I had been refusing to even admit to myself up until this moment.

"Yes," I whispered. "I guess the truth is if I were to ever–somewhere far, *far* down the road–be interested in dating again, Ahmet would definitely be the kind of man I was looking for."

Evie started making a quiet crooning sound and then giggled, "Oh, hon, I'm afraid you're already long gone."

"I am not!" I sternly resisted. "Ahmet and I really are just friends. We are both happy being just friends. We have both had enough heartbreak to last us a lifetime. I understand why you and everyone else in the world seem to want to partner us up, but the truth truly is—while we might be compatible, neither of us is looking."

"Okay," Evie said slowly, slyly, and noncommittally. She leaned back in her seat and looked at me for a long time, then smiled again and returned to finishing her sandwich, cream cheese smearing above her upper lip making her look like an eight year old imp.

CHAPTER 5

"FUCK YOU, FUCKERRRR!" I yelled at the truck driver who had just cut me off and nearly prevented me from taking my correct exit. I had once heard that people who swore were more trustworthy, and I latched onto that little tidbit like a fly on stink. Ever since I caught Doug in his affair, I had taken my art form of swearing to a new level. Nona did not flinch, her zen-like presence presenting the yin to my yang as we sat side by side in the big cab of the U-Haul. There were a couple of things about this situation that had me in a highly stressed state. Not only had I never driven a vehicle as big as this U-Haul (Note: I got the smallest one they had available but it still felt huge to me), but I had rarely driven in New York City at all. Even though I had lived most of my adult life in the city, I never owned a car while living there and only occasionally rented one. And even when I did that, it was because Doug and I were going out of town and he had done most of the driving. That being said, I loved driving and was certain that once I could get this beast of a truck out of the city, Nona and I were going to have spectacular fun. There is nothing like a road trip for the best conversations.

"Do you miss being an interior designer?" I asked her, easing back in my seat, finally relaxing a bit. That was my last exit to catch before it was smooth sailing for a bit. Nona made a small "hmm" sound as she thought about it for a moment.

"Honestly, I really don't. I did it for so many years that I think I was ready for the change. That is why Geraldo and I had discussed my getting into the coffee game in Austin. So it was the obvious next move for me when I left Texas. Whenever I get an itch to design a new space, there has been something for me to do. Of course, the remodel turning the old bank into a coffee shop was a monumental project to start with. Then I bought my little place and completely gutted and decorated it. Then I redid the space above the coffee shop as an Airbnb and my next project—" She paused for effect and because she knew I didn't know that she had a new project brewing, "-will be the building that is falling apart next door to me." Nona said excitedly.

"Wait, what? How do I not know about this?"

"I don't know when I'll get to it honestly with the baby coming, but I put in an offer on the building next door before I knew I was pregnant and they took it."

"Nona, the roof is caving in! Is it even salvageable?" I was so surprised by all of this. The spot next to Nona's lovely coffee shop, Coffee 'O Clock, that resided in an old bank that Nona had completely restored was the weak link to her place because it was caving in and looked like it was almost dangerous to walk by. It was sad to have such an eyesore right next to her lovely space, so it did not surprise me she wanted to purchase it. I just couldn't imagine how much time and money it would take to restore it and wondered if she had enough business to merit the expense. Not that it was any of my concern.

"It is not salvageable. That's why it is so perfect. It will have to be torn down and I can make it into an outdoor courtyard, kind of like what we sat in at The High Life." Nona was grinning from ear to ear at the thought.

"Oh, my GOD! How did you not tell me this? This is amazing."

"They sold it to me for next to nothing because the city was going to make them tear the building down and the owners didn't want the expense of that. So I've been talking to local construction companies about the cost of tearing down the building and it's not as much as I thought it would be. News of the baby has kind of slowed me down, but I was thinking. Now that I have a little one coming, there's even more reason to do it. I can create a little outdoor play space in one corner so when the baby comes to work with me, they will be able to go outside and play safely." My heart was about to explode at the adorableness of a little Nona-Vance baby coming to work with her and playing outside in the courtyard kid's space.

"I love it! This is the best idea I've heard in ages. And here you are with another major design project to keep your creative heart happy."

"Yep." Nona smiled a satisfied smile. "The baking does that too. I really love finding new pastry recipes and creating new drink options for the different seasons. My creative heart is pretty happy. How's yours? Do you miss Detective Rainey K. Moody?" Rainey K. Moody was the main character in the series of gritty detective thrillers I had been writing for nearly two decades. "I know writing what Sookie kept calling 'thinly veiled memoir-turned-novels' about bigfoot is not what you had planned."

"It's not, but I'm having fun. But you asked if I miss Rainey and I really do. I've been making notes and when I get back, I'm starting my next one. I will keep going with the bigfoot stories if they take off and it looks like they are accomplishing our goal of rebranding bigfoot and cutting back on people who see them as vicious predators, but I've been thinking a lot about my mom lately. Maybe it was seeing you with your son. I was thinking about doing a little poking around again in my mom's case and giving Detective Rainey K. a cold case to solve." Nona knew all about my mother's disappearance when I was two. She also knew that I had tried to find out what happened on multiple occasions, with no success. "I've never actually put my character on the case. I don't know, maybe it's the thinly veiled bigfoot memoirs that have got me wanting to turn the mystery of my life into a story. And maybe nothing will come of it. But I would really, really love to see my mom's case solved once and for all—even if I find out she just abandoned me. Even if I find out she met a horrible end, maybe at least I could get her some justice. I don't know. It would just be nice to have some resolution." Nona was nodding with a sad, contemplative look on her face.

"I'm so sorry you had to grow up without your momma. I've missed mine every day since the car wreck that killed her and my abuelita."

"I'm sorry you lost your mother and grandmother at the same time. I can't imagine." I sighed. "Maybe this time I will have more luck. And maybe all the research I have to do on how detectives approach cold-cases will help in my search for my mom." I shrugged. "It's worth a try." Nona nodded and then spoke.

"I'm sorry, Ele. But I have got to pee—again."

"Alright by me. I could go for some hot fries." Something about a road trip made me crave strange and somewhat disgusting gas station treats that, under normal circumstances, I don't eat. I guess I got it from my Aunt Becky, she would always load us up with cheese waffies, vanilla cokes and every strange snack you could imagine on our road trip adventures.

"Ooooh, yeah, hot fries sound amazing. I haven't eaten those since I was a teenager. And snowballs! Those pink coconut-marshmallow covered chocolate cakes!" Nona exclaimed with complete enthusiasm, like the very idea of these gas station treats was the best idea in the history of humanity.

"I love those too, but why the hell are they pink? It's like the wires got crossed and the marketing department was told marshmallow and coconut and said, 'We've got it! We'll call them snowballs!' and ordered up the packaging. While some other goober said, 'We can't leave 'em white. White is boring,' and ordered up the pink food coloring. And they were on the shelf before someone realized the screw up. And yet, we all just accepted it and love to eat us some pink snow balls."

"You're such a weirdo," Nona said, laughing as I rambled on. We pulled into the truck stop. It was then that I noticed the car that had been trailing behind us pull in, too.

I yawned and stretched as the two of us climbed back into the cab after a night in a small town motel that was clean but ancient. Before falling asleep, I spent an entire hour using a sharpie marker to color the orange plastic dart gun I bought at the truck stop last night, black—making it an almost convincing handgun. I'd kept the fact that I thought we were being followed to myself until then and when Nona heard my suspicions; she was all for me making a phony gun. It was day two of our drive back to Oklahoma from NYC with all of my earthly possessions in the back of a little U-Haul—all of them, that is, that did not come with the cabin I had bought sight unseen about eight months ago. We managed a full twelve hours yesterday. As well as two bags of hot fries, several snowballs apiece, and more orange crush and vanilla cokes than any sane humans should ever willingly consume. Oh, and lots and lots of M&M's, and a few delirious giggling fits—sugar induced, no doubt. Depending on how many pit stops we made today, we should make it home by bedtime. Originally, we had intended this to be a slow, luxurious trip home, but we had confessed to one another that we were both simply ready to sleep in our own beds and what was originally supposed to be a four-day, sight-seeing adventure was consolidated into two fun-filled epic days of nonstop driving, aside from the times we stopped to relieve the middle-aged pregnant lady's bladder, of course.

"So, Ahmet said Jojo could go at any minute, huh?"

"Yeah, I'm so glad we decided to fast-track our return trip. I'm sorry I didn't just ship the shit to myself. I don't know why I thought driving it would be so fun."

"Because it is! Don't apologize to me," Nona said indignantly. "I've been looking forward to our road-trip home as much as any of this crazy trip. Even if we are fast-tracking it."

"You're right. I'm having a ball being trapped in a vehicle with you, too." I smiled at her. "But I would be heartbroken if I missed the birth. I know there's a chance JoJo will deliver on her own and she won't need Ahmet and I, but something tells me we are going to be needed. Well, at least Ahmet is going to be needed and I will do my usual tagging along."

I kept my eye on my rear-view mirror and occasionally thought I was catching glimpses of the same car that seemed to be following us yesterday and if I wasn't mistaken; it was being driven by old ferret-face. The car following us was an old boat of a Chrysler from the eighties. I'm sure it was now considered a classic, but it just looked like the stereotypical undercover detective car from every cop show of my childhood. I still couldn't be quite sure. If they were tailing us, they were good at it. If they weren't, then all the craziness I had experienced since moving to Oklahoma had taken over my brain and I was now in full-on conspiracy mode. Part of me hoped that was the truth, but a bigger part of me believed that the ferret-faced asshole was tailing us. When I pulled a last-minute exit to get to the gas station, I saw the car clearly move over two lanes to take the exit about a quarter of a mile behind us, I finally knew.

"Okay, Nona. I do believe it's showtime." She was watching her side mirror and was seeing what I was.

"It's O.B.G. time," Nona said nervously, but with a chuckle. Last night, when we were slightly delirious with exhaustion, we had developed a plan. Nona came up with the abbreviation O.B.G. which she found hilarious since she was pregnant and all it was missing was a Y and an N.

"Yep, Operation Bad Guy is on like Donkey Kong," I said, smiling and shaking my head. My stomach fluttered nervously as I put the truck in park and my "gun" into my pocket. "Let's get into position." We made our way to the side of the cinder block building to wait.

CHAPTER 6

"Alright, you sorry sack of shit! Spill it! Why the hell are you following us?" I was holding my sharpie painted plastic dart gun on the man like Bert had taught me to hold my real one. I had a gun at home that Bert had made me buy and taught me to shoot when I first moved into the wilderness and was having problems with some local rednecks who wanted to hunt bigfoot on my property, but of course I hadn't brought it with me on the plane.

"What the hell, lady?" Ferret-face dropped his cigarette to the cement sidewalk and stamped it out. He was acting far too casual for a man with a gun pointed at him. You could hear the flies buzzing in the dumpster behind the gas station where I had cornered him. The bathroom had a concrete block vestibule providing a visual barrier to the doorway of the men's room. It was there that I had been laying in wait for him. We were both in the vestibule. I suppose if he wanted, he could dart back into the restroom, but he couldn't move forward because I was standing there "on him" with my gun. He must have caught the look of fury in my eye because Ferret-face held his hands up cautiously. "Now let's not be rash here, Ms. Carmichael."

"Who the fucking hell are you? And *why* do you know my name?" I asked, pointing my gun more purposefully right at his crotch.

PSA #35: If you are going to hold someone at gunpoint with a fake gun, whatever you do, be sure and commit. And a direct aim at the crotch is a sure-fire way to rattle your captive.

"Watch where you point that thing!" He held his hands up higher. "And what makes you think I'm not just a Rainey K. Moody fan?" I looked him up and down. He did actually look like he could be a fan.

"Well, if you are, then you're my first stalker. Are you my first crazed-fan stalker? Because I don't think you are and besides, I'm not down for that shit. I will shoot you right in the nuts if you don't back the fuck off, you understand me?" He looked like he was trying to decide if he believed me. I could tell he wondered how far I was willing to take this. Little did he know that I was more than willing to shoot his ass, were it not for the minor problem that I was holding him hostage with a toy gun. "But you're not a stalker, are you? You're something else. Now tell me who the hell you are and what do you want?" As I said this, I stretched my arms more exaggeratedly directly at his ball sack.

"Listen, lady. I can't tell you any of that. What I can tell you is that you are in no danger from me, alright?"

"NOT. GOOD. ENOUGH! Why are you following us? Did somebody hire you?" It was then that Nona's voice came from around the corner of the concrete block wall.

"Ele! I think someone's coming!" I had on a big cardigan sweater so I placed the gun under my sweater and told "old ferret-face" the back-up plan that Nona and I had worked out if this were to happen.

"Thanks, Nona! Meet us at the picnic table."

"Okay, dude. There is a picnic table about twenty feet behind this building, in the patch of grass by the little doggie run area. We are going to walk there and you are going to tell us what we want to know. I have my gun trained on you and I know how to use it, so I suggest that you go quietly, got it?" I saw something like a look of amusement cross his face, but hoped I was misreading him.

"Got it," he said soberly, and the two of us made our way to the picnic area quietly and calmly. As we came out of the vestibule, a father with his small son crossed our path and gave a disgusted look, no doubt wondering what the two of us had been up to in the restroom. Ew! I gave him a disgusted look right back, hoping to make him doubt his original assumption, but smiled at the boy who was clearly doing a pee pee dance all the way to the restroom. I was so thankful that Nona had been watching. It would not have been cool if they had caught me holding this man at gunpoint.

"Sit down." I commanded, and the man sat down on one side of the table while Nona and I took the other. "I have the gun directed at your nut-sack again, buddy, so don't get any ideas." Nona burst into spontaneous giggling at this comment and I worked hard to hold a straight face. Why was I enjoying this so much? Clearly I had issues. "Now, why are you following us?"

No reply.

"Okay, let me tell you what I know. I know you were at the ISPS conference. I know you were in the restaurant where we met with Mildred Spencer. I know you were in the courtyard coffee shop at The High Life Hotel near Chelsea Market. And I know you have been trailing us since we left NYC yesterday. What I do NOT know is why? And who the hell you are. So unless you want to lose Leftie, I suggest you get to talking. And just to be clear, by Leftie, I mean your left nut." A small nervous snort escaped Nona at the mention of the man's left testicle, and I honestly felt like I was with a junior-high boy for a moment. That is probably why I liked her so much, my humor quite often ran in junior-high boy territory.

"Wow. You're pretty observant. I was also at the Suddenly Sparrow concert and enjoyed a piece of cheesecake while observing you all at Sonny's the other night, but you were having too much fun to notice me then. And I know this is not what you are hoping to hear, but you are going to be seeing much more of me, that is, if you keep paying such close attention."

"But why? Who hired you? And what on earth do they want with Nona and I?"

"Lady, I wish I knew. No offense, but you're not that interesting. I *have* gained a few pounds, however, following you ladies around." As he said this, he rubbed his belly good-naturedly.

"Hey! Hands where I can see them!" I raised my voice, and he obeyed. He seemed harmless enough. I decided to take a different approach. "Okay, okay. I can see you are a reasonable guy. What *can* you tell me? Tell you what, I'm just going to ask yes or no questions for you to respond to."

"You've been following us since the bigfoot convention. Yes?"

"Yes." But there was something about the way he said his 'yes' that made me wonder.

"Wait, were you following us before the bigfoot conference?"

"Yes."

"Shit. Shit! Shit! SHIT!"

"They weren't kidding though, you are a spitfire." Spitfire—wait, suddenly I knew. That is what Agent McGee had called me. "Have you been on us since we caught the Sasquatch Serial Killer?" I asked cautiously, my eyes narrowing, watching for even the slightest micro-expression. And there it was. "You have!"

"Yes."

"So you're with the government." I stated it as a fact. "Mildred said our governments were watching, but I thought maybe she was just paranoid. You must be with some sort of woo-woo division." Seeing that I had unraveled so much, he held his hand across the picnic table to shake mine and introduce himself properly, while holding the other hand up to indicate he meant no funny business. I hesitantly took his hand.

"Rhett Barrett—APA—Agency of Paranormal Affairs."

"Elena Carmichael—wishing you would crawl back under the rock from which you came—but I guess that's just wishful thinking on my part, isn't it?"

"Afraid so, Ms. Carmichael. But there is no need for us to be enemies. Our government simply likes to keep tabs on the people regularly engaging paranormals."

"Why Rhett, I haven't the slightest idea what you are talking about!" I said in my best southern belle accent. I wasn't sure where the hell that came from, but Nona laughed while Agent Barrett ignored me and held out his hand to shake hers as well.

"Nona Baker,"

"Pleased to formally make your acquaintance, Ms. Baker."

"And yours." Nona smiled warmly. "I feel much better about being followed by someone whose name I know."

I didn't like it. I didn't like it one bit, but it was out of my hands and there was clearly no reason to continue holding my pretend gun on his ball-sack so I pulled open my handbag that was draping over my shoulder, pulled the toy gun out from under the table and put it in my purse. "If Agent McGee sent you, I guess I can deal with that." I threw him a look. "I don't like it. But I can deal with it." I sighed. "Well, we better all get some coffee. We're planning on driving straight through until we're home," I told Agent Barrett. "So it's going to be a long day." I guess if he was going to be with us, there was no sense in keeping our plans from him.

CHAPTER 7

I was lying in my bed with Biffy snuggled up beside me, deliriously happy I was home. I could not wait until morning to see the little guy and even though it was after ten pm when we finally rolled back into Oklachito, Oklahoma, I dropped Nona off at her house and immediately went to Ahmet's place to pick up my pup. At some point, Agent Barrett had parted ways with us, so I had no idea where he was hanging his hat in our fair town or how the hell he had been able to do it thus far without us noticing or the local gossip mill getting a hold of it, but I was relieved to be rid of him for the time being.

> Thanks again for watching Biffy for me.

I texted Ahmet and immediately saw the ellipses flash on my screen while he answered.

> No problem. I think by the end he and Frank Sinatra Jr. were friends.

I laughed at this. When I picked Bif up, we caught the two of them snuggled together in a ball fast asleep and Ahmet told me of the pure fury his large yellow blue-eyed tabby cat, Frank Sinatra Jr. had displayed initially at having Bif around. At first, the cat had declared war on my poor overgrown puppy, but eventually Bif wore him down with his slobbery love, much as he does with everyone he meets. My intention was for Bif to be a bit of a watchdog for me and I like to think he will have enough of a doggy sixth sense for his inner guard dog to activate if anyone comes around intending us harm, but his big happy smile with his tongue hanging out at nearly every human (or other critter, for that matter) that he meets gives me reason to doubt this.

> Well, I'm glad they became friends. We will have to get them together for playdates.

Ahmet immediately sent back the laughing emoji and a thumbs-up. I told him goodnight and drifted off to sleep.

"HELP!"

I heard it in my bones, not with my ears. The pressing urgency pulled me from my slumber and, as I stirred in my sleep, Bif put his wet nose on my cheek to see if I was okay.

"HELP!"

It came again even more desperately, not as an actual word but as the essence of the feeling of the word—for as much sense as that makes—and this time I startled awake and sat up. Just then, my phone pinged. It was a group text from Vance to both Ahmet and me.

SASQUATCH SAVES THE DAY

JoJo needs help.

I felt instant gratitude that Nona and I had decided to push ourselves and drive straight through instead of spending another night on the road. We had all been eagerly awaiting the birth of the bigfoot twins, and with great relief, because since the capture of the Sasquatch Serial Killer a little over a month ago, all the crazy-asses that had been storming the woods to try and kill bigfoot had thankfully cooled their freaking jets. When it was uncovered that what the media had dubbed the "Sasquatch Serial Killer" was not a sasquatch after all but someone who was trying to make the murders look like a sasquatch was doing them in order to get a bigfoot hunting business off the ground (while simultaneously fulfilling his sick lust for blood), people kind-of backed off on their hunt. Especially when the rumor spread that it was actually a bigfoot that had saved Barnett Weathers, one of the last victims, from the murderer.

I'm on my way to your place, Ele. Can you meet me there, Ahmet? JoJo has already delivered one baby but she's having trouble with baby number 2 and Bob doesn't want to leave her. He's going to try and direct me through the woods mentally without coming to get us.

Vance had been friends with the bigfoot the longest, having first forged a friendship with the creatures in his early teens. He was pretty much fluent in their "telepathic tongue" or, I guess, "wave" was more accurate. If anyone could listen to Bob's instructions to weave their way through the dark forest to Bob and JoJo's home, it would be Vance.

I'll be right there.

I could imagine Ahmet throwing on his clothes and grabbing his doctor's case that I knew he was keeping stocked and ready for when the time came. I was already out of the bed, pulling my jeans on over my long johns, and adding a flannel. It was unseasonably cool tonight and felt more like winter than fall. I hated thinking about JoJo delivering her babies in the cold, but Ahmet assured me that their internal thermostat was different from ours and that she and the babies would be fine. Suddenly, I remembered it might be possible for me to send JoJo and Bob a little peace. I was learning their odd telepathic way of communicating, so I started sending thoughts of peace and joy and well-being to them as I pulled on my hiking boots and heavy canvas jacket. I grabbed the flashlight and bag by the door that I had put there just for this occasion. It was agreed upon that even though Ahmet had been attending JoJo through the last bit of her pregnancy—if JoJo could do it alone—she would. After all, this would be her third pregnancy but, of course, none of the others had been multiple births and Ahmet had warned them (with Vance's help, of course) that multiple-births could be complicated and that it might not be possible for JoJo to do it on her own. I heard Ahmet's jeep coming up my driveway and Biffy was beside himself with excitement. "You can't come with us this time, boy." I patted his head and told him to get in his crate. He dropped his head and sadly, yet obediently, went into his crate to lie down on the cushy bed inside as I closed the door behind him. "I'm sorry, buddy. Maybe next time."

I opened my front door and stepped out just in time to see Ahmet's headlights round the last bend into my driveway and to hear Vance's truck coming close behind. Just then, the excitement hit me. JoJo was having the babies–had actually already delivered the first one. Oh, my God! Oh, my God! Oh, my God! It was finally happening. I'd been having silly fantasies of being an auntie to bigfoot babies ever since we had discovered JoJo was pregnant shortly after she and I had forged our odd new friendship. Ahmet jumped out of his jeep, case in hand. He furrowed his brow and nodded as he saw I had the backpack of supplies we had prepared for me to bring. His serious expression made the silly smile on my face fade, reminding me of the seriousness of this. Vance screeched to a halt in the driveway and jumped from his door practically before his truck reached a full stop. "Let's go!" He called and Ahmet and I ran behind him, following him into the woods between our houses. We had, of course, been to Bob and JoJo's dwelling place many times in the past few months so Ahmet could check on the progress of the pregnancy, but it was so deep in the woods that we were hopeless to find it again on our own, especially at night, but apparently, Bob was leading Vance to them. I focused on two things: following Vance and Ahmet through the thick forest in the dark night, and sending peace, hope, and love to my furry friends in their time of need. We heard JoJo's cries of pain before we reached them and we picked up our already rushed pace. Finally, we were there and Bob pulled back the brush that covered their opening to let the three of us in.

It shocked me to see the room was lit by glowing orbs of light hovering near the top of the room above where JoJo lay in pain. "You have GOT to be fucking kidding me!" I thought. "The crazy lady at the conference was right?" There was no time to ask questions or even wonder at the absolute nonsense of what I was seeing. We were there to help deliver twin bigfoot babies and there was work to do. At what point does one draw the line on accepting the bizarreness of it all? Ahmet was down on his knees pulling things from his bag, asking me for items as he was already feeling around on JoJo's stomach. His eyebrows furrowed so closely together they nearly knit into each other. He looked up at the little one who was lying on JoJo's chest. A perfect miniature bigfoot lay there wriggling on its mother's chest and JoJo seemed evenly split between attending to it and to the pain of the contractions that had begun again for the second baby's birth. Ahmet examined JoJo and then looked at Elena, Vance, and Bob.

"This one is going to be a breach, but I think she can do it. Elena, could you lay out all the items like we practiced? Then I'm going to need you to hold the first baby while she delivers the second. That way Bob can help JoJo." I wasn't sure if Bob was understanding Ahmet or if Vance was translating, but Bob appeared to be keeping up to speed on everything. JoJo moaned as her contractions for baby number two worsened and Ahmet and I quickly set up the birthing area so that anything Ahmet could need was within easy reach. Then I walked up to JoJo's head and smiled at her and the baby. She gave me a weak smile back and seemed to understand that it was time. She handed the first baby to me.

SASQUATCH SAVES THE DAY

PSA #36: When given the chance to hold a newborn bigfoot—TAKE IT!

As I pulled it up to my chest cradled in my arms, its bright black eyes looked up into mine and I nearly started balling. This tiny living creature was alert and beautiful and I was already in love. It surprised me that the baby seemed to be roughly the same size as a human baby. I had expected that bigfoot babies would be bigger, but I guess there was more than one in there! The sound in the background faded as I simply comforted the small one as its mother moaned in pain. Ahmet was talking softly and kindly to JoJo, encouraging her, and giving instructions to Vance to translate. "Wait, while I make sure the baby is in a position to move forward... Okay, now push. Push. PUSH!" JoJo cried out, and I focused on the little black eyes that had locked onto mine.

"The baby's butt is out. Now, tell her to rest and breathe and when the next pain hits, to push with all her might!" commanded Ahmet. He was so determined to deliver healthy, happy babies and to get JoJo and Bob through this ordeal. We all needed good news. No more tragedies in the Kiamichis (the mountain range on which we all live). The recent murders and the public backlash had wearied us all. It was only a few moments before there was a tremendous roar that escaped from JoJo, followed by the crying of another tiny bigfoot. Ahmet laughed aloud in relief. "Well, look at you, little guy! It's a boy! What was the first baby?" asked Ahmet. "I was so busy trying to focus on getting this little fella here, I forgot to look!" I had forgotten too. I looked between the infant's legs and saw that I was holding a sweet little girl.

"It's a girl!" I said happily. JoJo and Bob were now touching and admiring their new son and Bob turned to me with a soft gaze and held out his arms for his daughter. He placed them together on their mother's chest and it was about the sweetest, most heartwarming thing I had ever witnessed. The twins were both healthy, and the mother was doing fine. Things were going perfectly, but then there was a look on JoJo's face that made us all realize something was wrong. She was in pain. "Of course," I thought, remembering that she would have to deliver the afterbirth, but as Ahmet went to work, he cried out.

"Oh momma, I think there is another one coming." Everyone's eyes went wide. And Vance told JoJo and Bob what Ahmet had said. JoJo started nodding furiously like it made sense to her and Bob immediately handed the little boy to me, then lifted his daughter from JoJo's chest and held her in his arms while JoJo and Ahmet went back into high gear to deliver a third infant. Triplets! I knew even twins were very rare in the bigfoot community, but triplets were unheard of. Bob looked like he might faint, and Vance put a hand on his back to steady him.

"You alright, there?" Vance said kindly. The little boy snuggled down into my arms. He looked like his sister but maybe a tad larger and he had more of a copperish tone to his fur. Triplets! Holy mackerel. I could hardly believe it.

The next thirty minutes were intense for us all, but they were grueling for JoJo. Ahmet had to turn the baby so that it would be in the right position and sweat was running down his face as he was manipulating her abdomen with his hands. I knew he was way, *way* out of his comfort zone on this one, but other than the sweat, he kept his cool and kept a steady stream of comforting guidance coming as

SASQUATCH SAVES THE DAY

JoJo prepared herself to push yet again. JoJo looked exhausted—weak even—and suddenly I worried about her well-being. There was no way Bob could raise triplets on his own. "Lord in heaven, please help JoJo!" I prayed instinctively. I had never been very religious, but Grandma Goosey had instilled just enough of her faith into me, that it would come out in times like this and I always found comfort in it. I watched in awe as the little baby boy bigfoot in my arms started sucking on his thumb, holding my gaze the whole time.

"That's right! You can do it! You've got it. Push! Push one last time, JoJo. You can do this." Then JoJo let out a much less ferocious roar than last time, but thankfully, with the burst of sound, a tiny being came forth into the world. But with this one there was no cry.

"Ele! Get me the small portable oxygen generator out!" I thrust the baby into Vance's hands and dug into the backpack. As I pulled it out, I flipped it on and attached the tube and the nosepiece. Meanwhile, Ahmet had evoked the smallest sound out of the tiny being's body. It was alive! Relief flooded over us all. I stole glances as I got the machine ready. It was noticeably smaller than the other two, but now that it was breathing, it was really wriggling about on JoJo's chest as she caressed it, holding it close. "Another boy," came Ahmet's relieved laughter. "And he's little but mighty!" I handed Ahmet the oxygen generator and he put the hose around the baby's ears and the phalanges in the nostrils to be sure that the baby who was originally struggling to breathe got the oxygen he needed.

I took in the room before me, if you wanted to call it that–it was really just an overgrowth of reedy weed trees that had been woven together and filled in with reeds of tall grass to make a shelter, but I had to admit it protected from the cold wind that whistled through the trees. And in the thicket of overgrown bush where their home was positioned, I realized it was almost toasty in here with all of our body heat to warm the place up. It really was rather weatherproof. I saw Ahmet's look of relief as he took the vitals of JoJo and the babies, Vance's joy-filled expression as he gazed down at the little boy I had given him to hold who was still happily sucking his own thumb, and Bob and JoJo whose heads snuggled together as they took turns gazing down at the newest addition to the family and then at the baby in Bob's arms and then over at the child who was with Vance. Vance moved closer and held the little one in so they could see him fully. Once Ahmet had determined that everyone was healthy, he started wrapping things up. Bob, Vance, and I moved out of the way, each holding a child, while Ahmet assisted JoJo in delivering the afterbirth. And before I knew it, JoJo seemed to be revitalized by finally having her expected little ones with her, and an extra one to boot! She was alternating nursing two at a time while Bob held the third when we excused ourselves. Vance gave them instructions to reach out if they needed anything. I would have stayed longer, but the truth was we were lucky to have been here at all. It was time for them to do things their way, without human intervention.

As we came out of the hut, the dawn surprised me. "You think you can get us back to my place?" I asked Vance, and he told me that in the light he was more confident that he could, but that Bob was listening in case we got confused and he would guide Vance when necessary.

We walked in companionable silence. I looked over at my two friends, who each wore soft contemplative smiles. We were all a bit in our own worlds after such a strange sacred experience. As we broke out of the woods into my backyard, I realized I was far too excited to go back to sleep. Vance was texting, with Nona most likely. "You guys want to stay for breakfast? Or at least for a cup of coffee?"

"Nona's one step ahead of you! She offered to bring the extra batch of pumpkin cream cheese muffins she just pulled from the oven. Chloe came in this morning to bake with Nona so that she could learn the fall recipes, so Nona asked her if she would mind running the shop while she slipped out for a bit. I think she and Bert are dying to hear everything." I unlocked the back door, and we all sighed at the cozy warmth. "Oh my God, that sounds amazing. I'll start the coffee, tell her and Bert to hurry up!" Ahmet was tending to the whimpering, quivering crate in the corner. He opened the door and Bif leapt into his arms. Or at least tried. I could hear Ahmet chuckling and loving on my puppy, who was really more of a gangly teenager, as I started making coffee and pulling coffee cups, cream, and sugar out, and placing them on the table. I still like to use a French press but I bought a second larger one since I was having guests with fair regularity these days. It was so strange that since moving from NYC to this small rural Oklahoma town, I seemed to have a bigger friend group here than in all my years there. I guess that's one thing being involved in a secret society devoted to the preservation of and service to bigfoot will do for you; it creates an instant bond and a tight friendship. Because you sure-as-shit want to keep that bit of crazy a secret. Before I knew it, we were all sitting around the table–me, Nona, Vance, Bert, and Ahmet–drinking coffee and eating the best pumpkin cream cheese muffins known to man while Vance, Ahmet, and I took turns telling them of our morning's adventures.

"Oh Nona, they were so sweet. Tell her, Vance! He held one too." Vance and Nona were holding hands, and Nona's other hand was resting on her baby bump that was becoming more and more pronounced by the day, by the minute, if you asked Nona.

"It's true." Vance said with a tired smile. "They are very sweet."

"I just can't believe she had triplets." Nona said again in disbelief. "No wonder she was so big. You called it—Ahmet—last summer. You said she was growing much more quickly than seemed right. Lord, I can relate to that. They say older mothers often have multiples. If bigfoot standards compare to humans, I would say JoJo is an older mom as well." Ahmet laughed.

"Well, thank you for recognizing my astute medical awareness. But I think you're growing just right. And yes, JoJo is an older mum as well. You guys will have fun raising babies alongside one another. Vance, did you ever tell Bob and JoJo that you all were expecting?" Ahmet asked curiously. Vance blushed.

"No, I haven't gotten around to it."

"I can't wait to see them," said Nona. "You think they will let me?" Vance shrugged.

"Your guess is as good as mine. JoJo, and by association, Bob, have been way more social since Ele moved to town. Anything is possible. Ele might just get that auntie fantasy she's been playing out in her mind."

"Oh, shush!" I knew my face was turning red. It was a tad embarrassing by how invested I had become in both JoJo's pregnancy and now Nona's. "I know... I know... I'm pitiful."

"Hey," said Bert with a smile and an encouraging wink. "No shame in a little baby fever, Ele. Libby and I could never have kids, but that woman would hold any baby that came within a hundred-mile radius of her if given the chance. And sometimes, the chance didn't even have to be given. She would see a weary momma and just end up with their baby in her arms, all the while offering them an encouraging word and whatever help she perceived they needed." A melancholy love-sick look covered Bert's face and then he shook his head, releasing whatever haunted him in the memory as his usual cheerful demeanor returned.

"Yeah, Ele. I'm sorry," interjected Vance. "I was just teasing. I don't really think you're pitiful." Vance seemed deeply mortified at the possibility that he had hurt my feelings.

"Oh, you didn't hurt my feelings, but thank you. And thanks, Bert. I was just embarrassed because it was true! It's ridiculous thinking JoJo is going to let me babysit and dress her babies like dolls." I admitted.

"Well, maybe not dress them," Ahmet ventured. "But there are three of them. I don't know what kind of community they have, but I can't imagine that they won't need at least a little help."

"I agree," said Vance. "I don't know what they will need or how we can help, but I feel like they might need us now more than ever."

"OKAY!" I suddenly remembered the glowing orbs of light hovering at the ceiling of the hut. "What the HELL were those balls of light?"

"What balls of light?" Ahmet asked sincerely.

"Yeah," Vance joined in. "What balls of light?" And I threw him a look that could kill. I could see Ahmet not noticing as he was a little tied up, but there was no way in hell that Vance hadn't had time to see them.

"WHAT BALLS OF LIGHT?! You have got to be kidding me!" Anger must have been flashing dangerously in my eyes because Vance immediately cut in.

"I am... I am... Yes, there were orbs there for the delivery." He said this with a special look to Bert that made me wonder what the two of them knew and were not telling me.

"Holy moly!" Bert said breathlessly. "Really? You got a good look at them this time?"

"Wait! *This time?* You guys knew about the orbs of light when I was mocking the lady at the conference, and you said nothing?" I asked incredulously.

"Well," Bert began slowly, "in fairness, we've only seen them once before and it was from quite a distance, so we thought maybe we were seeing something else, something that we didn't quite understand."

"Yeah," agreed Vance. "We are as baffled by the possibility as you are, Ele. Since we were truly not sure what we saw and it was from a time we don't like to dwell on, we didn't see any point in mentioning them—the woman at the conference was bat shit crazy, after all." At this, Nona laughed aloud. She had been listening intently to everything we were saying. She looked at me and shrugged.

"Further and further down the rabbit hole we go," she said and smiled at me happily as she popped the last big bite of her pumpkin cream cheese muffin into her mouth.

"When did you see them before?" I demanded. I wasn't going to just pretend like one of the freakiest fucking things I had ever seen did not just happen. "What 'time-that-you-don't-like-to-dwell-on' did you see them before?" I pushed further and Bert gave Vance a long look until Vance heaved an enormous sigh.

"After Mac died," Vance said stiffly. "Actually, right after Mac died and his family came to take him away. We were watching as his father carried him off and just as they were blending into the trees like they do—you know what I mean," Vance said assuredly. I did. I have watched it in utter bafflement many times now. It was almost like they would disappear, so skilled were they in blending into their surroundings. "We could still hear Mac's mom and JoJo crying, though, and just make out their figures when suddenly three yellow balls of light appeared around them. And then they all disappeared. Even the lights and so—" Vance stopped talking and Bert picked up where he had left off.

"So you can see why we couldn't quite trust ourselves. Even though we both saw the same thing. We had just suffered from the most traumatic experience of our lives. And it was just for a flash that we saw them before everyone was gone from our view." Bert shrugged. I nodded my head and finally whispered.

"Thanks for sharing that with me. Sorry I pushed." I saw Nona reach up and lay a comforting hand on Vance's shoulder. Even after all this time, Mac's death still haunted the both of them.

"I still can't believe there were orbs of light in the room with us for the deliveries, and I didn't even notice." Ahmet was shaking his head in disbelief. I smiled at him.

"You were just a tad bit busy."

CHAPTER 8

"I tapped on his window and Agent Rhett Barrett looked up from his Louis L'Amour book and rolled down the window and smoke rolled out at me. I coughed a little and waved the smoke out of my face. The cigarette hung from his lips and he placed his well-worn paperback novel on the dash. Nona sent me out to his car with a fresh cup of coffee and a muffin, which I handed through the window to him and he took gratefully. "You know, you might as well come in where it's toasty and warm since we already know you are out here."

"Nope."

"You did in New York City." I pointed out.

"That's because you were on foot. I had to be too. You might have jumped on a subway at any moment and lost me. I needed to be able to follow you easily."

"I still don't understand why you are even here. You have got to be bored out of your gourd."

"Listen, don't you worry about me. It's a pleasant break from chasing rogue vampires down the back alleys of New Orleans at 3 am." My head snapped back to look at him and he smiled. I couldn't tell if that was a joke or if he was serious. I shrugged.

"Well, if you get tired of sitting out here or just need a bathroom break, Nona says you're welcome inside." Agent Barrett pulled a ten-dollar bill out of his wallet and I turned away without taking the money. "She also told me not to take your money. Guess she likes to feed her stalkers." I said over my shoulder, shrugging again, and walked away. I glanced back to see the smallest hint of a smile on the smoking ferret's face. Nona was waiting for me at the front door when I came back in. She had been watching the whole thing.

"He won't come in, huh?" She asked as the door closed behind me, the bell tinkling as it did. It was just the two of us. I had been writing and when I got up to take a break, she mentioned taking the agent out some coffee, so I offered.

"Nope. He says not to worry about him. He said this is a much better gig than chasing rogue vampires through the streets of New Orleans at 3 in the morning." Nona's eyeballs leapt out of her head just as mine had. "I think maybe it was a joke... I couldn't really tell. And well, hell's bells. After the orbs, I don't know what to think anymore. Maybe vampires are running the streets of New Orleans at night."

"Do you think he is watching Burt, Vance, and Ahmet, too, or do they have their own agents? And have you noticed him out at your place at night? Because I haven't ever noticed him around mine. You think he is off duty in the evening? Maybe since we live here, they're confident we're not going to pull a runner or anything. Maybe he gets to rest nights." Nona pondered.

"Maybe he uses drones to watch us at night." I speculated.

"Why?" This alerted Nona. "Have you seen drones around your place?"

"No. But they would be less noticeable than a dude in a car now, wouldn't they?"

"I'm not sure how much they even knew about Bert and Vance—until the conference, anyway. But surely they have someone watching Ahmet. Since he was the key to the Sasquatch Serial Killer case. If someone's watching us, someone has to be watching Ahmet."

"I'll have to ask him if he's seen anyone. Our land shares a property line, but his property is further up the mountain than mine and his driveway goes out on the opposite side of the mountain. I'm never over there so I wouldn't notice a surveillance vehicle even if it was there. Unless, of course, they decided to spy on us from our own properties, but they would have to walk in and I don't think even the government is likely to do that. Not unless they really thought we were up to something."

"Like setting up a 'Sasquatch Sanctuary?'" Nona said with a smirk.

"Shit! You think they know about that?"

"You said he was there at the restaurant when we met with Mildred." Nona pointed out. She looked thoughtful for a moment. "What do you think it would take to break him down? He was smiling when you walked away today."

"I saw that too. Maybe if we, well, if you–keep feeding him. He'll soften and tell us what we want to know."

PSA #37: When you are being followed by the Agency of Paranormal Affairs, it is a safe bet that giving the agents free pastries and coffee will eventually win them over. Worst case, you fatten them up and they can't catch you when you run.

"Maybe..." said Nona. "I don't have any better ideas. Hey, have you heard anything back on all of that? Is the guy going to sell you the land or what?"

"I haven't talked to Bert about it yet since we've been back. He said he would call him again, though. I'm also dying to go see the babies again. I wonder if Vance has heard anything from Bob and JoJo."

"Not that I've heard, and I always forget–I haven't told him about Agent Rhett Barrett yet," Nona laughed. "I sound like Dr. Seuss."

"I know, get this! Before I knew his name, I started calling him ferret face and the smoking ferret and then he introduced himself and he was suddenly Agent Rhett Barrett, the smoking ferret. It's too lyrical and just too weird, don't you think?" I asked as Nona chuckled and nodded her head.

"Some things are just meant to be, and with that face, I'm afraid that man's name was his destiny," Nona said with a big, lopsided grin. Just then, Chloe and Abby came in.

"You wanna see if Chloe will keep an eye on the place while we go talk to Bert and Vance?" I looked out the window and saw that both of their vehicles were at the office.

"Chloe, do you mind watching the place for a little bit?" Nona asked.

"Sure thing," Chloe said. She was already behind the counter making the two of them drinks. Nona gave both Chloe and her partner all their drinks and pastries on the house, which I thought was a very generous perk. So, of course, they came in every day, but in fairness, they were nearly coming in every day before Nona hired Chloe. That's what made Nona think of her when she was looking to hire her first barista.

Nona and I headed out the door and she waved to Rhett, who lifted his cup to her and nodded. Mountainside Realty was just a short small town block away from Nona's place, and we walked over. When we came in the door, the two of them looked up and Vance stood up to embrace Nona and give her a quick peck.

"With the excitement of the birth of the triplets, we forgot to tell you about the special agent who is following us." I decided not to beat around the bush. Bert laughed, at first thinking it must be a joke, until he saw the look on our faces.

"Holy smokes! You're not kidding, are you?" I walked to the door and looked down the street. Agent Rhett Barrett, the smoking ferret, was still sitting where we had left him. I crooked my finger at the two of them and all four of us stood looking out the door as I pointed him out. Just then, he rolled down his window and the cigarette smoke billowed from his car. As the smoke cleared, we could see that he was looking right at us and so we all waved.

Agent Barrett lifted his hand in a wave and went back to his Louis L'Amour book.

"Who is that? And why is he following you guys?" Vance asked protectively. "And why do I think there must be a story to why he doesn't seem to be surprised that we know he's there?" I gave him my most mysterious grin.

"That's because there is."

By the time we finished telling them about our hijinks with the smoking ferret 70s private eye following us in NYC and then home—leaving out none of the juicy bits about holding him at sharpied dart-gun-point—they were wiping their eyes from laughter and shaking their heads. "One damn thing is for sure," said Bert.

"There has not been one dull moment since you got here, Elena Carmichael." I smiled because I could tell Bert didn't mind the mayhem that had apparently arrived with me.

"So we were just wondering if you had noticed anyone following you guys?" Nona asked. "He said he's from the Agency of Paranormal Affairs and we were wondering if they had men on you guys and Ahmet as well." They both shook their heads.

"Nobody," said Bert confidently. Vance nodded to confirm this.

"What about drones?" I asked impulsively. And Vance's head bobbed up and looked over at me.

"I have been seeing one of those around town, but I'm pretty sure that it belongs to the McFarland boy. They are getting so affordable. I know I would have wanted one when I was a kid if something that cool had existed."

"That might be all it is. It probably is just kids. I don't know... I was just thinking that if they were going to manage any spying on Ahmet, they would almost have to use a drone since he rarely leaves his place and they couldn't bring a car on the property or even near the property without him being aware. That and Nona and I noticed that Agent Barrett is nowhere to be found at night, so we wondered if he might watch via drone then. I'm probably just being paranoid now, but we do not want them spying on us with drones in our woods. I don't want them to be aware of the babies."

"Well, I think we are probably fairly safe on that front," Bert interjected. "A few years back, I looked into using drones to make videos of these mountainside properties we sell and found out that our forests here are not conducive to drone footage. They can film from above the trees, but just seeing a bunch of treetops didn't seem to help our sales any, certainly not enough to merit the cost. The woods are just too dense, and the kinds of trees that are growing have too many spindly branches that can get in the way." Nona and I heaved a visible sigh of relief, and Vance and Bert both smiled at us.

"Okay," I said. "Well, that makes me feel better. The idea of them finding out about Bob & JoJo's triplets terrifies me, or worse yet, that they already had. Speaking of which, have you all heard anything? And more importantly, when can we go see them?" I was dying to see the little ones again. I picked up flowers this morning for JoJo when I ran to do some big shopping to restock after being gone. "Poor Nona hasn't seen them at all yet."

"I reached out to Bob this morning and received back an 'all's well.' So as far as I know, all is well." Vance told us, smiling. "I don't know if they want company or not, but I will ask and see what Bob says." Nona's eyes lit up at the idea and I can only guess that mine must look like a kid in a candy store. Pitiful. I had never been one of those women who swarmed babies. Middle-age was doing a number on me.

"Great!" I said. "Now, Bert. Have you heard anything about the land?" At this question, Bert came to life.

"I just got off the phone with Ron Dobson a few minutes ago. I was about to call you when you all walked in. He's been looking into it and he says that the only reason he hung onto the property after his father died was for the tax break and to honor his father's wish that the land be kept pristine and undeveloped. Well, since I told him the first time we talked, that was your wish as well, and since he discovered that the tax break wasn't much of a break at all, he said to tell you he has to check one more thing with his accountant but he just might be willing to sell. So you are one step closer and a whole helluva lot more likely to get it than before." Bert said with a flourish. This was a man who loved real estate. He loved wheeling-and-dealing. He loved bull-shitting. And he simply loved the good earth that made up the Kiamichi mountain range he most often sold. I was thrilled.

"Well, I guess we just stay the course and wait and see. Thanks, Bert, for being persistent."

"Well, of course. It's usually just a matter of letting someone sit on the idea of selling for a bit, let it simmer and before you know it, it was their idea!"

"So," Vance said, changing the subject as he looked out the front window at the agent down the street. "What are we going to do about him?"

"Our tactic has been to try to befriend him," said Nona. "But I don't know how well it's working. He does occasionally crack a subtle smile, but he is by no means our BFF yet." Vance smiled at Nona's use of the best friends forever acronym.

"Well, then we will follow your lead. Why don't you ladies introduce us?" Bert put on his cowboy hat and the four of us headed out the door down the sidewalk, directly to Agent Rhett Barrett's vehicle. He laid his western novel down on the dash and snubbed out his cigarette in the car ashtray when he saw us coming, grabbed his jacket from the seat beside him, opened his door and got out of the vehicle pulling his jacket on as he walked to the front of his car. Bert, in true Bert fashion, walked toward him, held out his hand, and started chatting him up.

"Well, how the hell are ya?" Bert was in full good-old-boy mode and it cracked me up. Not that he isn't a good old boy, he is. But watching him turn on the charm to a special agent was somewhat amusing. "The girls here were just telling us we have a new friend in town." He held out his hand for a handshake as he approached Agent Barrett. "Bert Russell, Mountainside Realty. It's damn nice to meet ya." They shook hands and Agent Barrett introduced himself stiffly, but cordially. You could tell he was much more comfortable being invisible and the over the top friendliness of Bert seemed to put him off his game.

"Rhett Barrett. Nice to meet you, Bert." He turned to Vance and held out his hand. Vance reached out and shook his hand.

"Vance Hill, nice to make your acquaintance."

"And yours," said Agent Barrett.

"I've got to get back to work, gentleman. You coming with me, Ele?" Nona looked at me as she turned.

"Yes, ma'am. These books don't write themselves." I smiled and nodded a farewell to the three men. Two of which) Vance and Agent Barrett) looked incredibly awkward while Bert seemed happy as a clam.

"Agent Barrett, you need a top up on your coffee?" Nona asked before we headed out.

"No thank you," he replied quickly, "but thanks for asking." I could tell he was not sure quite what to do with all this hospitality. He looked a bit like a cornered animal. Ha! Served him right–stalking us as he was. We walked across the street and entered the coffee shop to find Finnegan O'Leary at the counter. Finnegan's ancestors migrated in the mid-1800's to the United States during the great potato famine in Ireland, information I knew because I was often still working when he would come in and let me tell you, that man has the gift of gab. Nona always says, "Bless his heart. His wife died a few years ago, so the poor soul must be terribly lonely." Finnegan had to be hitting ninety, but he had recently discovered Nona's coffee shop and had quickly become a regular. Coming in every afternoon before closing for whatever pastry Nona had left and a cup of black drip coffee. About half of the time, Nona gave him the coffee for free because she would be throwing it out soon, anyway. And she would usually throw in an extra pastry or two if she had leftovers. He was chatting Chloe's ear off and it was amusing to watch Chloe and Abby as they interacted with the older man. They were nice kids, you could tell by the way they visited with Finnegan. Chloe was talking to him about his grandson, Jacob. Apparently, Jacob was a "good egg", at least according to Chloe and Abby, which seemed to please Finnegan immensely.

"Chloe, thank you for covering me!" Nona pulled the day's tips from the jar. You mind if I just give you the tips instead of clocking you in? I knew the tips for the day would far outweigh what she would have paid Chloe hourly and Chloe tried to refuse them saying it was no big deal and she didn't have to pay her at all, but Nona would hear nothing of it and forced the cash on the young woman.

"Well, thank you!" she told Nona. "It was nice seeing you, Mr. O'Leary," Chloe said as she grabbed her coffee and pastry to go and she and Abby headed for the door. Watching them go, I noticed that Bert, Vance, and Agent Barrett seemed to be in a deep discussion across the street. "Leave it to Bert," I thought with a smile and glanced at the clock on the wall above the counter. There was a little less than an hour before closing time to wrap up the research I was hoping to finish today, so I sat down and put my nose to the grindstone.

I just started my new Rainey K. Moody novel and the in-depth study into how investigators approach cold cases was already proving to be enlightening. I'd been thinking so much about my mother who I couldn't remember–a mother who I knew loved me but had disappeared when I was only two years old, leaving me in the care of my Aunt Becky. How can you miss someone you have no actual memory of? I had no idea, but you could. And I did. I had always missed her and it was this deep sense of loss that had always been a part of my very being that I had channeled into my writing when I first started writing the Rainey K. Moody novels. But somehow, I thought that by now, nearly twenty years after publishing my first book, I would have some kind of resolution, some kind of peace about my mother's death's death, but there was no resolution. No peace. Just quiet resignation. Shitty things happen to good people. Shitty things happened to my mother. Shitty things happened to me. But for some reason, I could not stop believing that if I could only know what "that shitty thing was" that took my mother from me, that it would bring some kind of redemption to me. I longed for the redemption I gave the characters in my books. I hoped against hope that when Rainey K. Moody solved this cold case, I would have some kind of peace about the cold case that had overshadowed me my entire life. Pulling out my phone, I dialed a number I had memorized as a child–the Boone, Iowa police station and asked to be put through to the detectives.

"Detective Puckett," came a deep baritone voice.

"Hello," I said, suddenly uncertain of my impulsiveness to call. "Umm... My name is Ele Carmichael, and I wanted to check in on my mother's cold case."

CHAPTER 9

Matilda Finch was standing at the top of the stepladder. All ninety-six pounds of her stood directly on the little warning label that said NOT to stand on the top step of the ladder. I was handing her the last of a pile of books to place on the top shelf of the newly improved reference section she was working on. When I had arrived to drop off some new bookshelves for the children's section, she had been scrambling up and down the stepladder. She was placing the older, more out-of-date encyclopedias up there. They would likely make it to the annual library book sale before too many more years, but for now, they would go to the top shelf. Encyclopedias were an outdated format for information now that we had the internet, but were they, really? Is it not nice to have this information somewhere in printed form? And believe it or not, in this small slice of rural Oklahoma, there were still people who did not have internet service in their homes. And of course, there were people like me living deep in the woods that could only get very expensive satellite internet that was sometimes hit or miss. When I saw my first bill, I wondered how on earth people here could afford it, anyway. The simple answer was–they couldn't. And so they used their phones, which were also spotty. And when they needed to get on the internet on a computer, they came to see Matilda to use the library's computers, or they resorted to doing things old-school and looked for what they needed in the reference section–in (gasp) books. Ever since the "I Love Bigfoot Festival," I had been volunteering as often as I could at the library. When I first offered, Matilda wasted no time giving me a slot to show up and work in and it had become a ritual I looked forward to.

"Birdy!" I heard Bert's voice ring out right after the tinkling of the bell over the door. "You in here?" He sounded so happy. "I've been missing my little Birdy!" He called out again, and I watched as Matilda's face and neck turned red as she scrambled down from the stepladder, wasting no time, calling out.

"We're back here! Elena and I are in the reference section!" She had said my name rather forcefully. It was almost as if she were telling him to shut up, that they were not alone. It was Bert's turn to blush as his head popped around the last row of the nonfiction stacks.

"Well, hello there, ladies! Ele, I didn't see your car." It looked like perhaps Bert was finally moving forward after losing his wife over five years ago and the color of his face indicated he was not quite ready for anyone to know. I decided to have mercy on him and refrain from teasing. As much as I wanted to start crooning, "Bert and Matilda sitting in a tree—K-I-S-S-I-N-G…" I would resist. The last thing I wanted to do was to spook my friends out of the potential of newfound love.

"I parked in the back so we could unload the new shelving for the kid's section that came to my house by accident because I forgot to change the delivery address from my place to here when I was ordering." I explained, feeling very pleased that he was unaware of my presence until it was too late to reveal what the two of them were up to.

They were looking quite uncomfortable, so I said simply and directly, looking from one to the other.

"I'm not exactly sure what I'm witnessing here, but if it is even remotely in the realm of what I hope it is, all I can say is—I'm tickled pink. Now Bert, since you're here–would you help Matilda and I unload the boxes? You, my friend, showed up in the nick of time." I smiled at Bert and then the three of us got to work unloading boxes.

I walked into Coffee O' Clock to see Nona and Vance leaning in together over the countertop, talking intently with one another. They startled as the bell rang.

"Hey, Ele!" they chorused when they realized who it was.

"Hey yourselves!"

"Guess what?" the three of us asked in unison.

"What?" Nona asked, laughing.

"No, you guys go first." Nona looked at Vance and nodded for him to tell.

"Bob and JoJo invited us all out to see the babies. Bob reached out to me just a little bit ago. I messaged him the other day asking if we could come sometime." It cracked me up that Vance used the word "messaged" regarding his telepathic outreach to Bigfoot Bob, like he was sending him a text, but I was too excited to tease him about it.

"Really?" I had been dying to go see them and also trying very hard to respect their privacy and not to nag Vance. "When?"

"Nona and I were just talking about whether it would be better to go today at 5 when she closes or at daybreak tomorrow morning."

"Oh, let's go tonight! Have you talked to Ahmet or Bert? Speaking of which–" I said suggestively. I was now smiling from ear to ear, and I could tell both Nona and Vance wondered what the heck was up.

"Oh, yeah! You had something to share, too. I forgot," said Nona. "Was it about Ahmet?" she was now the one being suggestive.

"No, silly! It's about Bert."

"Bert?" Vance's head turned at that. He had been texting the two of them to see if they were available tonight. I smiled.

"Yep. And Matilda," I said this last bit in a sing-songy voice. Nona gasped aloud and then grinned from ear to ear. "Really?" she asked excitedly.

"Well, I don't know for sure–" I told them the whole story, and they both agreed that it did indeed seem as if something was going on. Vance was smiling too.

"Matilda is a sweet one. She makes sense," said Vance. "It also explains where he keeps mysteriously running off to."

"She does make sense, doesn't she?" agreed Nona. "I think Libby would approve."

I heard Vance's phone buzz. "Well?" I asked.

"Bert and Ahmet are in for tonight. We will meet at your place at 5:15 if that's okay with you, Ele. I don't think sunset is until about 6:30 so that should give us plenty of time and the nightfall will keep us from overstaying our welcome," answered Vance. He seemed as excited as we were, which made me smile.

"I don't know–if the orbs are there again, the darkness might not be a problem," I joked while simultaneously in a mental battle over whether I hoped the orbs were there or were not there. They definitely pushed things into an even deeper realm of crazy. Vance was shaking his head in a way that indicated that he believed the orbs would most certainly not be there. "Well, I'm going to head home and make a big pot of stew and some crusty rolls, then. We can all have dinner after we go see Bob, JoJo and the babies! I'm glad I bought dried flowers this time. I'm going to take JoJo a bouquet. You think we should take them some meat or something?" I asked.

"That's a nice idea," said Vance. "I'll see what I can come up with." I waved farewell to the two of them and headed home to get ready for the night.

As I came out of the door, I couldn't help but glance nervously in Agent Barrett's direction. I did not want him to know what we were up to this evening. Inspiration struck me with an idea that I felt just might keep him away. It was a bit risky, but Bert and Vance said that Agent Barrett had been very cordial yesterday until Bert had tried to push things into more friendly territory by asking him to join them at the local diner for dinner that night. Agent Barrett had gone extremely cold and said, "I am not here to make friends." If I did NOT want him to come watch us, maybe the best thing to do would be to invite him to. After all, we wouldn't be up to anything with paranormals if we were inviting him to join us, would we? I headed in his direction and saw him release an aggravated sigh and start rolling down his window. I could see one of Nona's to-go cups on his dash so I knew she had been moving forward with our plan to woo information out of him by plying him with food and drink.

"Hello, Agent Ferret, I mean–Barrett." Holy fuck, Ele! Get your shit together. If he noticed, he was choosing not to acknowledge my mistake.

"Ms. Carmichael."

"I was just wondering–I'm having a few friends out for dinner tonight and wondered if you wanted to join us." He heaved another big sigh.

"Ms. Carmichael, it's like I told Mr. Russell yesterday. I am not here to make friends with you. I am not your friend. I wish you all would go back to ignoring me. I swear if headquarters knew how much you all were engaging me, they would take me off your case in a heartbeat. So, no. No, I will not be joining you for dinner this evening." I paid close attention to my poker-less face and intentionally put on a disappointed expression to avoid looking too pleased that I had accomplished what I wanted.

"Well, alright then. We don't want to get you in trouble with your bosses. Does this mean you don't want Nona to bring you out coffee and treats?" At this he looked startled and I could tell that this was not what he meant at all and I gave him a big grin.

"Don't worry," I winked at him. "I won't say a thing. If I know Nona, she'll keep 'em coming. But the rest of us will try to stop being so friendly." At this, he gave me a curt nod and started rolling up his window. I turned my back to him and couldn't help but let a grin overtake my face, but I focused very intently on not allowing a spring into my step as I made it over to my old lime green FJ Cruiser. As I headed out, I noticed his car pull out behind me, but it turned and went west so it looked like my inspiration really had worked!

On my way home, I stopped to get gas, and I was filling my tank with my head in the clouds when I heard a lazy drawl I hadn't heard in a while. "Well, if it isn't the uppity, Ms. Carmichael," came Abner Crawley's voice from the next pump. Why the hell wasn't I paying more attention to what I was doing? "Better be careful. I might get ya'. Aren't you breaking your own restraining order? Or maybe you like me more than you let on?" What a fucking creep this guy was!

"Nope. My bad." I immediately stopped pumping gas and put the nozzle back on the pump. I was waiting for my receipt to print out when he poked his head around the corner.

"Just so you know," he said, in a cross between a growl and a whisper. "We're not finished with you." Just then, my receipt printed out, and I grabbed it, jumped in my vehicle, and drove away. As I looked in my rear-view mirror, I could see him watching me go and laughing, and a chill ran up my spine.

Biffy barked happily, and I knew that my first guest must be coming down the road. I decided to put that afternoon's experience in a box and look at it later. There was too much to be excited about right now. We were about to see those beautiful babies. Cooking always calmed me and the house was filled with the delicious aroma of the stew that was warming on the stove. There was a pan of crusty rolls sitting on the stove ready to be popped into the oven to warm when we returned. The table was all set and two bottles of my favorite red wine were sitting on the island, ready to be opened. I loved entertaining. I looked at the clock and saw that it was 5:14. As I glanced out front, I saw three cars coming up the drive, one after the other. Apparently, everyone was as eager as I was to go see the babies. I grabbed my bouquet of dried flowers with a piece of jute wrapped around them in a bow and headed out front to join my guests. Biffy tried to push past me as I opened the door and I just barely kept him from slipping through my legs. "Sorry buddy. You better get in your crate for this." I knew if I let him stay outside there was no way he wouldn't follow us and if I let him greet our guests, I would play heck trying to get him back inside.

"You'll see everyone soon," I said as my dejected pup whimpered with his head and tail drooping to the floor as he went into the crate and I shut the door behind him."

I greeted my friends, who all looked as happy as I felt. Ahmet was carrying his doctor's case. I had my bouquet of dried flowers for JoJo, and Vance had a big lump of something wrapped in butcher's paper.

PSA #38: When invited to Bigfoot's home, always bring gifts.

"Are you all ready?" Vance asked. "JoJo is excited that we are coming." The sun was just starting to make its way toward the earth, but there was still a good hour or so of daylight left as we made our way into the woods. We all followed Vance, who I could only assume was following Bob's lead. After a bit of a trek through the woods, I heard Nona let out a little shriek in front of me and looked up to see what had inspired it. Bob was suddenly standing there before us, with an infant in his arms. He motioned for us to follow him as he headed into what I was now recognizing as their home, but what to the untrained eye simply looked like a very overgrown thicket of trees, bushes and brambles. I knew from my previous visits that it was hollowed out on the inside. Bob pulled at the opening that was completely undetectable unless you knew where it was and we followed him inside. When we entered the dimly lit space (there was an opening at the top where light could enter) JoJo greeted us warmly. She sat on a fresh mat of dried grasses that I was guessing they replaced regularly, like one would straw in a stable. It was odd to imagine what their everyday life looked like. It smelled mustier (and honestly, a little stinkier) than I had noticed before, but there were three new little bodies living in the space now.

In her arms were two beautiful tiny bigfoot that were close to the same size. I looked at Bob and realized he was holding the smaller son. JoJo and Bob both looked exhausted, but happy. I lifted my flowers to show JoJo and then laid them at the foot of her mat and she smiled warmly at me and I was flooded with a sense of joy.

Bob motioned for us to sit, which varied greatly from any previous visit. This was clearly a social call. We had never had a social call with them before. Bert, Vance, and Ahmet looked around awkwardly and then lowered themselves to the ground. Just then, JoJo's eyes rested on Nona's steadily expanding middle and opened widely. She looked at Nona and then Vance and then Nona again and then beamed. Nona nodded shyly, smiling in return. It was then that JoJo motioned for Nona and me to hold the babies if we wanted. There was no need to communicate telepathically. JoJo could easily tell that I did from the eagerness I exuded. We each took a baby from her arms and lowered ourselves to the floor closer to JoJo and then Bob sat across from us, so we formed a lopsided circle around the room. As JoJo released a baby into each of our arms, she leaned her head from side to side as if stretching a sore neck and shoulders and I heard her neck pop. It was such an oddly human gesture that it took me by surprise. I lowered myself to the floor and sat in what we used to call "Indian style." That was certainly no longer a politically correct term, however. What was it called now? Criss-cross, applesauce? When I gazed into the eyes of the little one who was intently gazing back at me, I let out a giggle of delight. And everyone in the room laughed. Even Bob and JoJo heaved silently in what looked like laughter, but was soundless. I could tell Bob was engaging Vance in conversation. And by the way he was looking from Vance to Nona, I had a pretty good idea what it was about. Nona looked as smitten by the tiny bundle in her arms as I was. Bob offered the baby he was holding to Vance to hold, but Vance was already holding a package, so he offered the child to Ahmet, who grasped the little guy and began looking him over real good. Just then, Vance remembered the bundle in his arms and handed it to Bob, who unwrapped it. It was a giant uncooked brisket. Bob's eyes went large and I could have sworn I heard his stomach growl. He nodded in thanks to Vance, who took the paper Bob was handing him back and folded it and put it into his back pocket as Bob rose and worked the piece of meat into some branches that they appeared to use as a shelf of sorts. I had a pretty good idea the two of them would feast when we left, and that made my heart happy. JoJo picked up the bouquet and looked at it admiringly, and I felt another rush of warmth and goodwill wash over me.

The little girl I was holding had taken hold of one of my fingers and was clinging to it for dear life. It was the cutest thing I had ever seen. I hadn't been around many human babies in my lifetime. I babysat briefly in my teen years for a neighbor but the child had been a toddler and I'd had a few girlfriends over the years whose babies I had held, but as is usually the case when people have kids, our lives headed in different directions and I hadn't ended up spending very much time with them after their children were born. Neither Sookie nor Evie ever had children and so I was very inexperienced. The baby wriggled in my arms and so I lifted the tiny form onto my shoulder and JoJo nodded encouragingly. It snuggled in and as I cricked my neck to look down at her, I watched in utter fascination as she began sucking her own thumb. I watched as Ahmet passed the little one he was holding to Vance, who gingerly took it into his arms. Nona had a look of total bliss as she cradled the small infant in her arms, and then she looked at Bert.

"You want a turn, Bert?" Bert looked afraid, but eager, and both Nona and Bert looked to JoJo for permission. JoJo smiled at Bert and nodded, and Nona carefully transferred the small being into Bert's awaiting arms.

Vance and Bob were clearly communicating with one another, even though Vance didn't take his eyes off of the child. And it looked like Ahmet was engaging with JoJo, but since most of our communication with them was telepathic, it was hard to tell for sure.

"You want to hold the little girl?" I asked Nona.

"Yes, please!" Nona answered eagerly, and I transferred the baby to Nona's arms. I found myself stretching my arms and rolling my neck as well. How were the two of them doing this 24/7? They had to be utterly exhausted. Before too much longer, two of the three babies started to grunt and squirm, and we realized they must be hungry. Their hunger coincided with the realization that the room was much darker than it had been when we arrived.

"We better get going," Vance said as he handed the squirming little bundle of love to JoJo, who eagerly scooped up her child and began caressing its little face with her fingertip. Bert handed over his bundle to Bob and Nona gently placed the little girl into JoJo's other awaiting arm.

"Thank you for having us," I said to Bob and JoJo aloud, but also trying my best to send the telepathic equivalent to them. They both nodded warmly to us as everyone extended the same thanksgiving for their hospitality. We exited their home and Vance headed assuredly and quickly in what I assumed was the direction of my home. We were all silent for a while as we followed Vance. Finally Nona said reverently what we were all thinking.

"I can *not* believe that just happened."

CHAPTER 10

We were all leaning back in our chairs, our stomachs full of beef stew and crusty rolls, our wine glasses empty, and our hearts full.

"This evening was like–," I paused, searching for the right word, "–*sacred*." As it passed my lips, heads bobbed up and down in agreement around the table.

"It really was." Vance spoke, which since he usually kept his thoughts to himself, we all listened especially intently. "I don't know if you all realize how unique the last few months have been." He was addressing this mostly to Nona, Ahmet, and me. "I mean, Bert and I swore ourselves to their service. What—nearly forty years ago?" Bert was listening intently, looked contemplative, and then nodded and shook his head in disbelief at how much time had passed. "And they have certainly reached out to us off and on over the years. As Ahmet knows, Doc Crenshaw helped us over the years when there was a medical emergency and when he died, it left us in a real hurt until Ahmet started helping. But the truth is, our interactions with the bigfoot were always very brief–just long enough to deal with the wounded foot or whatever the problem was–we haven't experienced friendship with them since Mac died." Vance's eyes were brimming with tears as he spoke. "I never thought we would see a day like today." He quickly rubbed one eye with the back of his hand in an attempt to mask his tears. Nona's arm was on the back of his chair, her fingers running circles on his back. There was such an intimacy there. Had I ever felt that kind of intimacy? Aunt Becky was physically demonstrative. She was a hugger. And I'd had one boyfriend in college that was a toucher, but while Doug was warm and I knew he loved me, I didn't think he had ever made such an intimate act of physical comfort toward me. It made me happy for them and a bit melancholy for myself, which was absolute silliness. Bert was nodding reflectively and spoke.

"Vance is right. This is not normal, folks. Nothing has been normal since JoJo first brought you flowers, Ele. It's like the child JoJo, who used to spy on her big brother Mac and us playing in the woods, intentionally decided to befriend you, Ele. And we are all getting to experience the fruit of that friendship. I mean, I've heard a lot of stories from a lot of people over the years and I read things–but I've never, ever heard or read anything like this. Usually the stories don't get past the interaction you had on your first night here, Ele."

I laughed. "What? You mean them scaring the shit out of me?"

"Yeah," said Bert. "Things like rocks being thrown on the rooftop to scare people away. Maybe even a small rock hurled at a person walking through the woods in a warning. Of course, there are the tales of trees broken across pathways in the woods to block the ATV's being able to get through. I once even had a fella tell me about waking up and discovering that they had placed his ATV in the tree branches above their tent during the night. But people almost never interact with them. Most are rarely even 100% sure that they've actually seen one, their interaction having been so brief that they begin to distrust their own minds and memories. There are the tales of seeing them for a split second as they cross a road or path in front of someone but never intentional interaction with people. Like Vance said, I've never experienced or even heard of a friendship with the creatures since our friendship with Mac forty years ago and since that didn't end well, I don't think Vance or I ever expected anything like that to happen again, at least not for us."

"I am glad to be hearing this." I said, shredding my napkin to keep my hands busy. "Since my relationship with JoJo and Bob escalated so quickly and has been quite hands-on in nature. I mean, Bob did rescue me from my kidnappers and carry me twenty miles through the woods while he was bleeding out–I think my perception may be skewed a little." Nona giggled at this and everyone around the table smiled at me, not mockingly, just amused.

"Maybe just a little," Nona said.

"Bob said their relatives are on their way. They are planning on setting them up on the Dobson's place, so they will be close by, but not directly in the woods between Ele and Ahmet." Vance said, filling us in on a little of what he and Bob had been discussing.

"I was catching some of that," Bert said, nodding. "I wish I was better at picking up their language. I feel like I'm hard of hearing when we talk to them. Vance can hear every word and I'm like a half deaf old man with them."

I wasn't sure if JoJo and Bob lived on Ahmet's place or mine. I think it was pretty close to the property line in the stretch directly between our two cabins, regardless. There were no fences out here. It's difficult to build a fence on a mountainside. And it should be unnecessary, but

I was seriously considering it when the Crawleys and other bigfoot game hunters kept trespassing on my property a few months back.

"The Dobson's place is perfect. Hopefully, they will agree to sell to me soon. Bob and JoJo's family may be our first unofficial sanctuary transplants. Have you told Bob what I'm wanting to do?" I asked Vance, suddenly wondering. It had never occurred to me that Vance may have spoken to them about this.

"Actually, I did today. When Bob told me where they were going to recommend that their relatives stay."

"What impression did you get from him regarding that?" I was curious.

"Mostly confusion," Vance said honestly. "They still have a hard time understanding the concept of owning land as it is. To them, it's just the earth and no one can own it. They get that people's houses are theirs, but I do not think they see the woods they live in as belonging to you or Ahmet and so for me to explain that someone else far away owns that property and that you are going to try and buy it was a very abstract thought for Bob, I could tell. But they definitely understand the concept of more and more people encroaching on land that for centuries they have been able to roam freely on. When I got through to him that you wanted to keep it free of people so that bigfoot could live there and more bigfoot could come if need be. He seemed to feel positive about that."

"I got to tell you though, Ele. I hope you don't think your sanctuary is going to be like your life with JoJo and Bob."

"I don't!" *Did I?* God, I was starting to wonder what I thought. This whole sanctuary thing had really been more an act of intuition than anything else. That, and preservation, both for myself and for my bigfoot friends. I like that I can hole up like a hermit in my cabin in the woods when I want. I don't want more neighbors, whether they are friendly or not, and I sure as shit did not want bigfoot hunters for neighbors, so if I could somehow get the Dobsons to sell me the property, then I could maintain my "hermitude" when so desired and also help keep my furry friends safe.

"I don't think most of the creatures are going to want to interact with you in any way." Bert said, and I nodded, taking it in. I think it's possible I have a strange view of what a sanctuary would be like. My God, they weren't my pets. I don't think I was letting my brain go there, but the whole thing was so damn weird. I needed to be sure that I understood that I was buying land so that I could leave everyone the hell alone. That my role would simply be occasionally restocking the pond or woods with game if need be. I wasn't opening a paranormal zoo. I wouldn't be building them huts and throwing neighborhood parties. I thought I should probably give Mildred Spencer a call sometime soon and talk to her more in depth about what running her sanctuary entailed. Biffy had had quite enough of this serious talk that did not involve him getting loads of love and attention from my friends, so he started yipping and wagging his tail and making the rounds around the table, asking for the affection he so rightly deserved. Of course, everyone was glad to oblige him. He was currently getting a good rubdown from Ahmet, who looked up to Vance and asked a question as if he had just remembered it.

"Did you ask Bob yet?" Of course we were all wondering, 'Ask Bob what?' except for Vance, who answered.

"I did. He said he thinks he will do it, but he's still working on him." Finally, I couldn't stand it any longer.

"Ask Bob what? He thinks he will do *what*?" I sounded like a nosy child, and Bert and Nona's smiles implied they thought so too, but I could tell they were glad I was the one butting in so they didn't have to.

"Well, if you must know, Barnette asked me again to find out if the sasquatch who saved him would be willing to meet him so he could say thank you," Ahmet filled us in.

"You mean JoJo's dad? The big guy?" I asked incredulously. It felt a bit miraculous that he had intervened on Barnette's behalf at all. After Mac's death, it seemed he would refuse all interaction with humans. This time, Vance answered.

"Yes, it's actually pretty interesting and might explain a little bit why they let us into their lives today in such a personal way. Bob and JoJo believe the future is going to require human allies. They believe things are moving quickly in the direction where, in order to survive, they are going to need people like us who want to help. I think it is why JoJo befriended you, but that may have just been because she wanted to. It was certainly why Bob was okay with her befriending you and likely factored into his willingness to risk his own life saving you from the kidnappers. Bob said he thinks JoJo's dad is realizing the truth in it too. And every time Bob mentions to him how Barnette is doing and that he still wants to meet him, he seems to soften to the idea more." It was so strange to think about Bob giving his father-in-law (or the bigfoot equivalent of) updates on Barnette. I hadn't even realized that Ahmet and Vance were giving Bob updates on Barnette. It also made me feel good that Bob and JoJo were seeing a need to make human allies. I mean, it was sad that it was coming to this for them, but I was happy to be an ally. And I was happy that I was already thinking of providing a sanctuary for them, because I apparently wasn't the only one who saw the need for it. It sounded like even the bigfoot thought it would be helpful. A wave of contentment filled the room.

"That was delicious!" said Bert, and the others voiced their agreement while I cleared the dishes. Nona jumped up to help, and I motioned for her to sit and gave her a wink. "Thanks, Bert. This evening has surely given me a lot to think about." Switching gears, I said, "Okay, I didn't have time to make a dessert, but I have coffee and a tub of ice cream if anyone wants any." Bert looked at his watch.

"I better get going," he said, not saying why, but I couldn't help wondering if it would involve a visit to a certain librarian. He must have read my mind, because he blushed ever so slightly before he stood up, thanked me again for the meal, and gave me a big hug and Bif a pat on the neck before he headed towards the door. I had a thought to offer to send a bowl of stew with him to Matilda, but thought better of it. It was getting a bit late for dinner and as far as I knew, Bert didn't know I had told Vance and Nona about him and Matilda and I didn't want to breach that topic now.

"We should get going, too." Nona yawned and stretched in her seat. I knew she had been up since the butt-crack of dawn. "But are you sure you don't want any help cleaning up?" She looked around and realized it was almost done.

"Nope. There wasn't much to clean up, anyway. I'll just put the stew pot in the fridge and eat the leftovers tomorrow," I said, smiling. "I'll deal with that pot later!"

Nona laughed. "What's the old adage? Never do today what you can put off until tomorrow."

"Yep." I said, smiling at my friend. Her middle was expanding daily, and she definitely looked pregnant now. It hadn't been any time at all since we had returned from New York City and in that brief period, she had gone from looking like she had an expanding middle-aged waistline to clearly being pregnant. Vance and Nona were on their feet now and Vance was bent over, giving Bif a good farewell rub. I hugged Nona and waved my hand in farewell to Vance as they headed for the door as well.

CHAPTER 11

"Well, looks like it's just you and me. Care to have a bowl of ice cream with me and watch that new British cop show that just came out?" I knew Ahmet wanted to see *DCI Dunkirk* as much as me because we had already talked about it. Ahmet liked British TV as much as I did, and so he readily agreed. "Coffee?" I asked as I was pulling out the tub of ice cream and laughed. "It's English toffee. Looks like it'll be a proper British evening–perhaps I should offer you tea instead." I was doing a crap accent and laughing as I started scooping ice cream into bowls.

"I'm good–" Ahmet smiled. "No coffee or tea for me. But absolutely yes to the ice cream." I carried our bowls into the living area and sat down on the sofa with Ahmet, carefully placing our ice cream bowls onto the coffee table in front of us, just as Ahmet was clicking onto the *DCI Dunkirk* episode playlist. "Have you watched any of it yet?" Ahmet asked before clicking on episode one.

PSA #39: If you have not yet partaken of the pleasure of British television, give it a good go. You might just discover that the slow burn is your favorite kind of burn. I know it is mine.

"No, have you?"

"Nope, I've been going to, but I haven't had a chance." At that he clicked play and the slow melodic theme song set an ominous tone. Images of an everyday-kind-of-handsome Detective Chief Inspector Dunkirk filled the screen, flashing images of the character from different angles usually looking intense or introspective. It is one of the things I like about British television, everyone is not required to be movie-star gorgeous. They let everyday handsome people participate and still be leading men. Heck, they let just plain homely folks be *leading* characters—not just character actors—and I think it's fan-freaking-tastic. It seems in American television, if you are ordinary looking, or, God forbid, *"ugly"*—your only shot is to be a character actor. That's dumb. I happen to be a fan of everyday-handsome and homely and is anyone truly ugly, or are they just interesting to look at?

As the show started painfully slowly, I sighed. This was my happy place. I have no idea why I love the British detective shows like I do, but I glanced over at Ahmet as I scooped up a bite of ice cream and he had a child-like grin on his face which made me realize I too had a silly smile covering my mug. It had been a pretty exciting revelation to discover we both liked the same British programs. I, of course, did not limit myself to the mysteries and cop shows, but simply felt that I must have been born into the wrong country. If it was British, I probably liked it. Ahmet said he preferred cop shows but when I threw out the names of some of my other favorite programs from other genres, he enthusiastically said again and again, "Oh that's a good one too!" until I realized the man was as big of an Anglophile as me. Biffy came into the room and bounded up onto the couch in between us, seemingly afraid he was missing something.

SASQUATCH SAVES THE DAY

"Sit! Sit, boy." I instructed, and I noticed Ahmet giving him a hand signal and Bif immediately laying down and putting his head on Ahmet's thigh while Ahmet laughed and lifted his ice cream bowl out of the way. We settled down onto the couch and finished both our ice cream and the episode sitting this way. Unlike American cop shows, which involved a ridiculous number of explosions and unlikely car chase scenes, it was, of course, a slow burn. And I was already hooked.

"You want to watch another one?" Ahmet asked, hitting pause before it could roll right into the next.

"Absolutely, but–I wanted to ask you something," I hesitated, and he turned toward me, as did Bif, who laid his little doggie head on my lap now. "Do you think I'm crazy?"

"Crazy?" Ahmet seemed confused.

"Well, not crazy. But, like, dumb?" I was feeling a sudden overwhelming wave of insecurity regarding the bigfoot sanctuary idea. "Well, not dumb, I guess." For someone who made their living using words, I was being particularly inarticulate. "I feel like maybe I'm an arrogant fool for pursuing this sanctuary idea. Like who the hell do I think I am–*rescuing* the bigfoot? They have somehow managed to stay hidden to the point of being thought of as mythical creatures for all these years. I don't think they need my dumb ass trying to protect them and build them communities." Ahmet's face softened. I could tell he was starting to understand that I was being buried by my own insecurities and self-doubt.

"I don't think Bert or Vance meant to make you feel that way at all," said Ahmet kindly, "but—you weren't really planning on building a community, were you? Like constructing homes for them?" He placed a comforting hand on my arm that was resting on Bif, who was sitting between us. Ahmet took a deep breath and looked at me anxiously, perhaps afraid of what my answer was going to be. I laughed, shocked that he could even wonder that.

"God, NO! I didn't mean that. I just–" I was at a loss for words again. But thankfully, Ahmet wasn't.

"I think everyone who is brave enough to do something new, something unusual, something selfless—has moments of doubt like you are having right now. I do not think you have a hero complex and are trying to impose yourself into their world. And yes, you may have conflicting ideas of what creating a sanctuary is going to look like, but let's face it. We spent our evening as guests to a family of bigfoot, bringing presents and celebrating the birth of their triplets. You're receiving some mixed messages here, cut yourself some slack. You did just spend an hour holding bigfoot babies as the sun slowly slipped from the sky and the approaching darkness made us all realize it was time to leave. That is not normal, Ele!" Ahmet laughed, and I started feeling a little better, like less of an idiot. "Besides, you heard Vance—Bob and JoJo think they need allies like us." This thought made me smile.

"Thank you. Sometimes I get too 'in-my-head' about things. I just got to wondering why the hell I wanted to do this, anyway. When Bert tried gently to tell me that things would be different with the new bigfoot who would come to the sanctuary than they are with Bob and JoJo, I started to question what my actual expectations and motivations were. Truthfully, I haven't given much thought as to how it's all going to look and work."

"Well, I think that is because you don't need to. You are not building a community for them. You're not making a zoo. You're simply purchasing land that will be safe for them to exist on. Land that you will keep undisturbed so that they can get on with living their lives in safety. I think not thinking about it is the best thing you can do." I gave him a grateful smile. Somehow, he knew exactly what I needed to hear to be reassured. I suddenly remembered Agent Barrett.

"Hey, I forgot to tell you! I have someone following me."

"What?" Ahmet's head spun around and he looked me straight in the face in surprise.

"How could you forget to mention that?"

"Well, we haven't seen each other since I've been back. I mean, other than when you were a little busy delivering bigfoot babies and then tonight, so there hasn't been a chance."

Ahmet, who usually forgot he even had a cell phone, lifted his phone up and looked at me pointedly. "I didn't want to talk to you about it through a text or a phone call, because I wanted to ask if you've seen anything unusual. I think it is likely you have someone following you, too. Have you seen anything unusual?"

"Okay, wait! You can't just dump that on me without further explanation. Who do you think is following you?"

"Agent Rhett Barrett from the Agency of Paranormal Affairs,"

"Wait, what? You've talked to him?"

"Yeah," I launched into the entire story about seeing him at our lunch with Mildred Spencer and then again in New York City. "Remember when I was in Chelsea at the coffee shop and said I thought I saw someone—that's who I was seeing."

"That's why you suddenly acted so strangely, I wondered about that later," Ahmet listened and laughed as I regaled him with the story of Nona and I confronting him at the truck stop and then how Nona keeps sending me out to his car with coffee and pastries as he sits in his car across the street from Coffee O'Clock chain smoking and reading paperback western novels.

"So he actually told you that Agent McGee was behind this?" Ahmet was absolutely gobsmacked.

"Well, not exactly. But he mentioned that 'they' were right, that I really was 'a spit-fire' and I called him on it because that was exactly what Agent McGee had called me the night I lost my shit at the police station." By the look on Ahmet's face, I thought he was going to roll his eyes at the memory, but instead, he let out a big sigh and a chuckle.

"I would say spit-fire was putting it lightly. You were an atomic bomb. But–" Ahmet was now understanding why I suspected he was being followed as well.

"Now you understand," I said. "That's why I asked if you've seen anything unusual. If they put someone on me, they most certainly put someone on you." I could see Ahmet's wheels turning. Finally, he spoke.

"There is this lady," he said. "I keep seeing her and wondering what on earth she is doing? The first time I noticed her, she ducked behind a bush, which was totally strange, but I decided she must have dropped something. Then I saw her at the grocery store and it was like she was constantly in the same aisle as me."

"Anywhere else?"

"Actually," at this admission, I think Ahmet might have been embarrassed that he had not already figured out that she was following him. "She was parked at the side of the road across from my drive. When I stopped to ask if she needed help, she told me, 'No, no... I have someone coming.' So I went on my way. I feel like an idiot."

"Don't feel bad. It would never have occurred to me either, except we were traveling and you can't see the same person over and over in different cities and trailing your car on the interstate and not start to wonder. If it had happened here, I wouldn't have thought much about it. It's a small town. Have you seen her in the last couple of days?"

"No, not since you guys have been back, actually."

"Maybe Agent Barrett is officially on all of us and she was just covering you while he followed us."

"Maybe. This is so weird. Why do you think they want to follow us, anyway?"

"That's what I asked and Agent Barrett told me they like to keep an eye on people who they know are having regular interaction with paranormals."

"How do they know we are still having interaction? Can we just lie and get them to go away?"

"I don't know. I was wondering the same thing. Wait. Did Agent McGee ever give you a card?" I asked, struck with sudden inspiration. "Maybe we can ask him to–"

"Call off his dogs." We said in unison. Whether this was at the mention of canine-kind or the fact that we were saying things in unison, Biffy got quite excited about this and began moving from one of us to the other, licking our faces.

"Oh, good grief. Bif! Sit!" Again, Ahmet made a hand motion and Bif obeyed. "So are you going to teach me this sign language you've got going with my dog or what?" I asked, half amused, half annoyed.

"Oh, yeah! Sorry. I wasn't trying to keep it from you. This means–" he made a flat motion with his hand and moved it in a downward motion and Bif immediately laid flat on the sofa between us again.

"Not now. One thing at a time. Don't you at least have Agent Brothers info?" Bif's immediate obedience to the hand gesture impressed me, but I was also irritated by all of this. Why were we enduring people following us?

"I do. But let's think about this before we hastily contact McGee & Brothers to try to get them to leave. Have you ever seen Agent Barrett out here?"

"No," I said. "Which is weird, don't you think? I asked Vance and Bert if they had seen any drones around and Vance had seen one in town a few times, which really upset me because you know if they were using drones in the woods they could discover the babies," Ahmet was nodding, looking concerned as well. "But Vance and Bert seemed to think that was just a kid playing with a toy. Bert told me that he and Vance had tried to use drones for promotional videos for property sales a few years back, but the woods around here were too thick and all they could really get were aerial videos from above the trees. That they would end up damaging the drones trying to get footage from underneath the canopy of the trees. Anyway, have you seen any drones in our woods?"

"Don't you think I would have led with that?" Ahmet answered dryly. "Rather than with a slightly overweight woman in sweats following me around grocery stores and ducking behind bushes?" I laughed.

"I guess so. Yeah, probably. So—no drones, then?" He didn't deign to reply, but I could see that little dimple starting to quirk in his cheek, so I knew I was not not actually annoying him, but he was about to smile. "That would be a no then."

"No! For crying out loud, Ele. No," he was now openly grinning at me.

"That is a good thing."

"Yes, very good."

"So why don't you think we should talk to McGee and Brothers?" I asked seriously.

"Maybe the fact that we are not seeing drones is why. Neither of us has seen anyone in the woods. The closest they seem to have been to our properties is one potential instance of a would be spy or soccer mom sitting at the side of the road across from my driveway. If this is how they are going to watch us, then I think they are going to get bored pretty quickly, don't you?" I could see Ahmet's point. I was clearly someone who liked to address issues head-on, but I didn't want to make this worse.

"Maybe you're right. Agent Barrett seems to be far more interested in sitting across from Nona's coffee shop smoking and reading his paperback novels than anything else. Maybe the smartest thing we could do is continue to reaffirm that there is nothing worth watching. I got the impression that he was treating following us around like a bit of vacation. What is that? Better the enemy you can see than–er, the enemy you know–er?"

"Yeah, something like that." Ahmet laughed. "Do you want to watch another *DCI Dunkirk* or not?"

"Yes, but after all that talk, I think I want another glass of wine, do you?"

"I'm good."

"Hey, I forgot to tell you," I started as I set our ice cream bowls in the sink and poured myself a glass of wine.

"What?" Ahmet asked almost warily, like what else could I possibly pull out of my pocket after revealing to him that we were being followed?

"It's not a big deal, but they are reopening my mother's cold case. Well, *reopening* it may be a bit of a stretch, but I'm working on a new Rainey K. Moody novel about cold cases and when I was doing my research, I got an itch to check in with the Boone City Police in Iowa–where my mother's cold case is–and well, there's a new detective who seemed interested in taking another look, so," I shrugged self-consciously. I hadn't told anyone about this, not even Nona, but I wanted someone to know. It's not likely anything would come of it, but there was the smallest glimmer of hope that I might be closer to finding out the truth. I couldn't help being excited. Ahmet jumped up and made his way towards me. I was so startled I almost spilled my wine and I placed it on the counter as he wrapped me in a big bear hug.

"Ele, that's great! That's fantastic!"

"Really?" I asked, somewhat shyly. "You think so?"

"Yes, very." He replied as he let me go and I picked up my glass of wine.

"Are you sure you don't want anything else to drink? I think I still have a few beers."

"Nah, I still have some ice water, I'm good." He shook his head and muttered, "Not a big deal..." He smiled at me again. "This is a very big deal." We walked back to our spots on the couch and plopped back down but because Biffy had gone off to play, we were side by side and as Ahmet grabbed the remote to hit play on episode two, his arm brushed mine and I felt his warmth and my insides warmed as well with the contentment of this unexpected friendship.

CHAPTER 12

I was standing at the vanity in the bathroom putting on make-up when I heard a voice that made chills run up my spine. The morning talk show I was listening to had switched to its hourly news update, and it only took six words for my hair to stand on end as I rushed into the bedroom to see who was speaking. This was the face behind the Tortoise mask. It was a scrawny, sickly looking young man with dirty dishwater blond hair and dark circles under his eyes, thirty years old tops, standing before a judge on a murder case and for whatever reason they had shown the clip of him saying "Your honor, I plead not guilty." Those six words were all it took for me to know. It was him. It was Tortoise-boy. I was sure of it. He had been one of my kidnappers–the one with the blabber-mouth. The one who had sounded like the younger of the two. The one who was always asking questions. The last time I heard his voice was when Bigfoot Bob and I were hiding behind the door of the cabin, about to escape. I will never forget the words he said, "I don't know why you're so worried about me saying your name. I thought we were killing her." Well, if this man was pleading "not guilty," I would bet it was a lie. If it weren't for the perfect timing of Bigfoot Bob, I too would be dead by this man's hand.

I quickly scrawled down the words on the bottom of the screen, "Bradley Cox Pleads Not Guilty for the Murders of John and Megan Staples." I sat down on the bed for a second, mascara wand still in hand, and wondered who I should call. Sheriff Struthers had been the man investigating my kidnapping case, but he was dead. And because of Ahmet's role with the serial killer case, I now had contacts with the FBI. Not to mention my little ferret-faced shadow, Agent Rhett Barrett, who was probably sitting across from Nona's place right now, waiting for me to show up. The only time I had seen Agent Barrett parked at the end of my driveway was on a day when I'd decided to write from home and I suspected he had driven down the driveway just far enough to see my lime green FJ Cruiser through the trees and then backed his way back to the entrance because I had heard Biffy barking earlier that morning but never knew why. My mind bounced back to the issue at hand. "Who should I tell?" I asked myself, speaking aloud to an empty room, which made Biff's tail begin tapping the floor. He had turned his little head sideways as if to ask, 'Who ya talking to?' which made me laugh out loud. My heart was racing. I headed back to my bathroom to finish putting on my face.

Ever since our time in NYC with Sookie and Evie, I had been trying to make more of an effort with my appearance. I felt better about myself when I dressed a little sharper and put on make-up. As soon as I finished, I grabbed my bag, my phone, my keys and called my dog. Bif was finally getting big enough and obedient enough to come to the coffee shop with me. I only planned on working at Nona's until about noon today anyway, and then I was going to help Matilda at the library for a bit and Biffy loved it there. But before we went anywhere,

I wanted to talk to Ahmet. I dialed him as I opened the cruiser door for Bif and he hopped in.

"Hey, you got a minute?"

"Sure. What's up?" Ahmet sounded ever so slightly winded, like he was walking.

"Do you mind if I swing by? You're not going to believe what just happened."

"Sure, come on over," came his winded response. "I'm almost back to the house now. I've just been on my morning trek through the wilderness." Ahmet said good-naturedly.

"Trek through the wilderness, huh? Well, how did that go?"

"Like it does everyday. No new monsters to report."

"Excellent." I said, pulling out of my driveway onto the highway, turning the opposite direction from town so that I could head up the mountain towards Ahmet's place rather than down the mountain into town. "See you soon." I hung up smiling and patted my pup on the head, running my fingers through Bif's soft fur was an instant stress reliever. It was no wonder companion dogs were sometimes prescribed for folks with anxiety. As I rounded the bend and came nearer to Ahmet's drive, I noticed a standard issue 90s something four door Buick LeSabre parked by the entrance to Ahmet's driveway. Something told me the Agency of Paranormal Affairs must be extremely low on the government funding totem pole. These cars were tipping into vintage status. Sure enough, there was what looked like a chubby mom in a tracksuit bending over into the back seat, digging for something. She scrambled to attention when I turned past her into the drive and I saw her grabbing her phone to take pictures. I smiled and waved.

PSA #40: When given the chance to mess with the Paranormal Agents that are following you and your friends, just. Say. YES!!!

It was likely I was the first visitor Ahmet had had since she had been watching. After making my way down Ahmet's half-mile drive, I saw him standing out front, smiling and waiting for me. Bif was bouncing around the vehicle like crazy now. He hadn't been over here since his stay and he was clearly eager to be back to visit. As soon as I opened my door, he pushed his way across my lap and jumped out and ran up to Ahmet for his morning love. Good grief. If he wasn't so cute, I would find him terribly obnoxious. Ahmet didn't seem to mind though and, per usual, was giving him a thorough pat down.

"Good morning!" Ahmet called, standing back up to talk to me while Bif went running after his big yellow tomcat, Frank Sinatra Jr. who clearly was down for a chase. "So, what happened to you this morning? I've been racking my brain trying to imagine what could have possibly happened this soon in the day."

"I just heard Tortoise-boy on the news. His name is Bradley Cox, and he has just pleaded not guilty for the murders of John and Megan Staples."

"Wait! What? You mean one of the guys who kidnapped you?"

"Yes! I was listening to a morning show on TV as I was getting ready this morning when the news interrupted it as it always does and one moment I was putting on my mascara and the next moment I was having flashbacks to my time in captivity. I know it's him. I just know it."

"Did you call the police?"

SASQUATCH SAVES THE DAY

"No. I wanted to talk to you about that. Do you think I should just go straight to Agent Brothers and McGee? I mean, since Sheriff Struthers has passed away? I guess the deputy who took over for Struthers worked on my case too, but that guy doesn't seem like the sharpest tool in the shed, if you know what I mean. I just want to be sure that something gets done."

"There's another thing–" Ahmet interjected. "What if he tells the truth?" I was confused.

"Wouldn't that be the best-case scenario?" I was not following.

"The whole truth?" He raised his eyebrows and stared at me, waiting for me to understand. Suddenly, it hit me. If this Bradley Cox fessed up, he might divulge that a bigfoot was involved in my rescue, which would just further entangle me with the Agency of Paranormal Affairs, who I was currently trying to convince were wasting their time on me. If their suspicions were further confirmed that our little group was in regular contact, we would never be free of them and neither would Bob, JoJo, and the babies.

"Shit. I didn't think of that. Of course, he might not say anything. It will just make him look crazy if he does."

"Wouldn't being declared insane actually be an improvement to where he's going to go if they convict him of murder?" Ahmet was right, an insanity plea might be just what he was looking for right now and if this Bradley bozo had taken to murdering people, I did not want him to get off. And yet I wondered. I remembered how miserable the kid had sounded at the idea of killing me.

"He said he had never killed anyone before. Maybe he is actually innocent. Maybe they would let me see him and talk to him privately. I could try to convince him that mentioning Bigfoot Bob would be a big mistake. I can't bear the idea of not telling anybody, though. Especially if he really did murder those people. Which, honestly, what reason do I have to believe he didn't? If Bob hadn't intervened, he would have murdered me."

"I guess the advantage to talking to Agent McGee is that he already knows Barnett's account that a bigfoot saved him. He won't think you're crazy if the truth does come out. And let's face it, Sheriff Struthers all but told us they had found inconclusive DNA evidence on some of the blood and hair found at the crime scene. That's why he wasn't very helpful to you after he realized you were withholding information from them." I gasped.

"THE DNA! You're a genius. I can't believe I didn't think of it. I'm pretty sure the Sheriff told me there was DNA evidence from both me and another individual (aside from the dead kidnapper's body that was found) which should match Bradley Cox if I'm right. And of course, you're right. That mystery DNA of Bigfoot Bob's blood and fur from his gunshot wound seemed to give Struthers a license not to pursue my case further. How do I know his deputy won't see it the same way? But if they have DNA from this Bradley Cox guy in my case, they may have already linked the two cases together without my help."

"Maybe, but I wouldn't count on that. I think you're right, Ele. Your best bet would be to try and talk to Agents McGee and Brothers about this, since we already know them. This is so weird, just last night I was wondering if anything was ever going to happen in your kidnapping case or if it would forever remain a mystery." Ahmet had already pulled his phone out. He'd pulled up Agent McGee's number, so I took the phone and pushed the call button. It surprised me to hear a warm voice emit from the speaker on only the second ring.

"Dr. Pamuk. To what do I owe the pleasure?" Agent McGee asked.

"Oh, this is me, Ele. Elena Carmichael–Ahmet is here though. He just already had your number programmed in. Um.. I was wondering if it would be possible to discuss something with you. I think I might have evidence on a murder case. I don't know that the FBI is involved, but I would really appreciate your guidance." This seemed to surprise the agent. Maybe they hadn't pinged Bradley's DNA on my case then, or if they had, the FBI was unaware.

"Well, sure Ms. Carmichael. Oddly enough, I'm actually free later this morning. Wanna meet me for coffee at Coffee O'Clock?" Of course, he would suggest this. He knew I was there all the time anyway, and he probably talked to Agent Barrett occasionally too, if they were allowed to talk between agencies.

"Why, Agent McGee, how ever did you know where I was planning to be?" He rumbled a low chuckle at my cheekiness.

"One has their ways, Ms. Carmichael. One has their ways. I'll be by around 11:00 if that will work for you."

"It's perfect. Um–do you mind if—?"

"Dr. Pamuk is welcome, Ms. Carmichael," Agent McGee answered before I was able to ask my question. It made me laugh.

"Thank you. See you at 11." I hung up and turned to look at Ahmet's expectant face.

"He's meeting me at Nona's at 11:00." Ahmet nodded. "And he said you could come." I smiled, and Ahmet let out a small laugh.

"Do you mind? I don't have to... but I'd really like to if you don't mind."

"Now, who's the nosy one?" I joked. "Are you kidding me? I invited myself to every one of your appointments when you were dealing with the FBI. I went as far as to get myself arrested, if you remember."

"Oh, trust me. I remember."

"Of course I don't mind you coming. I was about to ask when he answered before I could. Anyway, Biffy and I better get going so I can get some work done before we meet. Bif?" My pup was nowhere to be found.

"Don't worry. I'll find him. I'm sure he's off playing with Frank Sinatra Jr." Ahmet said, looking around the yard. "Hey, do you want me to just bring him with me when I come to town at 11?" I looked at my watch. If I wanted to get some work done, I needed to get hoppin'.

"Are you sure you don't mind?"

"Not at all."

I headed into town, thinking how strange it was going to be to see Agent McGee again. Soccer mom agent at the end of Ahmet's driveway was gone when I left and I realized I forgot to tell him she was back. I pondered whether it was better to reveal to Agent McGee that we knew we were being followed or not. It's possible that Agent Barrett had revealed it in his reports, but for some reason, my gut said he had kept our encounters to himself.

Coffee O' Clock was swamped this morning, but the universe was conspiring on my behalf because the gentleman who I like to tag team with on "our" table was just gathering his things when I came in so I proceeded to put my things down as he picked his stuff up. After exchanging our usual niceties with one another, I headed for the counter. Nona looked tired but happy. "What can I get you?" She had those heavenly pumpkin cream cheese muffins in the case again, so I ordered one of those and a vanilla latte.

"I know you're busy, but I'll give you the short version so you don't flip out when you see me meet with the FBI in here later," I had Nona's attention. She stopped on the espresso machine and openly gawked at me, nodding for me to get on with it. "I heard the voice of one of the kidnappers on my morning news."

"What?" Nona asked incredulously.

"I know. It's crazy. But the one who would always wear the Tortoise mask and talked too much, who accidentally shot the Hare in the struggle when I escaped, was on the news pleading not guilty to the murders of two people. So, I went to see Ahmet, and we decided since Sheriff Struthers was dead anyway, that I should talk to the FBI first and see what to do."

"Wow–just—wow." Nona said again as she started back up on the espresso for my drink. "Good grief, Ele. That's big news, keep me posted on what happens with the FBI." I looked around the crowded room.

"You look busy."

"God, it's been a madhouse here all morning. All the people doing the Oklachito Scenic Drive to see the changing leaves must have seen that magazine article naming us as one of the fifty best destination coffee shops that are 'worth the road trip.'" I looked around as she said this and realized she was right. Almost none of the customers filling the place were locals. They were tourists. So weird. But apparently the Oklachito Scenic Drive was an actual thing that people did every year to see the beautiful changing leaves. I had to admit. It was beautiful.

"Thanks, Nona! I better get to writing," I said, glancing at the clock as I picked up my muffin and coffee. "I'll keep you posted." She winked at me, but was already talking to the next customer in line and starting on their order. Despite the rumble of activity in the full coffee shop, I was able to get down to business on my story. Detective Moody had just agreed to take on the cold case of a missing person's case from long ago. There was no stopping Rainey K. Moody, who had just found fresh evidence on the cold case, and the scenes dripped quietly from my fingers and dramatically to the page. I could already tell this was going to be a good one. I was so immersed in my work that over two hours later, when I heard the throat clearing next to me and looked up to see Agents McGee and Brothers standing before me, I jumped.

"I'm so sorry!" I said, immediately jumping to my feet and shaking each of their hands while I looked around. The place had emptied a considerable amount since I began working and the four-topper next to the little two-topper on which I liked to write was open. "Let's move to this table so there will be enough room." I said, closing my laptop and transferring my things from one table to the next. Agent Brothers, a woman and the younger of the two, looked at Agent McGee.

"The usual?" she asked quietly. He nodded and added.

"Get me something sweet too, a muffin or something if they have any. We won't tell Carol," he winked and Agent Brothers shook her head at him and turned to go up to the counter.

Just as she did, Ahmet and Bif came through the door and made their way over to us. Bif was wagging his tail and greeted me first enthusiastically and then looked cautiously to Agent McGee, who was shaking hands with Ahmet.

"Sit," I instructed, using one of the hand commands Ahmet had taught me and thankfully my pup sat right down by the chair where I was putting my things. Ahmet looked at my empty cup.

"Need a refill?" He asked as he took off his jacket and placed it on the back of the chair next to mine.

"Ah–just a black coffee would be nice." I smiled and Ahmet made his way to the counter to stand behind Agent Brothers and the two started chatting quietly. Agent McGee sat down across from me and smiled.

"It's nice to see you again, Ms. Carmichael. Are you working on a new book?" He asked curiously, motioning towards the closed laptop that I was now slipping into my computer bag and placing on the floor beside my exceptionally well-behaved pup.

"I am, and I wish I had made a list of questions for you. That's a missed opportunity. It's about a cold case." Agent McGee looked pleased with the idea that I might want to consult with him about my book. He nodded, clearly pondering what I had said.

"Cold cases are tough, but they can be the funnest to work on. Especially if you can come to it with a completely fresh perspective. And now, we have so much more technology to work with that cold cases that have been sitting around for decades waiting to be solved are being solved every day." I knew he caught the glimmer in my eye at this news. I also knew that he knew that it meant more to me personally than just for my character. And it really did, hearing from an actual FBI agent that cold cases were being solved daily was immensely encouraging when I thought of my mother's case. But also helpful professionally.

"Huh," I absorbed what he had just told me. "I never thought about cold cases being fun to work on. I figured they would just be incredibly daunting. I will have to let Rainey K. have a bit of fun with this one, then, now won't I?" I knew Agent McGee was familiar with my work and was actually a reader of mine as one of the last things he had self-consciously done as they were wrapping up the Sasquatch Serial Killer case was to ask me to sign a copy of my first Moody mystery. He told me that it was still his favorite, even though he loved all of them. He said he had read it on the tail end of working a particularly grisly case of his own and somehow the resolution and redemption in the book had helped him find a little peace in his own case as well, which was particularly kind of him to say and also very nice to know on a personal level. You do this work, this solitary slow work, and of course, if the books sell, you know someone is enjoying them. But to know that they have helped someone to process their own difficulties is what every author longs for. Agent Brothers and Ahmet were sitting down with us now and distributing coffee and treats. Ahmet, knowing my love for the muffins had gotten us both one as well, so it was muffins all around. I smiled over at Nona and watched as she pulled the empty plate out of the display.

"I did not need another muffin." I smiled at Ahmet and around the table. "But, my God, am I glad you didn't ask me before getting me one," I pulled the wrapper down and bit into the pumpkin spice goodness into that cool cream cheese center that was a little bit of heaven. Everyone laughed and joined me in digging into their coffee and muffins.

"So," Agent McGee began with a mouthful of muffin. "You said you think you might have some information on your case, it was a kidnapping if I remember correctly." I nodded. "Well, what is it?"

I dove into my story, recounting all the details of this morning's revelation, and I watched as Detective Brothers jotted down what looked to be thorough notes. "I know this isn't your case, but in light of everything you learned while working with us on the Sasquatch Serial Killer case, I thought you might be able to advise me. I'm sorry if that was presumptuous. I know you are both very busy," I said sincerely to the two of them.

"Well, you're not going to believe this because I barely do, but they pulled us into the Staples Double Murder case this morning. That was our meeting before this. You are looking at the two FBI agents on the case. So you just may get the two of us promoted if this DNA of yours pans out."

"There is another concern," I cleared my throat and glanced at Ahmet, who gave me an encouraging nod. "It is–possible—" I paused, weighing my words carefully, "that the alleged murderer may, just maybe, suggest that bigfoot was involved in my rescue. That, of course, would be a total fabrication on his part." I said pointedly, looking each agent in the face.

"Of course," said Agent McGee, as he and Agent Brothers made eye contact.

"It's just that I heard him rambling about bigfoot when he was holding me hostage, so I think he might be a bit obsessed." This was, of course, a bit of a stretch. I heard him scream bloody murder when he saw bigfoot during my rescue, but that was the extent of it. "What I'm afraid is going to happen is that he will end up getting an insanity plea because the bigfoot thing might tip him over the edge for people, and well, I don't think this man is insane. I think he is very dangerous and if he killed those people, I do not want him to get off just because people think he is crazy." I laid this information down methodically, trying to paint him as someone who was already obsessed with bigfoot, without indicating any actual reality in a bigfoot being involved in my rescue. "I mean, don't you have to be crazy to kill someone in the first place? I've never quite understood that. Anyway, do you think, if he were to imply bigfoot's involvement, that they would declare him mentally incompetent to stand trial?" McGee and Brothers looked at each other again and Agent McGee took a deep breath and paused before answering me as if he was trying to choose his words carefully.

"Interesting that you think he might suggest that bigfoot was involved." His eyes briefly flicked in the direction of the street where Agent Barrett sat in his car. I kept my face neutral.

PSA #41: Okay, so this one is not original, but very relevant. Never let them see you sweat.

"Hmmm... yeah well, you know how people are." I replied with a shrug. It was one of those vague things people say when they are actually not saying anything.

"Oh, I do. I know exactly how people are," he said this without taking his shrewd eyes off of me. I felt like I was being inspected, so I did my best to keep myself neutral. I had a terrible poker face, and I knew that if Agent McGee were to push me, I would fail. But my hope was that if I could appear nonchalant enough, he would decide I must not know anything after all. I either passed his test or he got bored with the game because he swung his attention to Ahmet and asked excitedly, "Have you talked to Barnette recently?" Ahmet was nodding, but McGee continued talking. "He is doing great! That kid is a wonder."

"He really is," agreed Ahmet. "And lucky!"

"Yes, he was. Lucky you lived in the area." McGee said pointedly. Ahmet just nodded uncomfortably.

"There's another thing Ele forgot to mention and that I don't know if Sheriff Struthers will have put in her file," Ahmet said and Agents McGee and Brothers listened intently. "The people who kidnapped Ele were not working on their own accord. Ele overheard them mention checking in with whoever had hired them several times." Agent Brothers furrowed her eyebrows together and nodded. "Whoever it was—" Ahmet looked at Ele, silently considering whether to name names and noticed a subtle nod from Ele, so he decided to tell all. "We have strong reason to believe it was Abner and Jeb Crawley. But regardless of who it was, they never found them and I can't help being concerned that the lack of a conviction in her case leaves her vulnerable."

"Thanks for telling us that, we will definitely look into it," said Agent McGee contemplatively as he picked up his cup of coffee and swigged down the last of it. "Well, we'd better get to work. Thank you for reaching out, Ms. Carmichael. We will be in touch. We're going to pull your case and that DNA evidence and see if Mr. Bradley Cox's DNA is as good a match as his voice. We may want to visit with you again after taking a look at your case, but we will be in touch." He handed me a card and Agent Brothers did as well. "Call us if you think of anything else, or if you need anything." At that, the two rose from the table and bid us farewell. Ahmet and I watched them head out to their car, barely looking in Agent Barrett's direction. Maybe I had imagined the earlier glance.

"Do you think he believed me? When he reads my file, he will see that I told the Sheriff I escaped in the middle of the night and followed the stream home. He didn't seem like he believed me, but that's my story and I'm sticking to it. It's really a 'damned if you do, damned if you don't' kind of situation I'm in, anyway. I'd be damned to being thought crazy if I had admitted Bob had rescued me (not to mention potentially damning Bob and JoJo into further investigation.) But I'm damned to committing perjury if I don't admit to Bob's involvement. I hope I didn't tell him too much." I sighed.

"You didn't really tell him anything, just now, Ele. It was a complete evasion. Do I think Agent McGee noticed and will believe, as Sheriff Struthers did, that you altered your account of events in your initial interview? Yes. Which, by the way, I don't think, is considered perjury since you weren't in a court of law. I think it's just falsified information or something like that. But regardless, we are just going to believe you're not getting into trouble for it." At this, he put his hand on my arm in comforting solidarity. "You couldn't let a kidnapper and potential murderer walk. You had no choice but to talk. Besides, hopefully they will finally get behind who hired your kidnappers. It really bothers me that they just left that mystery unsolved." Bif whimpered and put his head on my lap, offering up big sad puppy eyes to let me know he was on my side too. And somehow, it helped.

CHAPTER 13

Ahmet walked with Bif and me as we headed out of the coffee shop, where there were two big surprises waiting for us. One: the car I had seen this morning across from Ahmet's driveway was now sitting empty, parked across the street directly behind Agent Rhett Barrett's car. And when we looked closer, the aforementioned Agent Soccer-Mom was sitting in the front seat of Agent Barrett's vehicle, engaged in what looked to be a heated discussion. Ahmet and I were marveling at this and appreciating the confirmation that yes, indeed, soccer mom was likely the Paranormal Affairs Agent assigned to him. But then a second thing happened that blew both of our minds. When the two looked up and locked eyes with us as we were coming out of the coffee shop, Agent Barrett rolled down his window and beckoned us over to the clear and emphatic dismay of Agent Soccer-Mom. I could hear her clearly as we walked toward the vehicle—"What-the-actual-*fuck*-are you doing, Rhett?"

"Hi!" I leaned down and smiled at Agent Barrett and became tickled as Agent Soccer-Mom looked everywhere but at my face, clearly in an existential crisis about what was happening. My guess was that someone trained them to never, ever, engage with their target. And here Barrett was, breaking every rule under the sun. And mere minutes after watching the FBI agent that tipped them off on us, leaving the area after meeting with us. She clearly could not deal with what was happening.

"Hi!" Ahmet said in the same overly chipper tone as he leaned down and looked in at the two agents, mirroring my behavior, which, in itself, was pretty amusing.

"So?" Agent Barrett said to me, clearly in demand of an explanation, but I refused to make it that easy on him.

"So, what?" I asked, feigning naivety.

"So you bloody well know what!" He stamped his cigarette out in the ashtray, clearly over the game. "What the hell were you doing meeting with them? Are you trying to get us canned?"

"Wait. You mean, you haven't told them you've made personal contact with us?" I asked in mock surprise. Agent Barrett let out a long sigh, like he was trying to keep his cool, and began again with a different approach. Poor man. I was having far too much fun to make this easy on him.

"No. No... I didn't see that it was relevant information. I thought we had a friendly understanding," he said calmly. Agent Soccer-Mom's mouth was literally hanging open during this exchange. I started wondering if he had even told her. Maybe they weren't very close. She was clearly about to have a seizure over our exchange. I decided I had toyed with him enough, poor guy.

"Agent Rhett, we do have an understanding. I'm happy to have you be the one following me. I, of course, would rather no one be following me since it is completely unnecessary, as we have previously discussed. But, do I want them to bring in some new RoboCop to follow me? Abso-freaking-lutely not! Believe it or not, that meeting had nothing to do with you two—or the Agency of Paranormal Affairs—or anything of that nature. I did not even reveal that I knew you were following us." At this information, both agents let out a visible sigh of relief. "We were meeting with the FBI about a completely different matter and I will warn you, we may be meeting with them again, but I'm fully willing not to reveal yours and my relationship to them, if that is what you prefer."

"Well, YEAH! That's what we prefer!" Agent Soccer-Mom finally spoke in a fit of passionate angst and disgust. I looked her in the eye and reached my hand in the window in front of Agent Barrett, who looked mildly annoyed at my proximity.

"Nice to meet you. I'm Elena Carmichael. And this is Dr. Ahmet Pamuk, but we all know you are fully aware of that, now don't we?" I winked as she turned red, whether with anger or embarrassment, I could not tell. I could tell, however, that she really, really did not like for her cover to be blown.

"Agent Margie Hart," she said with a resigned sigh and reached up to shake my hand.

"Great!" I said as she shook my hand. "Now I can stop calling you Agent Soccer-Mom." The look she gave me clearly implied she was not amused. After our handshake, I pulled my arm out of the vehicle to give Agent Barrett the relief from me he clearly desired. Ahmet leaned down a little and made eye contact with Agent Hart.

"It's nice to finally meet you, Agent Hart," he said warmly. And her mouth pressed into a straight line as she nodded and finally said aloud.

"You as well." Just then Nona came across with a to-go box of two coffees and two cookies in sleeves.

"Oh, for fuck's sake," Agent Hart muttered under her breath, clearly mortified that they were engaging with so many people. Nona must have whipped up a batch of cookies when her muffins sold out because the cookies were steaming in the cool, crisp fall breeze. Bif got excited, and I told him to cool it. Agent Hart's eyes got as big as saucers when she realized the coffee and cookies were for them. Nona was making it very hard for Agent Hart to dislike us.

"Here you all go." She said, handing the to-go tray with the coffees and cookies through the window to Agent Barrett. She tucked her head down enough to see Agent Hart. "Hi there. I'm Nona. It's nice to meet you. I hope you like coffee and cookies." At that moment, I knew I was going to really, really like Agent Hart. Because she gave a small sarcastic snort, raised one eyebrow just as a large dimple popped into existence on her cheek and good-naturedly splayed out her two hands as if presenting her chubby body to us as exhibit one. I laughed aloud.

"I like you." I said. Agent Hart was shaking her head, smiling.

"We'll see how I feel about you." She said wryly and then looked at Nona directly, "But you, I like." Nona was laughing now.

"Well, thanks." Nona smiled warmly at Agent Hart. "I guess I'd better get back in there. It's finally slowed down, but now I've got to clean up the mess." She waved at us all and headed back across the street to her shop.

"Thanks for the cookie!" Agent Hart called out to her as she was already taking a bite of fresh-from-the-oven deliciousness.

"Well, I guess we better get going as well," I said, and Ahmet nodded.

"Wait," Agent Barrett finally spoke again. "Aren't you going to tell us what you were meeting with the FBI about?" I looked thoughtful for a moment and then replied just as dryly as he would to me if I was asking nosy questions, which I often do.

"No...I don't think so." I smiled and waved, and Bif, Ahmet, and I headed back across to Nona's parking lot to our vehicles.

Bif ran ahead of me into the library and I heard him bark, which was weird, because he had fallen in love with Matilda the moment they'd first met. "Bif! Hush!" I said as loudly as I felt comfortable to in a library. Lately, I had been training him to only bark when people were coming onto our property so I would know someone was there, and the only other time it was okay for him to bark was, of course, when he sensed danger (ie. saw a bad guy). I had no idea if the latter was working, but when we saw a coyote slip through the backyard the other day, and he had barked at the backdoor like mad trying to get out to protect the area, I had congratulated him and patted him and told him he was a very brave and good dog indeed. So I was hoping it stuck. But when I came around the large nonfiction stacks to where Matilda's desk was, I nearly laughed out loud, for there was Dorothy Struthers sitting with her, I realized my dog clearly knew a bad guy when he saw one. Dorothy had almost at first sight been my sworn nemesis.

Now you may be wondering if, as a middle-aged woman, I shouldn't have outgrown the notion of a sworn nemesis, and my argument would be, "Absolutely not, passion is what makes us feel alive." And I have a passionate distaste for Dorothy who, incidentally, looked as thrilled to see me as I did her. Thankfully, Bif had cut out the barking because Matilda was scratching him behind his ears and cooing about how good dogs don't bark in libraries and what a good dog he was. I watched as Dorothy began quickly gathering her things from where she was sitting across from Matilda. If I wasn't mistaken, she had just hastily wiped away tears, but the woman was so brisk and curt, I would never know.

"Elena," she said, acknowledging my presence with a complete void of emotion.

"Dorothy," I returned her greeting with equal enthusiasm.

"Dorothy, you don't need to go. Ele is just here to help cover some of the new books she ordered for the kids' section. We can still talk." Matilda encouraged kindly. As she said this, she had motioned to a large stack behind her desk and I picked one up to look at it.

"No, no, no. I must go," Dorothy replied briskly. "Busy, you know," she added as she jumped to her feet. I wondered if she realized she sounded like the early reader I was now holding in my hand. I was admiring its beautiful cover.

"Really, Dorothy," I said sincerely. "I'm going to be in the back room at the worktable back there, anyway." To prove my point, I grabbed a pile of books and headed to the workroom, but Dorothy wanted to be in the same building as me as much as I did her and I could hear her telling Matilda goodbye. It sounded like Matilda was giving her a hug and one last pep talk. I couldn't hear the actual words she was saying because she had lowered her voice, but it had the lilt of a comforting pick me up talk. Dorothy's thank you sounded like she was fighting tears and I started feeling bad for interrupting them, even though I was fifteen minutes past when I'd said I would be coming in already. I pulled down the plastic roll of archival book jacket cover material. Matilda had only recently taught me how to do this, and I found the process to be quite relaxing and at the end you were rewarded with a shiny, clean, plastic covered book. One that you knew would stay clean and undamaged thanks to the process you had just put the book jacket through.

A few minutes later, Matilda came into the room with Bif happily on her heels, his tongue lolling out, a smile on his face, looking up at her admiringly. If I didn't know better and that Bif was a dog, I would think he had a crush on this tiny, birdlike librarian. Regardless, he clearly adored her. "So what on earth is the deal with you and Dorothy?" Matilda seemed confused. "I've never seen her shut down like that before."

"I have no idea, Matilda. She has been that way towards me since day one."

"Hmm…" Matilda considered this and then nodded to herself as if she had come to some conclusion in her mind, but I could tell she had no intention of sharing, so I continued.

"I've come to think of her as my sworn nemesis." Matilda burst into laughter at this.

"Of course you have. You're not a writer for nothing. Every good protagonist needs an antagonist." I raised an eyebrow.

"And Dorothy is mine." I said, and Matilda chuckled again.

"Hmm, I wonder–"

"You wonder what?"

"Well," Matilda hesitated and looked like she had surprised herself with the thought, but continued. "I thought she would be enamored with you—she's such a fan, you know." At this, I threw my head back and roared with laughter.

"I'm quite certain you are mistaken. That woman has been nothing but haughty and rude to me since I first met her."

"Hmm... curious!" Matilda mauled this information over. "Well, believe it or not, she is definitely a fan. She would never fail to let me know when you had a new book coming out to make sure that I had preordered copies for the library. And whenever a donation of one of your books would come in for the annual book-sale, she would always be the first to grab it up. I'm pretty sure she owns all of your books and I'm *positive* she's read them." I was speechless. This could not possibly be true. Dorothy had never had one kind word for me since the day she met me. "I wonder—" Matilda mused.

"You wonder what?"

"I wonder if you intimidate her. That woman is the biggest bulldozer I have ever known. The only person I never saw her run over was her husband, Sam, but I think that's because he was her bulldozer. Anyway, she certainly behaves oddly with you, that's for sure."

"That's because she hates me." I concluded matter-of-factly, I had theories as well. "I did not, however, mean to interrupt you guys. It looked like she was needing a friend and I'm sorry that I chased her off."

"Yeah, she's going through some hard times. I remember how it was after Theodore disappeared. It was just so hard to be alone. She knows I've been where she is right now, and we've been friends—of sorts—over the years."

"I'm sorry." I was referring to her loss of Theodore but realized it sounded a bit like I was saying I was sorry she had to be friends with Dorothy, but if Matilda noticed, she didn't act like it. She seemed a bit lost in her thoughts.

SASQUATCH SAVES THE DAY

"You know, the strangest thing that upset me when he disappeared. I had caught up all our laundry that day–the day he never came home–even the bed sheets. He had been out on an 'expedition' as he liked to call them and was due back that day, so I was getting the house all nice for his return and in the process, I had washed away the scent of him. I didn't even have his pillow case. Although his pillow itself held a little of his scent and I would fall asleep crying every night with my face covered in his pillow." Good grief. I was about to start crying now too and it must have shown on my face, because she looked up at me and smiled serenely. "Now, now. Enough of that. I made it through. And Dorothy will find her way too. Libby and Bert saved my life back then. Libby, stopping by the house and picking me up for work even though I had no intention of coming in. I can still hear her. 'You cannot stay alone in this house all day withering away waiting for him.' That was the thing you see. Since he was just missing and not found dead, I became terrified that he would call and I would miss his call or come back home on death's door and I wouldn't be there to save him, so I was trying to become agoraphobic." At this she gave a little chirp of a laugh, her eyes to the floor but clearly her mind was in another time and place, then she shook her head slowly. "But Libby was not having it. I would not become agoraphobic on her watch. She learned how to forward the phone to the library and taught me how so that all my calls would come here just in case. And when I argued that Theodore might show up and I wouldn't be there, we agreed that every two hours I would run and check." There was a long pause here. "I did that for three and a half years," she said slowly. This poor, poor woman. Hearing her stories made me wonder what internal struggles my aunt and grandma had contended with when my mother went missing.

PSA #42: You are not alone in this world and probably the greatest gift of life is when friends bear one another's burdens.

"My mother is still on the missing persons list in Boone, Iowa." I whispered. Before I knew it, she had swept to my side and wrapped me in a hug.

"I know dear, I know." I wrapped my arms around her slight frame and hugged her back.

"I'm sorry about Theodore," I whispered again.

"I'm sorry about your momma," Matilda whispered back. We held each other for a moment longer and as we pulled apart, we were both wiping away tears.

"I have something kind of exciting about my mom's case though," I said and Matilda clapped her hands together and came to life.

"Well, do tell!"

"There's not much to it, but I've been thinking a lot about her case. Rainey K. Moody is working on a cold case in my new book and so I decided to check in with the police station in Boone, Iowa and there is a new detective. When I told him about mom's case, he said he would pull the file and go over everything and see if he could find something. He said so much has changed since she disappeared that maybe technology could help us. He made no promises, of course, with a case this old, it's highly unlikely. But something could come of it." I said hopefully. "At least I know it's being revisited by a new set of eyes."

"That is wonderful, dear!" And I could tell she was genuinely thrilled for me.

"Sam really tried hard when Theodore went missing." I don't know why it didn't click, but when she saw the confusion in my eyes, she added. "Sheriff Sam Struthers, Dorothy's husband, handled Theodore's missing person case, and I can honestly say he did his best. He kept searching the woods for his remains for three and a half years. He finally concluded that Theodore had gone into a cave on his own and must have gotten lost or injured or fallen to his death, as there are many deep ravines in these underground networks that, if you're not careful, you can miss. We used to fight about that–him going into caves alone. I would tell him the US Forest Service recommends having a minimum of four people in a group when you go caving. That way, if someone gets hurt, then one person can stay with the injured while two people can go for help. But that just wasn't Theodore's way. He was a naturalist. He was quite famous in his field," she added proudly. "When he was in the woods, he was not remotely concerned about what the US Forest Service recommended. Not to say that he was unsafe. He was actually an excellent outdoorsman and very aware of the dangers. It's just that if he was on a mission that led him into a cave, he wasn't going to wait and find three people to join him. He would move forward in the safest way possible–alone." She shrugged in resignation. "I knew he was stubborn when I married him. Anyway, Sheriff Struthers found a pencil just outside the opening of one of the larger maze-like caves in the Kiamichis. It wasn't much to go on, but it was a Ticonderoga pencil, which was Theodore's favorite kind, in the middle of the wilderness. It had to get there somehow and Sheriff Struthers' best guess was that my husband had dropped it before entering the cave. Of course, they searched the cave, but they never found anything. It's certainly not a clear resolution of the case, but I suppose it was better than nothing. It was when Sam found the pencil that I stopped going home every two hours." She shrugged again. I was familiar with the shrug. It is the default stance of people who have faced great loss. My whole life concerning my mother has been one big shrug. You would not believe how much our mothers come up in everyday conversations. Even though I never called Aunt Becky mom (although I always kind of wished she would have let me) I had to, for sanity's sake, mentally interject her into all those moments when friends would talk about their moms. Aunt Becky was my acting mom and so it was her I thought of in those times so I wouldn't constantly be sad–so my childhood was more than one long shrug. Aunt Becky loved her sister so much, I think she was afraid to let me call her mom–that if she did, it would somehow erase her sister and my real mom, and she could not bear that.

"So, you said Libby and Bert saved your life after Theodore's disappearance. Were you able to return the favor when Libby died?" I knew it was nosy, but I had no problem with that. I wanted to know the scoop on her and Bert's relationship. She smiled a soft smile.

"Honestly, no. Not until now, anyway." There was that shrug again. "I tried to be a comfort when Libby died. I took dinner to him like so many of us in the community did. I called to check in with him sometimes in the evening before bed, remembering how bedtime was always the hardest time for me and how Libby would often call me at bedtime after Theodore disappeared. He was always polite and nice, because he's Bert and he doesn't know how to be anything but nice," she smiled as she said this last bit. "But he would get me off the phone as soon as possible until I finally stopped trying. Everyone grieves in their own way, and Bert's way was alone." I smiled and asked another nosy question.

"Does this mean he's not grieving anymore? That he's ready to move forward?" I asked, and Matilda smiled.

"I don't know that we ever completely stop grieving the ones we've loved and lost. But yes, I think he is moving forward." And that was all I could get her to say on the matter. We spent the rest of the afternoon in companionable silence, mixed with the occasional patron coming in and needing Matilda's help to find something. In short, it was a perfect afternoon.

CHAPTER 14

I was raking up yet more leaves around the house when my phone buzzed in my back pocket. I saw it was Bert and quickly answered. "Hey Bert, what's up?" I asked cheerfully.

"Well, I'm afraid I have some not great news." Bert said, and my heart clenched.

"Spit it out then."

"The Dobson's have another offer on the table. A substantial one."

"How substantial?"

"It is double yours," Bert said with a sigh. I couldn't believe this. Bert had researched prices and made a more than fair offer. He had also been almost certain that they were going to be reaching out to us any day to seal the deal.

"How?" I stuttered. "Who?"

"Well, Ele–that's the even worse news," sighed Bert miserably. "Dorothy Struthers."

"What? Why on earth would Dorothy want the property next to–?" Then it clicked into place. Dorothy didn't want it. "The Crawleys? Again? Why are they such a thorn in my side?"

"Ele, I've got something to tell you. It's been weighing on me for a while, but I have been able to deceive myself into believing there was no reason to bring it up until now. You see—there was another bidder on your place before you that I turned down on behalf of my clients. And by behalf, I mean I didn't even tell the clients about the offer for fear they would take it. In full disclosure, they had told me to handle everything. That they didn't want to talk about the place until I had their buyer. And the Crawleys didn't offer the full asking price, so I used that as my reasoning for telling them no. In reality, I just didn't want them getting their grubby bigfoot hunting paws on your mountain."

"The Crawleys tried to buy my place, and you turned them down?" I couldn't believe what I was hearing. "Well, no wonder they hated me from the start."

"I know," Bert said miserably. "It was all I could think of when you disappeared. I was terrified that I had gotten you killed. When you called the day after I turned them down with a full price offer, I ran with it as fast as I possibly could. They were so pissed when they called me two days later with a higher offer and I told them we already had a buyer. I think they wanted to get a hold of your place because they knew they would essentially have your place and free access to the Dobson's place without having to pay for it. Everyone knows the Dobsons don't live anywhere near here. Poachers have been slipping in there and hunting deer for years until the game warden cracked down on them. The Crawleys are the only ones that have persisted to hunt on that mountain without permission. My guess would be that they've talked Dorothy into sinking Sam's life insurance policy into it." Bert whistled. "It must have been a helluva policy, though. Sam was a pretty responsible guy, so it makes sense he would be insured to the hilt." His voice dropped again, and he said softly, "I'm so sorry, Ele."

"Sorry? Sorry for what? For not selling my property to the bad guys before I had a chance to buy it? For not telling me sooner? Bert, you didn't do anything wrong. I'm so glad you did what you did. It does explain why you pushed the sale through so quickly for me, though." I was smiling a little now. "I mean it, Bert. Don't sweat it. I would have done the same thing. And there really wasn't any reason to tell me until now. It would have just made me even more paranoid. I'm glad I know now and if you hadn't told me in answer to my direct question of what they had against me, then I might have been pissed, but you told me as soon as I asked." I heard Bert's audible sigh of relief.

"Thanks, Ele. I really appreciate that." My predicament pushed itself back to the forefront of my mind.

"So, what should I do?" I asked, miserably. I wasn't sure I could comfortably double my cash offer. If I did, I would be worried about money and I wasn't sure I could face that again. In fairness, there was no reason to think I would not continue to have a successful writing career. So I probably could do it. It just scared me.

"Let's get everyone together to talk. Why don't you come out to my place tonight and I will make chili for everyone? Ele, they've given us 72 hours to make a counteroffer. I talked them up from the 48 hours they were offering us because I begged Dobson not to take their offer. I told him they would put up a bigfoot hunting business on the property, but as far as Dobson is concerned, that still honors his father's wishes that the land stay undeveloped, and unfortunately, money talks. He didn't really listen to me telling him the place would be full of fools shooting guns all willy-nilly. He promised me, though, that if we can beat their offer, he will take ours instead, since we were the first to approach him."

"Well, I guess that's something," I said, trying to sound hopeful, but without much conviction. "Bert, I gotta be honest with you, I don't know if I feel comfortable sinking that much into the property. I can't bear the thought of them getting their hands on it, though. Bob, JoJo and the babies will have to relocate. I guess I could get a loan…"

"Let's just talk it over tonight. I'll call everyone and let them know we've got an emergency meeting at my place tonight at 6 pm."

The rest of the day dragged on. I decided to write from home since I was getting such a late start after my morning yard work. Thoughts were swirling in my mind from my call with Bert and what on earth I was going to do? I didn't see how paying double the value of the land was in any way a good business decision. Especially when I knew it was a black hole that I was choosing to sink my money into. This was an investment that would never create any financial return, in fact, quite the opposite. I would continue to sink money into it through property tax and keeping the sanctuary stocked in game when necessary for the rest of my life. I sat with my fingertips on the keyboard of my laptop trying to work, but my mind was so distracted I was getting very little written and so I called to check on my mother's case. On the second ring, that same baritone voice boomed, "Boone Police Station, Detective Puckett speaking."

"Detective Puckett? This is Ele Carmichael."

"Yes, hello Ms. Carmichael, I've been meaning to call you." He said, and my heart leapt. Could he possibly have already found something? "I was doing some cross-referencing on details from your mom's case and there was another woman who went missing a few years later from a nearby town, and her last known location was the same bar where your mother met her date."

Now my heart sank. It was great. It was good news in that it was a lead, but it was a lead into a possibly terrible end for her, which of course, I had always known was likely, but somehow now that it was looking even more likely, my heart felt like shattering. Detective Puckett must have sensed my dismay. "I'm sorry. I know it's not much, and it certainly isn't the kind of lead you were hoping for, I'm sure."

"No, no, no." I insisted. "It's wonderful. It's great to have any leads at all, as old as her case is. Thank you for telling me."

"Well, they've re-opened the other case as well, and our two teams will be working together. Maybe we can get to the bottom of this once and for all and give you some kind of closure."

"That would be—well, it would be very much appreciated." My voice cracked as I responded to Detective Puckett, and we quickly bid each other farewell. God, today sucked! I decided to take a walk in the woods to clear my head. Biffy and I were enjoying a pleasant stroll through the woods when Biffy took off running with me close behind, calling his name. We broke into a clearing and there was Bif getting an awkward pat on the head from JoJo as he sniffed the babies she had shuffled in her arms in order to find a free hand to pet Bif. JoJo knelt down, holding the smaller boy and the girl. The bigger of the two boys was latched onto Bob, who was standing on watching with an amused expression. My heart filled with joy at the scene before me. I could not let the Crawleys get their hands on this land. I could not bear for Bob, JoJo, and the babies to be forced to move away or worse, be injured or killed before they had the chance to move away, especially when I could have stopped it. If it meant I had to sock all my money into that land, or go up to my eyeballs in debt to keep that from happening, then that is what I would have to do, good business decision or not. I watched Bif lick one of the baby's cheeks as it squirmed and JoJo smiled. I got a flash of the babies playing with Biffy and riding him like a horse, and I knew that there was simply no other choice. After a brief exchange of warm intentions and a quick look at each of the babies who were already growing and changing so much, we bid them farewell, much to Bif's chagrin. It was his first time to meet the babies and clearly he liked them as much as he liked JoJo and Bob. As we walked home, a strange peace enveloped me. I had never been one to make decisions based on good business sense or even logic, my heart had always led me and it would lead me in this matter as well. It led me to buy a crazy ass cabin in the backwoods of Oklahoma and apparently my heart was a masochist that intended me to become in debt to hold on to what I had found here. But if I was honest, I didn't believe my heart had ever led me astray. As I questioned the truthfulness of this, I remembered a flash of warning from my heart about Doug so many years ago. It all came back in a flood of memories. Initially, I was unsure about Doug, but he had been so charming and I was so ready to have someone to call my own that I ignored the little niggling uncertainty in my heart. And then, so many years later, I paid for it. Well, I would not ignore it this time. I would find a way to protect these creatures.

PSA #43: What's that old saying? Follow your heart. It knows the way.

When Bif and I got back to the house, I called my banker, who thought I was nuts for wanting to buy overpriced land in Oklahoma, but agreed there would be no problem in giving me the loan. I didn't really want the loan, but did not see another way. My mind was racing and so I made a peach cobbler to take with me to Bert's. Baking was soothing to me and I tried not to do it unless I had an outlet for said baked goods, otherwise I would (as was evidenced by historical record) eat it all by myself. The heavenly scent of peach cobbler hung in the air. I was curled up in the large leather chair with my laptop on my lap, trying to write. I had given myself a strict daily word count to reach, and I was only halfway there, and was hoping to get in a few good pages while the cobbler baked when Bif started barking and running to the front door. From Bif's behavior, it was not someone we knew.

I got to the door and peeked out the peephole to discover the Paranormal Agents Barrett and Hart standing on my porch, looking around awkwardly. I didn't want Bif to befriend these two because I wanted to always know if they were poking around and if I let them in the house without putting away Bif, my pup would certainly become great friends with the two. Cracking the door as Bif barked madly, I lifted my finger at them through the glass and said, "Let me put my dog away." Then I closed the door in their faces. "Bif, good boy!" I patted him to affirm that barking at these two was a good thing. "Now, get in your crate." Although Bif was noticeably displeased by this, he slunk to his crate and I closed the door behind him and even put the cover over it. He whimpered in protest. "I know, boy, they won't be here long." I ran back to the front door and flung it open, then opened the glass screen door to let them in.

The two agents looked fairly miserable, and I wondered what on God's green earth would bring them to my doorstep. "Come on in. Have a seat." We walked into the living room and they each took a seat awkwardly on the two sides of the large overstuffed sectional and I sat facing them in the leather chair I had been trying to write in. "Can I offer you any coffee or iced tea?" I asked politely, and they shook their heads. "What exactly can I do for you?" I asked cautiously.

"Ms. Carmichael," Agent Barrett started. "We'd like to make a deal." Well, I'm not sure what I was expecting, but this was certainly not it.

"Excuse me?" I asked, unsure if I had heard him correctly and not even sure what on earth making a deal could mean.

"What he's trying to say is, well, we like it here," explained Agent Hart.

"You like it here?" I was so confused, I still wasn't following. "I mean, don't you have homes to go back to?" They shrugged simultaneously. "Actually, a home," admitted Agent Hart, "but we've spent so little time there the past 24 years, it hardly feels like it. And despite the fact that we are trying not to meet people, every time we turn around someone here is greeting us and being all friendly and well, we're not used to that," Agent Margie Hart was turning red at this confession.

"Wait. Are you two—together?" I was gobsmacked. I had truly, not in a million years, seen this one coming. "Like together–together?"

"If 21 years of marriage counts as together, then yep," said Agent Hart plainly.

"Then why didn't you know that he had already broken cover the other day? It surprised you when he beckoned Ahmet and me over. I heard you chewing him out. Your face was not one of a person who was 'in the know,'" at this comment, Agent Hart threw her partner, in more than one sense, a glare.

"Because *someone* is a jackass," she answered without hesitation. "He knew I would be livid, and he thought he could keep it from me. You see, I stayed here to keep an eye on Dr. Pamuk while you were in Canada and NYC with your friends and when he was filling me in on details, he conveniently forgot to include your little pit stop confrontation."

"Okaaay..." I felt like I was slowly catching up. "But I don't think I understand. What do you mean you like it here? What does that have to do with me?"

"You see, we are only here because we are being punished by the Agency." Margie glanced at Rhett, unsure of how much to tell, but he gave her a subtle nod. "We lost someone in New Orleans and the agency did not take kindly to it," Agent Hart explained.

"You mean the vampire?" I asked excitedly. Margie's eyes got as big as saucers.

"OH FOR CHRIST'S SAKE, RHETT! You didn't?" Agent Hart murmured more obscenities under her breath and continued. Agent Barrett at least had the decency to look guilty. "What else did you tell her?"

"I think that's about it." I interjected. "He's honestly been quite tight-lipped when talking to me. I thought he was just joking about the vampire, though. Until–" I left it hanging there and the realization that she had been the one to reveal the truth of the vampire to me annoyed her even further. "So, what type of deal could you make with me?" I was still very confused. Agent Barrett cleared his throat here and interjected.

"You said something to us the other day that got both of us to thinking. You said you would 'rather have us as your tails than some new RoboCops to deal with.' Of course, we understand that you would rather have no one following you. Who wouldn't? But I'm afraid they are going to have someone on you guys for a while due to the information learned in the Sasquatch Serial Killer case, and especially after your little meeting with the FBI the other day. I don't know what you were talking to them about, but not a day after your meeting we got a tip off from them that they had reason to believe even more strongly now that you are in communication with bigfoot."

"Shit." I whispered. It had just slipped out, but both of them pricked up at it. It was practically an admission of guilt, at least by the looks on their faces. That was the problem of fraternizing with the enemy. I'm a what-you-see-is-what-you-get kind of girl and damn it, I was beginning to think I had no choice but to befriend this enemy for real. "That was NOT an admission, you two. It just pisses me off because I want to be rid of you once and for all. It was my ethical duty to talk to the FBI about–well, HELL–I'll just tell you! You see, I was kidnapped and held hostage several months ago now, and I saw one of my kidnappers pleading not guilty to murder on the news the other morning."

"You mean the Staples murder?" Agent Margie Hart asked curiously.

"Yes. I was putting on make-up in my bathroom and I heard the voice of one of my kidnappers on television–they always wore masks when they were around me–but I swear to God, that was him. Bradley Cox was one of the two men who held me hostage, I'm sure of it. So, since Ahmet and I had met Agents McGee & Brothers on the serial killer case, I gave them a call and they just happened to have been the FBI agents assigned to the Staples case that very morning. Anyway, there is likely something in my kidnapping file that is making them think I have contact with bigfoot." I heaved a large frustrated sigh. "You still haven't told me what the hell kind of deal you're talking about." Agent Barrett looked to his wife and long-time Agency of Paranormal Affairs Agent, Margie Hart and nodded subtly for her to take over where he had left off.

"Listen, we know you don't want to be followed, but if we don't give them something soon, they are going to replace us. Someone else will screw up and they will send them to the backwoods of Oklahoma on bigfoot duty as punishment. The thing is, we don't want to go back. We like it here. This is the first time either of us have slept well at night in I don't know how many years. Most agents consider bigfoot duty mind-numbingly boring, but we've been doing this so long, to us–it's heaven. We were in the same academy graduating class, Rhett and I, and we each have exactly 9 months and 3 days left until we can retire. We want this to be our last assignment. And well, we may even want to retire here as nice as everyone is–" She gave a slight shrug and looked at me almost like she wanted encouragement. "I mean, you've got a great coffee shop."

"I know, right?!" I answered enthusiastically. "I never in a million years would have considered moving here until, on a whim, I did. I bought this cabin sight unseen and moved here from NYC because my ex was a cheating bastard and I needed to get away from him, but I have never felt more at home anywhere in my life." This seemed to be just the encouragement Margie was needing.

"Please help us. If you have any bigfoot information that you can give us, then we can string them on—" Just then, Margie saw something out of the corner of her eye that made her stop talking. I had forgotten all about the prints being displayed on the big built-in bookshelves around the fireplace when I had invited them into my space. She jumped from her seat and before I could stop her; she was looking closely at JoJo's enormous foot and hand prints Bert and Vance had taken in my front yard. "Something like these! Where did you take these prints from?" I hesitated, trying to decide how much to tell them and just like that, an idea dropped into my brain that could help us all out.

"I didn't make the prints. My friends Bert and Vance did." Rhett was now standing with Margie, looking at the prints.

"Those are damn fine plaster casts," Rhett said admirably. "I can't believe they got a handprint too. Those are hard to come by." He made a second stab to get information. "Where did they find the prints in order to make these?" And that was when I found myself lying yet again to a government agent. At least it wasn't the FBI this time, but I wasn't sure this was any better.

"I think they made them out by the Crawley's place. Personally, I think they are the ones who hired the kidnappers who took me hostage. When I first moved here, they kept coming on my property trying to lead bigfoot hunts and I told them not to come back. They asked permission and then suggested that I should pay them to exterminate the bigfoot for me and I told them to get the hell off of my property and never come back, and well, that's when the anonymous harassment started and a month later I was kidnapped."

"Jesus," said Margie. "And you escaped?"

"In the nick of time. They had indicated that they would likely be killing me when they came back in the morning–they had to get the go ahead from whoever hired them. Like I said, I think it was the

Crawleys—and so I got a hold of a broken piece of glass and slowly sawed the zip ties off of my legs. When I escaped in the middle of the night, I followed the stream in the direction I thought home was, suspecting that it was the same stream that ran behind my house on my property and I was right." I could see that Margie's opinion of me had just gone up considerably.

"You're lucky they left you your shoes," Margie said off-handedly, and I was so surprised by that comment I prayed my face didn't show it. By the suspicious glint that had just entered Margie's eye, I suspected my poker face had failed me yet again, but I said nothing more and neither did she. Rhett interjected an astute observation as well that I was not expecting.

"Why would they want to hunt on your land if there were prints like this near their own property?"

"Beats me." I said, forcing my face into submission. "But that's what Bert and Vance told me."

"I can't believe those jackasses would want to hunt bigfoot. They are literally one of the few kinds of paranormals we deal with that just want to be left the hell alone," Margie said in genuine disgust at the idea that the Crawleys would want to hunt bigfoot. Her summation that bigfoot were the peaceful creatures I had found them to be was welcome news to me and also made me like her better. Maybe I could be friends with these two.

"Really?" I asked, interjecting as much naivety as I could into the question. "So you don't think I need to worry about all the stories about bigfoot around these parts?"

"Not at all. Every one we've encountered simply wanted to be left in peace. Now, don't get me wrong, they can be utterly ferocious when provoked, but overall, they are peaceful creatures. It's why the agency considers a bigfoot case punishment. Like I said before, in the scope of the paranormal, most agents consider them endlessly boring." She snorted a little laugh at this. "That's why Rhett and I like the case so much. We're ready for a little more boredom and a little less danger. We just want to serve out our 9 months and 3 days and retire peacefully." There was such a deep longing in her words that suddenly I wanted to help them.

"So, how could those prints help you?" I didn't really want to part with the prints, but also was warming to the idea of working with the two of them. I liked them both well enough and was pretty certain that they were likely to be better than anyone the agency might send after them, since they were not trying to prove themselves but simply biding their time. Margie must have sensed my hesitancy to part with them.

"If you let us borrow them, we could most likely return them to you when we retire," she said, her voice full of hope. "Do you think they would even pass as ours?" She directed this question to Rhett, who was holding one of the casts in his hand and turning it and studying it intently.

"I think so. It looks like they made it with the same kit we use. I was just wondering if they would be able to tell that it wasn't as fresh as we are saying it is." As Agent Barrett said this, I made a decision.

"Listen, if I let you guys take this. Can you tell them you made the cast at the Crawleys? Will they think it was odd that you were poking around there when you were supposed to be watching us and hanging around our properties? I really don't want people poking around here. I just want to live in peace. I'm not trying to hide anything, I just want to be left alone." This last bit wasn't entirely untrue. I wasn't trying to hide JoJo and Bob, they were quite capable of doing that on their own. Something about the weariness in my voice must have struck a chord with them and as they broke eye contact with one another, Margie answered with confidence.

"I think we can do that," she said. Just then the timer rang, and I jumped up from my chair to pull my peach cobbler out of the oven, and as I did, Agent Barrett seemed to take the olive branch I was offering—I would help as long as they would divert the attention elsewhere.

"The Crawleys, huh?" Agent Barrett said thoughtfully.

"Yep. Those bigfoot hunting bastards tried to kill me." I said with certainty, and whether Rhett and Margie believed that the casts were made on the Crawley's place or not, they seemed willing to follow my lead.

CHAPTER 15

Matilda answered Bert's door and my heart soared. "Well, hello there, friend," I said, grinning at her like the Cheshire cat. She rolled her eyes at me and laughed. I was so happy that Bert was finally comfortable enough to invite her into our little group. This was his version of an official announcement that he and Matilda were dating.

"Hello, Ele. Oh my goodness, that smells good." Matilda commented as I came through the door past her. It was true, I carried with me the scent of peach heaven.

"It's still warm. Nona and Vance are picking up some vanilla ice cream to go with it in case anyone likes their cobbler à la mode."

"Of course, we like it à la mode. 'Just add ice cream' is the magic secret of how to make almost anything better." Matilda said with a laugh. I followed Matilda into the large open room and placed the cobbler on the island, and another heavenly aroma hit me. The kitchen smelled so good my stomach growled loudly enough for everyone to hear and we all laughed.

"Chili's almost ready!" said Bert happily. Bif danced merrily from Ahmet to Matilda to Bert, who was stirring the chili and pulling down bowls from the cabinet. There was a bowl of grated cheese, a bowl of chopped onions, some saltine crackers, and even a bag of Fritos on the counter alongside my peach cobbler. Just then, Vance and Nona let themselves in the front door and called out their greetings. They were so cute together, Nona put the ice cream in the freezer and gave me a hug and when she did, I could feel her baby bump even though it had not been an extremely tight embrace and I looked down and her loose sweatshirt and realized I could see a round hard belly underneath. I laughed and bent down. "Hello my little friend. I love you," I said to her abdomen and then suddenly felt self-conscious, until I saw the joyful look on Nona and Vance's faces and realized it thrilled them that I already loved their child.

"Everyone, grab a bowl of chili and let's eat. We've got a lot to talk about," Bert announced cheerfully.

"Even more than you know! Something crazy just happened," I said and everyone's curiosity peaked at that and we quickly filled our bowls and sat around Bert's big wooden table. Matilda was passing around beers and glasses of iced tea like she had always been a part of us. It must have been strange for her to be in Libby's kitchen, but she and Bert both seemed incredibly natural and happy.

"So–?" Nona looked at me expectantly. "What happened?" I looked at Bert.

"Did you want to discuss the reason for calling this emergency meeting first?" I asked him.

"Aw, we can talk about that in a bit, go ahead," Bert encouraged, while crunching a bunch of saltines into his chili bowl.

"Well, first of all, I don't know if Bert and Vance know about Agent Hart. Or, Matilda, do you even know that since the serial killer case, people from the Agency of Paranormal Affairs have been following Ahmet and I?"

"Bert mentioned it to me," smiling, she nodded for me to continue.

"Well, Bert and Vance, you met Agent Barrett the other day, but while he was following us around Niagara Falls and NYC, Agent Margie Hart stayed here to watch Ahmet. Nona met her with us the other day when she saw Ahmet and I talking to two agents instead of one. Nice touch, by the way, bringing out coffee and cookies for two. You totally won her over," I addressed this side note directly to Nona. "Anyway, this afternoon the two of them showed up on my front porch." Everyone stirred around the table at this news. "I know," I said. "That was my response. So I let them in and they wanted to make a deal with me."

"A deal?" asked Ahmet. "What kind of deal?"

"Well, it turns out that they love it here—they've never been treated so well or felt so welcomed anywhere in their lives. And despite their efforts to be invisible, the fact that they are not only seen, but openly accepted is not lost on them. And, get this–" I paused for dramatic effect. "It turns out they are married!"

"What?" Nona exclaimed. "You are kidding."

"I'M NOT!" It was so unexpected it completely delighted me. I love a good surprise.

"Then why was she so clueless the other day? She clearly had no idea what he was up to," Ahmet asked, reasonably.

"That's what I asked." I chuckled. "Agent Hart's answer was that her husband was a jackass. But apparently, it is such a no-no to break cover that when Nona and I caught Agent Barrett and confronted him on our way back from NYC, he was hoping he could just keep it from her because he knew she would be upset, but he didn't count on us continuing to talk to him and to be so welcoming into the community with everyone coming up to him and introducing themselves and Nona treating him to coffee and desserts every day. Anyway, to make a long story still long, they think they may want to retire here, but unless they make some kind of progress in their case, the agency will replace them. I guess I said something the other day to them about how if I had to be followed, I wanted it to be by them and not some new RoboCop. It gave them the idea just to come clean. They are from the same agency graduating class, so they are both eligible to retire in 9 months and 3 days and they are hoping that this can be their last assignment. And get this! They believe bigfoot are harmless creatures who just want to be left alone. The agency sent them here as punishment, because most agents find bigfoot duty excruciatingly boring. But for them, it's a vacation. They are seriously thinking of buying property here."

"Well, I'll have to go talk to them then, I can think of several places just off the top of my head that might be a good fit." Bert said excitedly, and we all laughed because Bert, the realtor, was now in the building.

"Anyway, I gave them JoJo's footprint cast that you guys made in my yard. I hope you don't mind. They said they will get it back for me eventually, at the very least when they retire, if not sooner. But, get this! I told them you took the print over by the Crawley's place."

"Why'd you do that?" Vance asked.

"Because she doesn't want anyone snooping around our places," Ahmet answered for me while I nodded. I could tell he approved of my tactic.

"I don't know that they believed me because Agent Barrett's first question was 'if there are prints like that over by their place, why did they keep trying to hunt on your place?' I told him I had no idea, but

I made it incredibly clear that the only way I would make a deal with them was if they said they made the casts at the Crawleys." I looked at Ahmet and shrugged.

"Well, that was bloody brilliant," said Ahmet, which made me smile because his love of British media in his use of 'bloody' was coming out and I was also pleased that he thought I had done well.

"It is nice to know they have the same perspective on bigfoot as us," Vance mused.

"It is." I agreed. "Margie got really pissed that the Crawleys were so intent on hunting them. I don't know, but—" an idea had just dropped from the heavens straight into my brain. "We'd have to get to know them much better. And it will require some serious questioning of them, but I think–if they move here–they might be absolutely perfect candidates to join 5S. With their history, they will know how to keep the government off of our tails. And they already know that bigfoot is real. My guess is that is part of the appeal of our community. They know we know they are real, too." I let my mind wander on the idea and then shrugged. "It's worth considering, anyway. By the way, does your presence here mean you've joined our ranks, Matilda? Are you an official 5S'er now?"

"Yep. All for one–" Matilda answered with a giggle. Bert had clearly told her all his stories and even filled her in down to their juvenile slogan. I laughed aloud, and we all chorused back to her while lifting our cups.

"And one for all." Matilda glanced in Bert's direction, and he was gazing at her with sheer adoration. It was so darn sweet I could hardly stand it, but it filled me with joy for them. They both deserved happiness in their lives. They had each been through a whole heck of a lot.

Throughout my big story, people were getting up to get seconds and now we were all leaning back in our seats, satisfied with our chili consumption. Matilda and Bert were refilling drinks and passing out fresh beers to anyone who wanted them and I started taking cobbler orders and scooping up bowls of cobbler with "homemade" vanilla ice cream. It cracked me up when a store-bought carton of ice cream was labeled "homemade." As everyone settled back around the table with dessert. Bert spoke.

"Nona, why don't you tell her?" Nona smiled from ear to ear.

"Okay," she replied eagerly. "Ele, when Bert called us all to invite us over tonight, he told us what was going on. And we've all agreed. If you are willing to still make the offer you originally proposed to the Dobsons, the five of us want to invest in the other half in order to help you beat Dorothy's offer. Of course, it means you would have investors on the land so it would not be 100% yours. It would make the 5S group one-half owners of the sanctuary, but if you can live with that—" Nona beamed at me and my eyes filled with tears. This lovely group of humans was not only willing to help, but had already solved my problem before we even got together tonight to discuss it. It humbled me to be a part of this loving community.

"Are you guys sure?" I asked through my leaking face. "That's still a lot of money from each of you. I talked to my banker. He said they'd be happy to do the loan." I wanted to make sure they knew I had other options. I didn't want anyone to feel pressured into investing into my hairbrained scheme of a Sasquatch Sanctuary.

"We're sure," said Bert with a smile and everyone nodded in agreement.

"And you have the added bonus of not owning the sanctuary alone," Ahmet smiled at me. He knew that I was feeling silly the other night about the idea and, like maybe, I was crazy. Ahmet must have read my mind because he followed with, "So, if this sanctuary idea is crazy, then we're all crazy with you."

"Here's to the crazy ones!" Matilda lifted her glass, and we all toasted again.

"Thank you," I said simply. "Thank you all so very, very much."

"You're welcome." As Bert said this, I looked into the smiling, nodding faces surrounding me. The sanctuary was going to happen and we would be doing it together.

PSA #44: When choosing friends, never make the mistake of overlooking the eccentric, the ones that seem a tad bit odd. People who are just a little bit on the crazy side often make the very best of friends.

"Are you okay, Ele?" Nona asked, refilling my black coffee without asking. Usually, I started my morning off with a vanilla latte and then followed it with black drip coffee while I wrote. I woke up early and decided to go into Nona's and make an early start. I'd been writing for about two hours at this point and the cold case Rainey K. Moody was working on was so sad I had made myself cry. It didn't happen often, but occasionally, the emotion of what I was writing overtook me.

"I'm fine," I smiled up at her. "Just hit a sad part of the story. It happens sometimes."

"Well, I'm sorry you made yourself cry," she smiled a wry smile, "but I find it utterly fascinating that you can become overwhelmed by the emotions of your own story." I smiled back at her.

"I know. It's weird. Sometimes a story just surprises you. You know, writing isn't that different from reading, sometimes when you're reading a really good book you are just on this hell of a ride and you might have suspicions of where the story could go but you don't really know, and then it gets there or somewhere else you weren't expecting and you are delighted or devastated or whatever other emotion the story is leading you to. I freaking love reading. That's why I love writing. They are not all that different." Nona looked thrilled by this tidbit of information.

"I love that. Well, the world is glad you do what you do, Ms. Carmichael. Carry on," she winked at me and headed back behind the counter with her coffeepot in hand.

I went back to my work and an hour later; Agent McGee interrupted me by clearing his throat. He was alone. "Do you mind?" He gestured to the seat across from me, asking if he could join me.

"Of course." I motioned for him to sit. He laughed as he pulled out the chair and sat down.

"Of course you mind, but join you anyway, huh?" he smiled as he said it, and I laughed apologetically.

"I meant 'Not at all. I don't mind. Of course, you can join me.'"

"Sure you did," he teased.

"What's up?"

"Well, I've been looking at the file for that case of yours." He studied me closely as I put all my energy into appearing nonchalant. "You know, there was some pretty interesting information in there."

"Was there?" I asked innocently.

"There was." We sat together in silence for an uncomfortably long beat before he continued. "Like some unidentified DNA in the mix."

"Oh, no!" I feigned ignorance, pretending I didn't understand that he was talking about the bigfoot DNA that had been found at the crime scene. "It didn't match Bradley Cox? I was just sure he was one of my kidnappers."

"No, that's what I came to tell you. You were right. Some of the blood at the sight matched Bradley Cox, so we are charging him in your case as well. You will have to testify."

"Well, shit," I muttered. I hadn't thought about the fact that I would have to be involved in a court case. I just didn't want him to get away with the Staple's murders. I saw the odd expression on Agent McGee's face and corrected myself. "I mean, that's great news! I knew it. I just knew it. It's just that I hadn't thought about the fact that I would have to testify. But, I will, of course." I quickly added in case he thought I had plans to bail on him. I guess technically, with DNA evidence, they could probably get a guilty verdict without my testimony, but my testimony would cinch it and even if he got off on the Staple's murders, at least he would be charged with my kidnapping and with intent to kill. "So, has he told you who hired him?"

"Not yet, but we're hopeful that we can get it out of him. If he thinks it will help him in some way, I think he will eventually talk." He studied me again, and I tried not to fidget and took a drink of my cold coffee just to have something to do with my hands. "Are you really not going to acknowledge my comment about the mystery DNA?" He asked again, and I sighed and set down my cup.

"What do you want me to say?"

"I want you to tell me the truth. You and I both know that the account you gave Sheriff Struthers was not true. Elena–" He paused and looked thoughtful, like he was trying to decide if he wanted to say what was coming next. "We know the kidnappers took your shoes." I let out a small gasp and my face revealed the truth. How did he know that? "Sheriff Struthers reported barefoot footprints on the dusty floor of the cabin. There were also some very large barefoot prints as well," he looked at her pointedly. Well, hell. Why hadn't Sheriff Struthers said anything about this to her? I guess the stories were true. Law enforcement around these parts all knew that the bigfoot were there. They simply didn't talk about it. I had heard tales of officers answering calls of late night disturbances at properties and when they reported back to the station, they were simply asked, "Was it—?" and answered, "Yep," and yet none of it was reported. I don't know if the authorities usually kept it secret so as not to look crazy because they didn't want the backlash from others in the extended law enforcement community or what. In my case, I had theorized that Sheriff Struthers knew his cousins, the Crawleys, were guilty and used my withholding of evidence as an excuse not to pursue pressing charges on his relatives, but maybe there was more to it than that. I realized we were sitting in silence as my mind had been spinning on these thoughts and Agent McGee studied my face closely. Then I gave him the closest thing he was probably ever going to get out of me in the way of an admission.

"Are you going to charge me with something if I don't change my story?" I asked simply. This wasn't just about me, or Agent McGee. It was about keeping my friends safe. He sat there playing with a napkin that had been sitting on the table. He took a long time to answer, and

I was starting to be afraid of what he would say when he did speak, but finally my fears were put to rest.

"No. I just really want to know the truth–that's all." At that, he got up from the table, smiled, and gave me a little wave. "I'll be in touch, Ms. Carmichael," he said, and then he strolled out of the coffee shop at a leisurely pace. As the door closed behind him, I let out a long breath that I hadn't realized I was holding. Nona walked up to my table. The place was mostly empty.

"What was that about?" she asked under her breath.

"That, my friend, was an attempt to unravel the statement I gave to Sheriff Struthers at the hospital after Bob rescued me." Nona let out a long breath herself.

"Shit," she said.

I nodded miserably.

CHAPTER 16

I decided to drive out to Ahmet's place, mostly because I was having a hard time getting my conversation with Agent McGee out of my mind. And as I got to the driveway, Agent Hart's car was sitting there again. She looked up from what she was reading and waved at me as I waved at her, then I noticed she was motioning for me to stop and talk.

"Hey, how are you?" I asked, smiling at her. She seemed surprised and then smiled back.

"I'm much better today, thanks to you for letting us borrow your casts."

"That's what Rhett told me!" Agent Hart looked exasperated but quickly recovered.

"Don't be too hard on him. I'm always the one to instigate a conversation with him and he absolutely hates it when I do, and I promise, he never gives me more than the bare minimum of information I'm asking about." I smiled at her as I said this, and I saw the deep crevice dimple on her cheek pop before the smile hit her lips. "I just happened to notice he wasn't across from Nona's place most of the morning while I was working and when I was leaving, I thought it would be nice to let him know I was coming out here since you were likely watching

Ahmet's place, anyway. You guys know we're not really going anywhere, don't you?"

"Yeah, but we're supposed to watch for suspicious activity."

"Seen any yet?"

"No, but I have got a ton of reading done." I noticed a stack of paperback books in the backseat of her car. I couldn't help noticing my first two Moody books in the pile. "Thanks again for the plaster print, though. They told us they were about to pull us and send in someone else, instead we've been reassigned for six more weeks." Agent Margie Hart seemed pleased about this.

"I saw Bert heading over to talk to your husband as I was driving away. I bet he'll be trying to show you property that's for sale by tomorrow. I hope you don't mind. I told my friends you were thinking of staying." By the look on her face, she did mind, but was trying hard not to. "I'm sorry." I said, picking up on her trepidation.

"Oh, it's okay. It's hard to be seen after spending your lifetime being invisible. It is our job to be invisible, but you all have made that difficult."

"Sorry," I apologized again.

"Naah, it's okay—it's actually nice." She amended. "I'm just not used to it yet."

"So what kind of things do they want from you to let you stay on the case?" I asked curiously. "Maybe I can help you come up with more of it." It was her turn to look curious.

"Why are you helping us, anyway?"

"I thought we established that I didn't want to start over with new agents."

"Oh, yeah," Margie shrugged like, 'Of course, I remember that,' but for some reason I got the impression that she was disappointed. And I realized that it wasn't the whole truth.

PSA #45: Often in life, it is tempting to keep "would-be-kindnesses" to ourselves. I mean, no one wants to feel like the goober who is over complimenting others when they really should have just played it cool. But it's important to remember that everyone has a bit of insecurity in them and sometimes one small encouragement can make all the difference in the world to the person who needs to hear it.

"Which is true," I said. "But not the whole truth. I guess the whole truth is that I like you guys." I watched as Margie Hart's hard shell cracked just a little. "You are interesting. I mean, how many people do you know who spend their lives investigating paranormal activity?" I realized who I was talking to. "Don't answer that. Obviously you know scads–but for the average person like me, you don't get that."

"I hate to break it to you, but you are anything but average," Margie said with a smile.

"Fair enough, but not only have you had an interesting career, I'm hoping that you will eventually feel comfortable sharing your stories with us." I shrugged. "I can never resist a good story. And besides, you are clearly hilarious and as for Rhett, I sense there is more under that 1970s Private Investigator exterior he has going on." Margie barked a little laugh at that.

"I call it his Rockford Files complex," she said with a grin. "I have tried to update his wardrobe, but he always goes back to the same sunglasses, the same clothes." She shrugged, "It's not even like he just hasn't moved on. He was only a child in the 70s. That man has had to go out and dig up these outfits from vintage and thrift stores. Oh, and those flyers in the Sunday paper that show very outdated clothing that are clearly targeting old people. He just loves those companies because he is able to get the clothes he likes, but they are brand new." She laughed again and was shaking her head in happy resignation. "I finally had to give up and let him be."

"Well, not that he will care if you all are planning on retiring, but part of it was his personal style that made me notice and remember him." I decided not to mention that I thought he looked like a smoking ferret in 70s private eye attire. "He was too memorable to me and as a writer, I collected him in my storage bank of characters. I saw him in Niagara Falls in a restaurant and so when I spotted him again in New York City and I recognized him, it freaked me out. That's when my suspicions that we were being followed became founded."

"Well, if for some reason we stay in the game and don't retire, I will let him know that his look makes him more visible than invisible these days." She paused for a moment and then answered my original question. "The agency likes anything we can get that shows that we have made contact with or are observing contact being made with the paranormal world. That's why your print was so perfect. It is the kind of thing the agency considers evidence." I was starting to second guess my decision to share.

"So, do you think it will make them want to stick around permanently?" I hadn't thought about the possibility of the whole thing backfiring and being stuck with them forever!

"If they do, Rhett and I plan on asking to be assigned here. We will tell them we plan to become a part of the community and work undercover. It would be the best of both worlds for us really, we could still get paid but live in an environment that we enjoy and can feel at home in—maybe even make some friends." She sighed. "We could finally put down some roots."

"Do they do that?" This surprised me. "I mean, let people permanently locate somewhere? And you would be okay with waiting to retire?"

"Oh yeah, if we worked here, we wouldn't need to retire. And yes, to answer your question, they've got a lot of agents permanently stationed on the ground. The south has them largely for hauntings and vampires. Savannah, Georgia, has one agent on the ground there and New Orleans, of course, has several. We've got a few agents in permanent residence in Washington state since they have such a high number of extraterrestrial visits and, of course, they have sasquatch, too. We're all over."

"Roswell, New Mexico?" I asked only somewhat jokingly.

"Sure, but totally overrated." Margie said matter-of-factly. I realized this was the perfect conversation to find out if we even wanted Agents Barrett and Hart permanently assigned to the area.

"So, you seemed upset on a personal level at the idea of bigfoot being hunted, but what is your agency's end goal with this thing?" I asked cautiously. "I mean, if there were actually bigfoot around this area, is the ultimate goal to round them up and kill them? To imprison them? To protect them?" Margie pondered how to answer my question, or maybe she was just pondering as to whether or not to answer.

"The unofficial motto among the agents is 'To Protect & To Protect', the idea being that we are protecting both sides–both humanity and the paranormal. Most of us became agents because we are interested in all things paranormal and we don't want to see harm come to any beings unnecessarily. We don't want to see people endangered by paranormals, and we don't want to see paranormals endangered by people."

"So you're telling me the government wouldn't hold an extraterrestrial or a bigfoot captive to research them or experiment on them?" I asked suspiciously. Again, there was a long pause.

"No, I'm not telling you that," she whispered. "I'm telling you that Rhett and I wouldn't." Was this her way of saying that we could trust the two of them more than the agency they worked for? Just then, we heard the buzz of a motorbike engine getting louder as it drew nearer to us. Ahmet came around the bend of his long driveway and came to a stop in front of our two cars.

"Well, hello, ladies. Having a good chat?"

"We are actually. Were you feeling left out?" I joked. Ahmet laughed.

"I didn't even realize you all were down here. I just felt like going on a ride. You wanna come, Ele?" The last time I had ridden on Ahmet's motorcycle with him had been initially terrifying, and by the end, really fun. Margie's phone buzzed, and she looked at the screen and then lifted her finger in the international "just a minute" hand position and answered it.

"Hmm..." I said quietly to Ahmet, pondering his question, "I came by to talk to you about something. But sure," I shrugged. "A ride sounds fun." Agent Hart put her phone down beside her and let out a small chuckle.

"That was Rhett. You weren't kidding. Bert has a place he wants to show us right now and since you guys are together and going on a ride?" She raised her eyebrow to verify I had said yes.

"Yes," I replied happily, "I guess we're going on a ride."

"Well, I'm not going to learn anything new from that. I think I'll meet Rhett and Bert in town so we can go look at the place." Agent Margie Hart almost seemed light-hearted. She usually had the countenance you would expect from a government agent with just a hint more quirk, which was, of course, accounted for by the fact that she was with Paranormal Affairs. She wiggled her fingers in a little wave, started her engine and pulled out onto the highway and headed toward town.

"Let me park my car," I told Ahmet.

"Just take it up to my place. I'll follow you." I drove up Ahmet's driveway, parked my car, and as I was getting out, I saw Ahmet go into his garage and get a second helmet. It looked brand new. Then I noticed the one on his head looked new as well.

"Those are pretty. Did you get new helmets?" I asked, even though I could tell that he had.

"Yeah, now we can have our talk while we're on our ride," he seemed so pleased with himself. I was confused.

"What do you mean?"

"They have headphones and speakers in them. That way, we can talk to one another while we ride." He switched something on and then handed the helmet to me and I put it on my head.

"That is so cool," I understood his excitement now. I immediately started talking to see if it was working. "Breaker one nine, breaker one nine–you got your ears on?" I asked in my best C.B. lingo truck driver voice. Ahmet laughed softly, but I could hear it so clearly.

"Are we truck drivers now?" His warm voice was right in my ears. It felt a tad too intimate. I might have to keep up the truck driver persona in order not to get weirded out by it.

"Copy that, good buddy," I smiled and shrugged. "Or maybe not," I went back to my regular voice, "since I have now exhausted my entire truck driver vocabulary." He laughed aloud at this.

"Good. I have a feeling that would have become annoying fairly quickly."

"What? Are you saying I'm obnoxious?" I asked indignantly.

"Not you–but truck driver Ele may be a bit much. We both know those are two very distinct personalities." It was my turn to laugh.

"And now you are accusing me of having multiple personality disorder! I don't know if I want to go on a ride with you or not!" I joked as I climbed onto the bike seat behind him.

"Aww...come on. It'll be a blast." At that, Ahmet revved up the motor and did all the little ankle and wrist motions involved in making a motorcycle go. It seemed quite an elaborate feat. And then we jetted forward, I let out a little squeal and immediately heard Ahmet's soft laughter in my ears. I wrapped my arms around him and held on tight. Well, these stupid helmets were going to be embarrassing. I was able to make all sorts of terrified sounds before and now I would have to try and maintain my cool so he wouldn't hear every gasp.

"So, what did you want to talk to me about?" He asked once we were on the highway.

"Agent McGee surprised me at the coffee shop today."

"Really?" Ahmet sounded as surprised as I was.

"Yeah, it was so weird. He basically came to tell me that they know my account to Sheriff Struthers was a load of bunk. It turns out Sheriff Struthers did, too. He had written in his report that I was barefoot, so they knew it was impossible that I had run all that way home in just a few hours, at least not without my feet being considerably more cut up."

"What did you do? Did you tell him the truth?"

"No. I wasn't sure what to do, so I asked him if they would charge me with something if I didn't change my story." Ahmet let out a long slow exhale, understanding that this question was practically an admission that my original account had not been entirely true.

"What did he say?"

"He said no, that they wouldn't be charging me with anything, he really just wanted to know the truth."

"Wow, did you spill the beans then?" Ahmet asked as if he already knew I had and my answer surprised him.

"No—but probably only because he got up and walked away after saying it." I admitted. "I wanted to tell him everything, but honestly, I cannot see one good reason to reveal what really happened. It could only put Bob, JoJo, and the babies in jeopardy. Best-case scenario, nothing would happen. But the risk is not worth it just so I can be up front with an FBI agent I like. I think there is a possibility I may eventually tell Rhett and Margie, though."

"Yeah, you seem like you are really hitting it off with them." Ahmet mused.

"I don't know if I would put it that way, but I do think they're the real thing. I mean, I think they're just like us. I think they know that supernatural beings are real and they want to keep them safe. She told me that the unofficial slogan of the agents was 'To Protect & To Protect,' kind of like the policeman's 'To Protect & To Serve.' The idea behind it is that their goal is to protect both sides–the humans and the paranormals."

"Huh, that's oddly sweet. Not what I would expect from any government agency, if I'm being honest." Ahmet replied.

"That's what I thought too. Anyway, I guess Bert is already working on selling them a place—so that's hilarious."

"The man loves real estate, and he loves these mountains. I think he must feel good about them too or I can't imagine him intentionally bringing government agents to our front doors permanently. He must see an advantage here somewhere." I could tell Ahmet was not entirely sold on the idea, but he was remaining open-minded.

"I guess we will see," I said, and we were silent for a while as we took in the sheer beauty of the day. The leaves were all shades of orange and gold, red and purple. It was incredible, really.

"I had something I wanted to tell you too." Ahmet was suddenly excited as he remembered he had news to share.

"What?"

"Barnette is coming tomorrow to meet JoJo's dad."

"WHAT?! Are you kidding me? The big guy really agreed to meet with him?"

"Yeah, can you believe it? Vance organized it all." I wanted to ask if I could be there, but I wasn't sure if I should. Ahmet must have sensed my unasked question.

"I'm pretty sure you are welcome if you want to come. We're meeting at the treeline behind my house tomorrow at sunset."

"I would love to be there. Is Joyce coming?" I was wondering how Barnette's mother, Joyce, was handling this. She had been understandably trepidatious about the whole bigfoot angle of Barnette's rescue at first assuming it was a hallucination, but after our visit, begrudgingly accepting the truth of it.

"No, Barnette decided not to invite her. He said she hates it when he even brings bigfoot up, so he decided it was kinder if she didn't know what was going on." I could see that. It made me kind of sad though, because here was a woman whose own son was saved by sasquatch and she was still having a hard time warming up to the idea of the creatures. How the hell were my books supposed to rebrand bigfoot if someone who had every reason in the world to like them was still scared? I shook it off, there was nothing I could do about it. I must have physically shuddered in my effort to shake away those thoughts.

"Are you cold?" Ahmet asked with concern. "I should have grabbed you a jacket from the house."

"Oh, no. I'm fine. I've got my cardigan on and the sun is so warm today. This is so beautiful, Ahmet. Thanks for taking me."

"You're welcome," he suddenly sounded a little shy, which made me feel shy.

"Where are we going, anyway?" I noticed we had turned down a side road I had never been down. It was a gravel road that didn't appear to be particularly well maintained and it ran congruent to the river.

"Vance was telling me that there are a series of little waterfalls down this way. I'm hoping I can find them. I'm sure they're not going to be terribly impressive, but I love waterfalls all the same."

"Oh, me too." We made our way around a bend in the road and I could see a whole area where the river widened and there were rapids. Ahmet slowed down as we passed, and I looked back over my shoulder as the bike headed downhill. "Oh, Ahmet. It's beautiful!" I said quietly and sighed. He pulled off the road and turned off the motor.

"Well then, this must be it." His voice came out muffled as he pulled off his helmet and climbed off the bike. He held the bike steady so I could climb off as well and we each placed a helmet on a handlebar, so it was nice and balanced. We turned and took in the terrific view. The tree covered Kiamichi Mountains jutted up behind the river, but in the river itself were a series of drops and rapids that made a series of small waterfalls. There were some deer on the other side of the river drinking and one of their heads popped up, followed quickly by the others. They were inhaling the scent of us and their ears moved about on their heads, searching for a sound from us. Though their eyes had yet to find us, they were clearly determining whether to run.

"Aw, the poor things look frightened," I whispered. Their large, dark eyes finally landed on us on the opposite side of the bank. We had been making our way to the riverside as we talked. Ahmet and I sat down in silence and the deers must have decided that we were not a danger to them because they went back to drinking the water, although they kept a watchful eye on us as they did.

"They're beautiful, aren't they? There are a few deer who live in the woods between our houses that will get within an arm's length to me now. I walk through the woods so often, they have accepted me."

"Do you pet them? Or feed them or anything?" I had been wondering about putting food out for the ones I see behind the house sometimes. Likely, the same ones that Ahmet sees given the proximity of our homes.

"No. They say feeding them can make them more vulnerable and, as much as I would love to reach out and touch them, I don't." He smiled at me and then looked back across the river at the group of deer that looked like they were about to go on their way.

"Just seeing them is enough. When I was a kid, I would never have imagined I would live in such a place that I could wander the woods every morning. I didn't want to live anywhere but the city. But life changes you, doesn't it? Heartbreak changes you." The sharp and sudden pain of sadness at the mention of heartbreak surprised me and I realized that I after the initial window of grief that I had allowed myself when I was staying with Evie before moving to Oklahoma, that I had shoved all my heartache into a box, an angry box, and tried to never let myself feel any of the pain. When I did, I likely disguised it as anger—fuming anger with a very foul mouth.

"I guess it does," I mumbled. "I've been trying very hard to ignore heartbreak and get on with things, but I suspect all I've done is hide it away. I suppose it would be good if I tried to process through it rather than repress it."

"We all have our own way. I walk. I told you it was to stay in shape after leaving the city, which is partly true, but a lot of my morning hikes involve trying to outrun the thoughts that plague my mind. It's not as bad anymore, not as constant anyway, but sometimes it's still a struggle. For a while, I couldn't see a pregnant woman or a baby without weeping. Which, as you can imagine, was awkward as a doctor. No one wants their doctor to burst into tears when they are coming in for a checkup." I couldn't help but smile.

"No, I suppose not." I realized that being around Nona, or possibly even JoJo, might have been triggering for him, so I asked. "How has it been being around Nona and caring for JoJo?"

He smiled at the mention of JoJo. "And before you say anything, I am fully aware that JoJo and the babies aren't human."

"I wasn't going to say anything, because you are right. When you first noticed she was pregnant, I became a little obsessive- compulsive about it. I was overly concerned about her and the baby's well-being. It was something that I thought I had long ago overcome, but the triggers were probably always there. I think over time it becomes a matter of whether you let yourself pull those triggers and spiral into those dark places again. But, oddly enough, in caring for JoJo through the pregnancy and through delivering the babies, I have felt a huge release. Like after all these years, I am able to heal. And when I see Nona, I feel nothing but excitement and joy for her and Vance."

"That's really wonderful, Ahmet." We sat watching the water swirl in the river before us. I noticed there were tiny fish popping up to the surface, doing what I didn't know. Suddenly, the words came tumbling out of me. "After I found out that Doug had cheated on me, I ran. Until he came here to try and get me back—" I saw the confused look on Ahmet's face. "I guess that was before you knew me—he came here shortly before they kidnapped me to try and talk me into coming back to New York with him." Ahmet made a small sound of acknowledgement as he nodded for me to continue. "I had not even had a proper conversation with him since I had left him. You see, he didn't know that I had caught him. Evie and I just happened to go to the same restaurant that he had taken his assistant to for lunch that day. So naive was I that I had even been about to call out to the two of them when I noticed his hand on her leg slipping up her thigh under her skirt. I was absolutely shocked. I didn't see it coming. Evie and I immediately went back to the home I lived in with Doug and moved out every one of my things to her storage unit and by the end of the day, I had moved in with her. I had completely moved out before he was even aware that I knew about the affair. He came home that night to discover that me and all of my things were missing and when he tried to talk to me about it, I told him I had received all the information I needed when I saw him at lunch with Sarah that day. I let myself mourn during the time I was at Evie's, then I came here and put Doug and all his nonsense out of my mind."

"God, Ele. I'm so sorry." I felt a rush of embarrassment that I had just bored him with my life story.

"Don't be. I love my life here." I said this with certainty, because–it was true. I did actually love my life in Oklahoma, of all places. Although I wondered if the words 'of all places' would ever stop being the words that automatically followed 'Oklahoma' in my mind. "I'm sorry for blabbing on and on, boring you." Ahmet put his hand gently over mine for just a moment.

"Don't," he said softly. "Part of being friends is knowing each other's story." He gave me a gentle pat and then took his hand away, leaving me aware of its absence.

We sat for a bit longer and then walked along the river for a little while, stopping in front of each of the little falls to appreciate their beauty. In the crisp fall air, with the trees all around us a varying array of colors, I felt oddly content.

CHAPTER 17

I woke up to my phone ringing. "Good morning, sunshine!" came Bert's cheerful voice when I groggily answered it. It was barely seven. I couldn't help but be reminded of a time in the not so distant past when I called and woke up Bert at the butt-crack of dawn. I'd just spent hours wide awake after Bob and JoJo had tried to chase me away by throwing large rocks onto my roof in the middle of the night.

"Why on earth are you calling me so early, Bert?" I rubbed my eyes and looked at the clock. 7:03.

"Aw, hell, Ele! I'm sorry. I didn't realize how early it was. I just got up and saw that I had received an email from Ron Dobson. He's attached a sales contract. He says it's ours." I jolted awake in excitement.

"Really? You're not kidding?" I asked excitedly.

"Now, why the hell would I–?" Bert started to answer me but I interrupted him.

"You wouldn't! You wouldn't call me at this time of the morning if you were pulling a prank. Bert! You did it! You found a way. I knew you could. We're going to get our sanctuary!" I was so excited I didn't even give him a chance to answer me. My brain was firing ninety to nothing, realizing that all the crap of trespassers and jackasses trying to hunt in the woods around my house was potentially a thing of the past. I let out a whoop and Biffy went nuts barking and yipping and licking my face. He was excited because I was excited. I could hear Bert laughing.

"I'll let the others know. I'm glad you're happy, Ele." Bert said sincerely. He sounded happy as well.

"Hey, Bert," a sudden inspiration had just hit. "Do you think we can ask Mr. Dobson to hold off on telling Dorothy until everything is a done deal? I think I would feel safer that way." I hadn't mentioned Abner's threatening me at the gas station the other day to anyone, but suddenly I realized I didn't want the Crawleys to get wind of our purchasing the property until papers were signed.

"Yeah, of course I can ask. If I tell him they've been pretty ugly to you, he'll understand. But Ele, you haven't been having any more problems with them, have you?"

"Just a little run-in the other day, but nothing I can't handle."

"Ele, you have to tell us these things! You can't be facing these two alone. Especially since you still have that restraining order. We can have them arrested for breaking it."

"It's okay, Bert. I was actually the one who broke the restraining order."

"ELE!" Bert seemed even more alarmed now, what the hell did he think I would do, anyway?

"It was an accident, Bert. I wasn't paying attention, and I accidentally pulled into the pump next to Abner to get gas. He just said some nasty things to me, that is all. I hurried the hell out of there and then we went to see the babies that night and I kind of forgot about the whole thing until now."

"Well, okay. But don't do it again. If you have any contact with them, you tell us, okay? Especially if they are threatening." I could hear the concern in Bert's voice, so I chose to be comforted to have friends who cared rather than annoyed that he was bossing me around.

"Okay, Bert. I will. Thank you," I said sincerely. Then I screamed again in excitement, "ACK! Bert, we're getting our sanctuary!" I squealed one more time into the phone and I could hear him laughing as I hung up. I wasn't about to let the Crawleys ruin this moment for me. I hopped out of the bed with Bif hot on my heels and decided to go to Nona's early today. It was already an exciting morning, my pup couldn't wait to see what was coming next.

The novel was going incredibly well. Nona greeted me with a giant hug, a vanilla latte and a blueberry muffin on the house in celebration of the news. Bif was being such a good boy, just sitting at my feet chewing his bone as I wrote. I was deeply entranced in my scene when my phone buzzed. I normally ignore calls while I'm writing, but it was the Boone Police Department, so I grabbed it as fast as I could before it went to voicemail.

"Detective Puckett?"

"Yes, ma'am. Is it safe to assume, then, that this is Ms. Carmichael?"

"Yes, it is. What's up?" I could almost feel the buzz of electricity coming at me through the call. Something had happened. I could tell from the energy in the detective's voice. Instead of his usual, slow calm baritone rumble, he was speaking more quickly with a tinge of excitement dripping from every word. I jumped up from my seat and began pacing around the table. The place was empty except for the three of us, since it was well past the morning rush and late enough that even the dawdlers had gone, but both Nona and Bif were watching me intently.

"I have news,"

"Well, no shit Sherlock! Spit it out!" I don't know why I become an utter smartass when I get anxious, but apparently Detective Puckett was not offended, because a deep rumble of a laugh echoed in my ears. "Sorry, but why else would you be calling me? What is it?" I asked impatiently.

"We've found your mother." You could have knocked me over with a feather. I thought he would have news, a lead or something, but not the news I had been waiting to hear my entire life. I suddenly felt faint and lowered myself back into my chair. My head was literally spinning. Nona and Bif knew something was up by the look of me and were both almost instantly by my side. "Well, we've found her car and a woman's remains were inside. I just got the confirmation back from forensics and it's a match. Are you there, Ms. Carmichael?" My breathing was shallow. My head was swirling. Nona put her hand on my shoulder to steady me.

"Yes, I'm here." There was another long pause as I tried to regain my composure. "But, how?"

"They found the other missing woman I called you about the other day alive and well in Los Angeles. It turns out she had simply run away, changed her name, and no one had run her case again since the onset of the internet or they would have discovered it by now. So when that thread closed, I started combing through your mom's case file again, trying to see if there was anything that could have been overlooked. I was using google maps to try and retrace all possible routes to and from the bar that night based on what your aunt had told the original detective and I got to thinking, what if she decided to take the scenic route home? That bar was only a mile from Lake Merryweather. The more scenic route home around the lake was not her obvious path home, but would only take her about fifteen minutes out of her way. And I thought that it wasn't a total impossibility that she might have done this because I often choose to take the long way around the lake when I'm close by. It's calming. Anyway, there is that one curvy spot in the road that runs right along the southern bend of the lake and I just got that tingle you get when you're on to something." A small whimper escaped me and Detective Pucket paused for a moment.

"I'm okay. Keep going."

"Well, further inspection of the case file revealed that they had never dragged Lake Merryweather after your mother's disappearance, so I ordered a sonar search. They discovered a car on the first day. I didn't want to call you until we were able to pull the car out of the lake to get more details–it was such a long shot. But when they pulled it out, it was your mother's vehicle–the make, model, and tag number match the report and there were the solitary remains of a female body–still buckled in–which would indicate that she was knocked unconscious in the accident. I knew it had to be her, but decided to wait for confirmation. After waiting this long, the last thing I wanted to do was give you false hope. But this is not a false hope, Ms. Carmichael. We have finally found your mother." At this, I burst into tears. I laid my forehead on my laptop on the table in front of me and silently wept. "Er–on behalf of the entire police department here in Boone, I offer our deepest condolences. I'm gonna let you go, ma'am. You have a lot to process. I'll be in touch."

"Thank you, Officer Puckett. Thank you." The words escaped me in a whisper. I placed the phone on the table next to my computer and then laid my head down and cried some more.

Nona, sweet Nona, was kneeling beside my chair on one side, just patting my back and rubbing circles with her fingers as I had watched her do to Vance the other night. Bif was on my other side with his head in my lap, offering his own brand of comfort and an occasional whimper. Finally, after a few minutes of weeping, I raised my head from the table and turned into Nona's open arms and cried for a little while longer on her shoulder. "It's my mom." I finally said between breaths. "They found my mom." I heard Nona gasp.

"Oh, honey," was all she said, understanding that I just needed a little time. She continued to comfort me wordlessly as I cried some more. Finally, after I was all cried out, I pulled away from her and she moved to sit in the chair across the table from me as I scratched Bif behind his ears.

"Detective Puckett was studying her file when he realized that they had never dragged a lake that she might have passed on her drive home. It wasn't her most likely path home, so I guess they didn't think of it. I don't know how that's possible, but somehow it is. Oh, Nona. It's the best I could have hoped for, aside from maybe them finding her alive somewhere with amnesia, but that would hold its own sorrow. Nona," I heaved a heavy sigh, realizing suddenly what a tremendous relief this new knowledge was. "It was just an accident—a tragic accident. There wasn't any foul play. She didn't suffer at the hands of evil." I started crying again, but continued to speak through ragged breath and tears. "Every time in my whole life that I have ever heard of a crime committed against another human that ended in their death, I couldn't help but place my mother in the scenario. Was that how she died? I would always wonder. It was horrific, but I couldn't help it. The torment of not knowing is bound to the imagination, and the imagination can be cruel." I looked at my friend and found myself smiling. I inhaled so deeply I felt almost lightheaded from the infusion of oxygen to my system, I wondered if I had ever breathed so freely before. It was like, for my whole life, I had been just a little bit suffocated by the not-knowing and now that was gone. The weight on my chest that I hadn't even known was compressing my lungs had lifted.

"Hey, you okay?" Agent Rhett Butler said with concern as he rolled down his window. I must have looked a mess, because the fact that I had been crying was clearly not lost on him. I approached his vehicle with a smile, a cup of coffee, and a cookie from Nona.

"I am very good. I just got some news that was quite emotional," I replied. I didn't elaborate further. Nona and I had been talking for several hours and I was all talked out. I also wasn't ready to share it with anyone else yet, although I knew it was possible that by tomorrow's papers the news could be widespread. I didn't know if the national news would pick it up because of my author status or not. I hoped not, but needed to prepare myself for "Remains of Best-Selling Author's Mother Found" headlines. "Nona wanted me to give you a cup of coffee. I'm just heading home now, but since I know I have no choice in the matter, you're welcome to follow." I hoped he wouldn't. As far as I could tell, they almost never followed us in the evening and even though it was still early afternoon, my hope was that by telling him my plan, he would give himself the rest of the day off. I decided not to mention that I was going over to Ahmet's later and I certainly didn't invite him to this one. Both Rhett and Margie were getting more friendly to us, warming up to the idea of possibly moving here. He might actually take me up on the invitation next time, and the last thing I wanted was Agent Barrett and Agent Hart to show up just when Barnette was finally getting his chance to meet the bigfoot who had rescued him from the Sasquatch Serial Killer.

"Thanks for the coffee," he raised his cup, looked across to the coffee shop and nodded a thank you to Nona as well, who was standing at her front door. She smiled and gave a wave back. "Bert showed us a beautiful property yesterday. He's lined up a few other properties for us to go look at later today. Now that guy is a boat-load of fun, isn't he?" When I first heard of the elaborate lengths Bert would go to show potential buyers the properties for sale, I teased him that he would never make the sales because people were having too much fun hanging out with him. On some of the more remote properties, he would take clients in to explore the property on his ATV or even occasionally on horseback.

"Bert is a lot of fun. He's a really great guy, too. I know realtors don't always have the best of reputations, but you can trust Bert. He's as honest as the day is long." I smiled at Rhett. "So he's taking you out to show you more properties today, too, huh?" It seemed that Bert and Vance had already thought of a way to ensure that our friendly neighborhood paranormal agents would not be anywhere near Ahmet's place this evening. Bert would be entertaining them.

"He is indeed," said Rhett. I smiled at him, a genuine Mr. Rogers Won't-You-Be-My-Neighbor kind of smile, and I felt it too from my heart.

"That's great, Rhett. So you guys are really thinking of taking the plunge, huh?" Rhett was smiling too and nodding animatedly and he reminded me less of a ferret at the moment and more of an otter—a happy-go-lucky otter.

"You know, we just might. Like I said, neither of us has slept this well for years." Again, I wondered where they were staying, but didn't think Rhett would welcome my asking. "There is a real peacefulness here, isn't there?" He sighed a contented sigh as he said it.

"There is." I agreed. "There really is." I smiled and realized that he was precisely right. I had loved my life in NYC, but the prevailing descriptive word for the city would not be peaceful. Maybe that was why I had felt so instantly at home here, it cocooned me in peaceful vibes. Aside from when I was being kidnapped or harassed by man or beast. I gave him a little smile and a wave and headed to my car. As I pulled out to head home, I was so distracted thinking about all the news of the day—my mom had been found and I was going to get the land for the sanctuary and I maybe even actually liked these crazy fuckers that were assigned by the government to spy on me–that I did not notice as Jeb Crawley pulled out and followed me. Nor did I notice when Agent Rhett Barrett pulled out and followed him.

CHAPTER 18

Barnette and Joyce were standing in Ahmet's driveway talking to him when I got there. Seeing the two of them sent my mind into a flashback to the hospital not so very long ago. Barnette lying in the hospital bed in a neck cast contraption, having barely escaped death at the hands of a crazed serial killer that was plaguing the area and Joyce, his momma, who was fiercely protective after the ordeal and infinitely grateful for her son's survival. They had wanted to thank Ahmet for his role in Barnette's rescue just like they were here today to thank JoJo's father, the bigfoot who had intervened in the knick of time to stop the thrust of the murderer's knife into Barnette's chest and prevent the removal of his heart. I felt like I was running late even though we didn't have an actual time set other than "sunset". We were on bigfoot time now. The sky was a beautiful peachy hue as the sun began to fall behind the mountain. As I got out of my vehicle, I looked around and realized that I had beaten Vance to Ahmet's.

"Hello you two!" I called out. "I didn't think you were coming, Joyce!"

"I almost didn't get the opportunity. This little turd here thought that just because the idea of bigfoot being real creeps me out that he would spare me. Good thing he's an honest kid, and I happened to be checking up on him last night and asked what his plans were today after he finished his big test. Since he couldn't lie to me, I got a chance to tag along. I don't know why he would think I didn't want to thank the creature who saved his life!" Joyce reached up and ran her hand over her son's head and I could imagine that she had been doing that same affectionate move since he was a young child. Barnette was smiling and looking sheepish.

"Hi, Ele. It's nice to see you again," said Barnette. Although Ahmet had been in touch with Barnette, I had not seen him since he shared his story at the bigfoot festival and I wondered if he got any flack at school after that. I mean, what freshman in college wants to be known as the crazy bigfoot kid? I knew a local news station ran a story on the festival and had shared part of Barnette's story, but miracle of miracles, the story did not run nationally. I would have thought that the sole survivor of the Sasquatch Serial Killer claiming to have been rescued by a bigfoot instead of being attacked by one would have been an international headline, but what the hell do I know?

"It's nice to see you, too. You're looking great," I told him. Barnette smiled and shrugged. It was true. His neck brace was gone and all signs of his very near death experience were gone.

The rumble of pick up truck tires on gravel reached our ears and Ahmet, Joyce, Barnette, and I all turned to watch as Vance came up the drive. It surprised me he was alone. He jumped out of the vehicle and called out to us.

"Sorry I'm late. Nona wasn't feeling well, so I was just staying to make sure everything was alright." Ahmet went to full alert.

"Is she okay?" Ahmet asked immediately. "Is she cramping? She's not spotting, is she?"

"Oh," Vance looked confused for a moment. "Oh no, I don't think it's the baby. She said she just had a headache." This didn't seem to ease Ahmet's mind.

"Was she dizzy?"

"No, I don't think so."

"Any changes in her vision?"

"Not that she mentioned." I could see that Vance was now getting anxious.

"A fever?"

"No, Ahmet. She just had a little headache. Should I be worried?"

"No... no. I'm sorry. I'm sure that's all it is. But if she starts having trouble breathing, or extreme swelling in the face or hands, or—" Ahmet stopped and took in all of our staring faces. "I'm doing it again, aren't I?" We all nodded. Joyce put her hand on Vance's arm.

"I got headaches all the time when I was pregnant with Barnette. It's fairly common." Vance let out a little sigh of relief and then looked back to Ahmet, who nodded encouragingly and smiled.

"It is common. I am really, really sorry I scared you. A severe persistent headache can be a sign of preeclampsia–I just wanted to make sure."

"It's okay, doc." Vance smiled at Ahmet, "But you did just scare the bejesus out of me." He looked up toward the tree row behind Ahmet's house. "They're here." Barnette began looking excitedly in the direction Vance was looking, but clearly didn't see anything.

"How do you know?" Barnette asked, curiously. Vance hesitated, then shrugged and said calmly, like it was the most normal thing in the world.

"They just told me." At that, he headed toward the treeline behind Ahmet's home with all of us hot on his heels. Although Joyce seemed a bit more reticent, I could tell she was still completely intrigued. Vance slowed his gait and, as if by magic, two giant creatures appeared from the trees and stepped out into the clearing of Ahmet's back yard. A little squeal came out of Joyce, it wasn't a scream or at all loud, just a short high- pitched squeal in the back of her throat that she had been unable to control. Bob's father-in-law (if I were to put it in human terms, and since I'm a human, this is just easiest) had a good foot on him and I was pretty sure that Bob was hitting nine or ten feet. He was simply massive. I wondered if this was an indication that bigfoot do continue to grow taller their entire lives as I had read. I looked over to see Barnette, who was grinning from ear to ear in recognition. JoJo's dad looked at us warily, taking us in each individually by slowly looking us up and down, and then his eyes finally softened as they rested on Barnette. He looked him up and down and kind of cocked his head to the right and gave Barnette almost a smile.

"He thinks you look much better than when he last saw you. He is pleased you are well," communicated Vance on the beings behalf.

"Is he talking to you telepathically?" Barnette asked.

"Yes, why?"

"Because I felt like I was picking up that same message. Can I try to tell him 'thank you for saving me?'"

"Of course," Vance was visibly excited that Barnette was understanding them. The key is to think in feelings, you are communicating intention instead of language. They won't understand the words 'thank you' but can totally understand the sentiment. It's kind of tricky but try to focus less on language and more on sending the intentions of your message. Barnette slowly nodded to the big guy, smiled, and then closed his eyes in deep concentration. I watched as the creature's eyes widened in surprise and then as an even wider grin spread across his face. Barnette opened his eyes and was thrilled to see that the big guy had received his message. Ahmet, Joyce, and I exchanged glances. We were hanging back a little bit, but then Joyce stepped forward to join Vance and Barnette to face the big guy and Bob. She looked at her son and Vance.

"Can you please thank him for me as well?" she asked and smiled directly at each of the giants standing before her and intentionally made eye contact and nodded. Barnette repeated his earlier motions and closed his eyes and held a look of deep concentration. As he did, the creature who had saved Barnette's life nodded and held up a hand, palm facing Joyce, and so intuitively she did the same. At that moment, I heard a zing, like a very fast wasp had just flown right by the side of my head and then there were two more. Bob and the big guy looked alarmed and turned and ran, disappearing into the forest as seamlessly as they had appeared.

"Get down," yelled Vance, as he simultaneously grabbed ahold of both Joyce and Barnette and pulled them to the ground just as Ahmet and I hit the ground beside them.

"Is someone shooting at us?" I asked incredulously. I truly could not comprehend it, but it seemed as though it was true.

"I think so. Is everyone okay?" Ahmet asked us, looking from one to the other to make sure no one had been hit. Each of us nodded and murmured assurances that we were not injured. I could no longer hear the footfall of Bob and the big guy. But I heard running in the opposite direction. And then it sounded like more running in the opposite direction.

"The shots came from the direction of Dobson's land," Vance said.

"Oh, for fuck's sake, when the hell are they going to give up?" I asked angrily. Joyce looked a little taken aback by my foul mouth and probably by the intensity of my foul mood as well, but I could not do it anymore. Vance's face held a look of deep concentration.

"They're both fine," he announced. "And so are JoJo and the babies. They made it back to Bob and JoJo's home. I'm so sorry," he said to Joyce and Barnette as he began helping Joyce to her feet. The rest of us stood up and started brushing the grass off of us. Frank Sinatra Jr. began weaving through my legs and purring and I reached down to pet him and could feel some of the tension flow out of me as my fingers caressed the soft fur of the big yellow tomcat.

"What was that?" Joyce was clearly on full momma bear alert. "And what did you mean, 'when the hell are they going to give up?'" Ahmet, Vance, and I exchanged a look and Ahmet took the lead in explaining.

"There are some local men who are trying to buy the adjoining property to Ele's and mine—the Dobson's place—so that they can lead bigfoot hunts." This information clearly distressed Barnette by the look on his face. "They don't know it yet, but Ele and a group of us found out today that we beat them out on their bid for the property. We are trying desperately to put an end to this." I could tell by the look on Joyce's face that this was not a satisfactory answer. I knew she must be thinking what would have happened if her son had been killed here tonight after all they had already gone through and I could see that Ahmet was perceiving this as well. "Joyce, we never would have asked you guys here if we had thought anything like this would happen. We haven't seen or heard any evidence of these guys on the Dobson's place for months now. And never near my property, only Ele's. I am so, so sorry that this happened." Joyce relaxed a little. One thing puzzled me.

"Is it just me or did it sound like there were two separate groups running apart from the bigfoot? I could have sworn I heard someone run away in the other direction after Bob and the big guy took off running—I'm assuming it was the shooter or shooters. But then, right after that, I heard what sounded like another runner or two going off in the same direction. Almost as if they were chasing the first—"

"I heard that too," said Barnette excitedly. "What do you think it means?"

"I don't know, but somehow, some way, we have got to put an end to these trespassers once and for all." I said with certainty, and Ahmet nodded in agreement.

"Well, let's go in the house. I made some bubble bread. Let's have some tea or coffee and a treat." We followed Ahmet to his back door. I think we all needed a little time to regroup after what had happened. It's not everyday you get shot at, or at least it shouldn't fucking be. Although, I'm pretty sure it wasn't us that were the targets. This really really upset me. How could we possibly make a sanctuary on property that was constantly being trespassed on by gunmen with a vengeance for the beings for whom we were trying to provide refuge? The last thing I wanted was to welcome displaced bigfoot so that they could be hunted. The conversation pulled me away from my worrying mind.

"What is bubble bread?" I heard Barnette ask, and Ahmet was very animated in his response.

"What is bubble bread?! You mean you've never had it? Oh, my friend, you are in for a treat!" Ahmet slapped his hand across Barnette's back as he said this and I saw the soft look on Joyce's face.

"It's sweet, isn't it?" I asked her softly. "The way the two of them have bonded."

"It really is," Joyce answered in a lowered tone as well. "And it came just when Barnette most needed it. Did you know he calls Barnette several times a week and has helped tutor him a bit in a class Barnette was struggling in?"

"I did not. But it doesn't surprise me. Ahmet is truly one of the kindest humans I've ever met." We watched as Ahmet instructed Barnette on how to start the coffee while he pulled out coffee cups. He sat a varied assortment of teas on the counter and started a teapot of water to boil on the stove. Then, when he had our full attention, he pulled the aluminum foil off of the top of a bundt cake pan in a 'Voila' fashion to reveal these gooey balls of brown sticky bread all stuck together in the pan. A heavenly sweet cinnamon scent hit our noses and there was a simultaneous sigh of satisfaction.

"I think you're right." Barnette said with a huge grin. "Bubble bread, where have you been all of my life?" He leaned over the pan, closed his eyes and breathed in deeply through his nose. Joyce, Vance, and I laughed and Ahmet just looked immensely pleased.

Ahmet served up dessert dishes of bubble bread all around and we each made our coffees and teas and sat around Ahmet's dining room table. His place was lovely. It was fairly minimalist in the decor but with a traditional flair of mission furniture handmade by the Amish instead of the modern design I usually associated with minimalism. It had a comfortable, homey feel.

"I can't believe they are real," Joyce said into her teacup as she took a sip.

"I know," I commiserated with her. I understood the overwhelm she was feeling.

Discovering that a mythical creature is real is a bit much to the logical mind. "I passed out the first time I saw one, so you're handling it better than I did," I said, laughing, remembering looking into Bob's face through my bathroom window when I had first moved into my cabin.

"You passed out?" Barnette asked in delight.

"Yes, sir." I told them the entire story—how Bob and JoJo had tried to chase me away at first by throwing big old rocks on my roof so that they would roll down and scare me. "I will never forget the sound of it. BOOM- rattle- rattle- rattle- THUNK! BOOM- rattle- rattle-rattle-THUNK! It was terrifying. I spent my first night in my cabin huddled down trembling, waiting for the first signs of morning so that I could call and chew out Bert, who sold me the place." Everyone was laughing at the thought.

"Bert felt terrible," interjected Vance. "He knew there were bigfoot on the property, or at least he very strongly suspected there were. And he would have done anything to keep the Crawley's from getting ahold of the place. When your bid came in and beat theirs, he was so tickled. I've never seen him so happy. But, of course, then he felt a great responsibility for you. And felt really bad that they had tried to scare you off so soon. On your first night, even!"

"Well, it worked for them with the couple who built the house. You can't blame them for trying. They had to have been so upset when the couple built it and moved in. I don't think they lived there more than a couple of months before putting it on the market." I said.

"I don't think they lived there more than a couple of weeks," said Vance.

"Why didn't you run away?" Joyce asked incredulously. "I would have been on the first bus out of town." She laughed.

"I'm stubborn." I laughed. "And they had done pissed me off. Once Bert assured me I wasn't in actual danger, I had no problem facing them off. They tried it several nights in a row, but I just put in foam earplugs and yelled out my window for them to cut it out. Eventually, they realized their tactics weren't going to work on me." I smiled at everyone around the table. "Then JoJo decided to befriend me."

"What?" asked Barnette excitedly. "I've got to hear that story. And did I hear Vance mention babies?" It was after 10:00 by the time we all left. We had such a nice time visiting, and we annihilated that pan of bubble bread, only leaving one serving behind for Ahmet to have for breakfast. It turned out that Barnette wanted to help out once we got the sanctuary going and Ahmet was excited about the idea of having help if any of the creatures needed medical care. A veterinary student and a medical doctor seemed like the perfect team for the job. How strange the world works! Sookie always likes to say that the Universe is conspiring on her behalf and lately, aside from being shot at, that sure seemed to be true.

PSA # 46: The Universe is conspiring on your behalf! Believe it!

CHAPTER 19

Hey, I didn't get a chance to tell you because we were never alone but something very HUGE happened today

I was laying in bed trying to fall asleep and my brain would not turn off. Three hugely significant things had happened that day and Ahmet didn't know the most important one. And it was possible that it would be in the papers in the morning and since I didn't know if Ahmet read the New York Times on his phone with his morning coffee, I just wanted to tell him myself.

What ELSE happened? You mean something besides getting the Dobson place and getting shot at?!?

Yep.

?!?!?!

They found my mother's car and her remains.

Oh my God, Ele!

I know. It's a lot. I can't sleep. And it's not because of getting shot at or thinking about our sanctuary. I can't stop thinking about my mom. I finally have the truth. It turns out she must have decided to take a strange route home that night that took her around the lake and she had an accident and ended up in the lake. They said her seatbelt was still on her, which likely means she was knocked unconscious during the accident. It's so funny. It was so long ago I would be surprised she was even wearing a seatbelt except for the fact that when the seatbelt laws started passing across the country, my Aunt Becky would always laugh and say that my mom would have been thrilled! That she had always harassed Aunt Becky to wear hers. It is such an odd detail to know about a woman I cannot even remember for sure. But now, that seatbelt is my clue that she might not have suffered.

Oh, Ele. <3

Every horrific death I have ever imagined for her at the hands of a murderer was not real! She just died in a car wreck and while drowning is terrible, she was likely unconscious when she drowned.

Ele, I don't even know what to say. It feels weird to say I'm happy for you, but I am. I am so happy for you to have closure. And for you to know the truth! <3 Thank you for telling me.

> I was afraid it would be in the papers tomorrow and I wanted to tell you myself.
>
> Also, you are nice to talk to.

That seemed a little forward of me and I wasn't trying to make advances. It was simply true. Ahmet was terribly nice to talk to. He always made me feel better. Whether I was sad or already happy, I always felt even better after talking to him. I hoped I hadn't weirded him out, though. I could see the little ellipses start and stop and start again. Finally, his text came through.

> You're nice to talk to too. How are you feeling? You weren't kidding when you said your news was HUGE!

> I feel lighter. Like a weight that has been with me always is lifted and I just might float away. But I feel happy. Happy to know the truth. Happy that I'm finally going to be able to give her a proper burial. Just happy. Of course, if I think about those bastards being on Dobson's land tonight—I mean OUR LAND!!!—and shooting at us, I am immediately pissed. But mostly, I just feel happy. I'm so thankful that no one was hurt.

> Me too. I realized later that we should have called the sheriff's office and told them we had been shot at, but what good would it have done? And it would have ruined the rest of the evening. At least we were able to salvage the night and have a nice time with Barnette and his mom.

Exactly! It was weird when I left your place though because Agent Hart was parked at the end of your driveway when I left and Agent Barrett was parked at the end of mine. I've never seen them here at night. I wonder what the hell that means.

?? I don't know ??

That is weird.

Well, I'll let you sleep. I just wanted to tell you my news.<3

Thank you<3

Night night.

Good Night.

As much as every feminist bone in my body resisted it, my soft insides couldn't help being pleased that Ahmet had used heart emojis in his text. Of course, I had used one too, but he had done it three times—and he made the first one. Good grief, I was ridiculous. Still, I went to sleep with a smile on my face.

I was about to go into Nona's the next morning when I saw Agent Barrett pull up across the street, so instead I crossed over to his car. He rolled down the window and looked a little worse for wear. I wondered if he had slept at all last night.

"Hey, you were out late last night. You know you didn't have to make up for lost surveillance just because you went and looked at land yesterday afternoon," I joked, hoping to get him talking. Something was super strange about him and Margie being at our places at nighttime last night, and I wanted to know what was up. Unfortunately, Rhett seemed in no mood to chitchat. "How did that go, anyway?" He looked confused. "With Bert, I mean. Did you like the places he showed you?" Rhett went all tight-lipped on me. Something was definitely up, I knew it. He seemed to be contemplating how to answer my question, but I suppose he realized that I could always just ask Bert about it if he decided not to be forthcoming, so he opted to talk.

"We didn't end up going with Bert yesterday. Something came up."

"Oh, really? What?" I asked, feigning indifference but dying to hear. He sighed a heavy sigh.

"I'm sorry, Ele. But I can't tell you that. It is official agency business, I'm afraid."

"Official agency business that involves me?" I pushed.

"I didn't say that."

"You didn't. But you were sitting in my driveway last night, for I don't know how much of the night. By the looks of you, it was all night, although you were gone by the time I left this morning, so I could be wrong. But I know I've never seen you or Margie before at night at either of our places, so I am pretty damn sure that this official agency business involves me in some way." He sighed again.

"Damn, you're pushy. You know that?"

"I've been told." I smiled, thinking about Agent McGee's choice to view me as a spit-fire rather than a giant pain in the ass, or at least I hoped he still held that opinion. The last time we spoke, he just seemed weary that I wasn't being honest with him. We both knew it, and yet I had refused to budge.

"Listen, Ms. Carmichael," so we were back to formalities. He'd been calling me Ele lately. "We've been put on full alert. You might see more of us than you would like and if so, I'm sorry. Both Margie and I will try to stay out of the way."

"Might I know why you've been put on full alert?" I asked as politely as possible, trying to keep my cool. Again remembering my granny's advice that you could catch more flies with honey than vinegar and yet again wondering why I would want to catch flies.

"Someone will be in touch." As he said this, he began rolling up his window. I was being dismissed, and it was very irritating to me, but I knew better than to fight it, so I pivoted on my heel and stomped into Nona's place ready to confide in my friend but Chloe was at the register which worried me.

"Good morning, Chloe," I faked cheerfulness. "Is everything okay with Nona?" I asked, concerned for my friend.

"I think so," Chloe seemed concerned as well. "She called me last night and said her headache was sticking around and she wondered if I would be willing to pick up a few more hours and cover her today. Abby and I are trying to buy a second car, so I'm happy to get the hours. But I hate it that she's not feeling well." I quickly texted Nona.

Missing you this morning. Are you okay?

A reply came quickly back,

Headache seems to be subsiding. Is Chloe doing okay?

She's killing it. Don't worry. Just get better! <3<3<3

:)will do:)

Chloe'd been making my vanilla latte without my even ordering, she went straight to work while we visited and also while I texted with Nona. I assumed she was working on someone else's order, so it surprised me when she placed it on the counter in front of me, with a perfect little heart on top. "Wow, look at you doing latte art!" I exclaimed encouragingly. "This is beautiful, Chloe." She blushed.

"Thanks," she flashed me a huge grin and looked so pleased with the compliment that it made my heart happy. Could I ever remember being so young? Yep. Heck, some days, I still thought I was a young adult. "Would you like a muffin or a scone with that?" Chloe asked and although I almost never got the scones, today's were slathered with a maple frosting and I couldn't resist.

"Thank you, Chloe," I smiled at her and placed a twenty in the tip jar as she handed me back my card. We gotta help this girl get a car. My table mate, who I typically tag teamed with for my favorite table, did not seem to have any intentions of leaving, so I had to settle for a table on the opposite side from where I usually sat. I was finding this incredibly irritating until I noticed that I could see out of one of the front windows from my new seat and that was a kind of nice change. I was gazing out the window, mindlessly thinking about what move

Detective Moody was going to make today. My story was at the height of the climax--in that "shit just got real" moment—and I was trying to work out in my mind how best to let things unfold when I happened to notice the same old pickup passing by for probably the third time. I looked closer and realized that the driver was Jeb Crawley.

Just as he passed, Agent Barrett pulled out behind him. This was an interesting development. I wondered if Agent Barrett had taken an interest in the Crawleys after all and exactly what that interest was. I forced my brain back to Detective Moody and the cold case my character was working on. The publisher had taken on my little bigfoot pet project, but they still wanted my next Moody novel to come out on schedule.

Finally, the man sitting at my table got up and left and as I was moving my stuff over to my preferred coffee shop office space, Agent Brothers walked through the door and headed in my direction. I put my things down at the table and looked up and smiled at the woman approaching me. Agent Brothers was tall and lean, but you could tell she was pure muscle. She looked like she had played women's professional basketball at some point, but she also had that girl-next-door prettiness to her face, so she wasn't as intimidating as you might expect a tall female FBI agent to be.

"Good morning, Agent Brothers." I smiled warmly at her and motioned to the seat across from me. "Would you like a cup of coffee?" I was still on my feet and started to head to the counter to get her one, but she declined.

"I can't stay. Agent McGee asked me to stop by and see if I could set up a time for us to meet with you." My eyebrows narrowed as I wondered why they wanted to see me.

"Am I in trouble?" I joked, only half serious. I mean, Agent McGee had told me no charges would be filed against me for falsifying my story, but I didn't know whether that was guaranteed or not. Probably not. Agent Brothers looked confused, and I wondered how much Agent McGee had told her about our last meeting, if anything at all.

"You could be in danger. And we want to make a plan."

"Oh." This stopped me dead in my tracks. "You guys can come over to my place this afternoon if you'd like. I can be home by 1:30." I wanted to do this sooner rather than later, so I knew what the hell was going on. Agent Brothers started texting, and a reply flashed on the screen almost as soon as she had sent it.

"That works for us," she finally smiled at me. "We'll see you this afternoon, Ms. Carmichael. Don't worry, we're on top of this." I nodded and returned her smile, wondering what "this," could be about.

Bif started barking, and I looked out the window to see Agents McGee and Brothers pulling up in their big black SUV. I told Bif to sit and I opened the door to greet them. I watched as each of them climbed from the vehicle and then headed toward my house. The smell of fresh brewed coffee filled my home, and I had purchased a half a dozen cookies from Chloe before I left. They were one of my favorites, with cranberries and walnuts, oatmeal and white chocolate, and were big and chewy and delicious. I didn't figure it could hurt to warm the two of them up with treats. I felt nervous, and I felt alone. Ahmet hadn't answered my text about the last minute meeting yet. He probably hadn't even seen it. I knew he had a tendency to forget to carry his phone with him. I could have dropped by his place on my way home, but decided not to be ridiculous. He wasn't my security blanket, and I was perfectly capable of meeting with them on my own. But now I was regretting how independent I had felt earlier and wished I had brought in back-up. Bert would have happily joined me as well if I had only asked.

"Come in!" I smiled at the two of them and Bif did, too. His tongue hanging happily out of his mouth as his tail thumped the floor beside me. I had told him to sit and to stay and even though he was clearly happy to have guests; he was obeying me and I was oddly proud of his behavior. Agent McGee bent down and rubbed him behind the ears before I led them to my dining room table and began pouring cups of coffee. I had placed three cups and three little dessert plates with pretty napkins around the table, and Agent McGee was clearly pleased.

"Cookies! You didn't have to do that, Ms. Carmichael."

"Well, I didn't bake them. I just brought some home with me from the coffee shop. Besides, it sounds like cookies are the least I can do, assuming that you and Agent Brothers have a plan to protect me from this danger she mentioned earlier." The two gave each other a look that made me wonder whether that was the plan after all. "What's the danger, anyway?" I asked hastily.

"That's what we wanted to talk to you about." He took a bite of his cookie and a drink of coffee while I exhibited exceptional self-control by not shouting out for him to spill the beans already. Finally, he swallowed and continued. "Bradley Cox has finally revealed who hired them to kidnap you. At first, he pretended that he never knew who hired them, that he had just been brought into the whole thing because his friend needed help on a job. But he's not the brightest bulb in the box and he couldn't keep his stories straight."

"Who was it?" I asked quietly. I was quite sure I already knew the answer, but wanted to hear it for myself.

"It was just as you suspected. Apparently, Abner and Jeb Crawley really want to get you out of their hair, but are trying desperately to do it without incriminating themselves." I heaved a sigh. It was almost one of relief, if that was possible. I was not relieved that I had enemies who clearly wanted to see me dead, but I was happy to know finally that I wasn't crazy and that my suspicions were indeed warranted. "Although you might be interested to know that you weren't the only one who suspected them. Sheriff Struthers had been building a case against them, keeping evidence against them in your file, but he was missing the proof he needed to file charges. Which is why we wanted to talk to you."

"Okay—" I looked at the two of them. Agent McGee was finishing off his first cookie and started to reach for a second before looking at me a little guiltily. "Knock yourself out, man. Help yourself," I smiled. "That's what I got them for."

"Thanks. I'm starving." Agent Brothers gave an affectionate eye roll over the rim of her coffee cup as she took a sip, and I smiled at her.

"A witness, someone close to the Crawleys, has come to us and told us that they are planning another attack on you. The witness has agreed to continue to spy on the Crawleys and let us know when they plan to strike." Dorothy. It could only be Dorothy. Who else could it possibly be?

"Is it Dorothy Struthers?" I asked, absolutely shocked at the idea that Dorothy would come to my aid. But I suppose it wasn't that out there. I would certainly never be the president, or for that matter, even a member of the Dorothy Struthers fan club, but if I found out someone was trying to kill her, I would do everything I could to help prevent it. They gave each other another look that told me what I needed to know.

"Nevermind, you don't have to answer that. I already know. So, why are you talking to me? I'm surprised you needed to reveal any of this to me to take them down now that you have Bradley's statement." Agent McGee nodded for Brothers to explain things to me while he had a third cookie. I topped off their coffees as Agent Brothers began speaking.

"That's the thing. We still need hard evidence. All we have now is the confession of a man who is hardly reliable, and hearsay. The witness has agreed to testify to what they have overheard, but without anything more substantial tying them to the crime, we are afraid they will walk or, at worst, get a suspended sentence of some kind. BUT–" she looked to Agent McGee, who stepped in at this point.

"If they attack you, it will be a sure thing." Agent McGee said bluntly.

"What?" I asked in surprise. "A sure thing that I'm dead?"

"No, no, no. We'll keep it from going that far. We just need them to go through with the attack. From what our witness has heard, they plan on either nabbing you or attacking here at your place, with the latter currently being the most likely. She, I mean, the witness, promises to notify us the moment they know. And if we keep people on you at all times, we will know when this goes down regardless so we can stop them from actually harming you, but not until they have already started the ball rolling so that we are able to charge them with attempted murder." I thought about what they were telling me. It sounded as if they were saying that my life was held in Dorothy's hands, well, Dorothy's and the government's. I wasn't sure that I could trust either of these options. But I knew for certain that I would have no peace, that neither Bob and JoJo nor any other of their kind that tried to reside in our sanctuary would ever be truly safe here until the Crawleys were out of the picture. I could see no other legal way to make this happen, so I agreed.

PSA #47: If the only way to put the bad guys away is to become the bait, then place yourself on the hook like a worm and wait!

"Okay." I said with resignation. "What do you need me to do?"

CHAPTER 20

For some reason, when Ahmet texted me back apologizing profusely for missing my text asking him to join me for my meeting with the FBI, I told him it was no big deal despite the fact that it all felt like a very big deal. I told him that Agents McGee & Brothers were just checking in to let me know they had a confession from Bradley Cox. He had finally come clean that it was the Crawleys who'd hired him. Ahmet, of course, immediately asked if someone had arrested him yet and I told him that the FBI had a plan. What I did not tell him was that I was central to this plan, or worse yet, that I was the bait. I guess I figured, "why worry him when there was nothing he could do?" There was nothing I could do either. As I lay in bed that night examining the situation from all the angles, I could think of no alternative. This was the only way to get rid of the Crawleys once and for all and if it required a little bravery out of me, then by God, I would just have to be brave. I fell asleep with my mind swirling about the impossibilities of finding another way.

"Thank you. Thank you so much." I placed my credit card back in my wallet as I hung up the phone with McFarley Mortuary & Crematorium in Boone, Iowa. Apparently, McFarleys buried my Grandma

Goosey, although I had forgotten that detail as twelve-year-olds rarely take note of such things, the woman who I had been talking to had helped with her funeral. It was so strange to talk to someone who knew my grandma, aunt, and mother when they were alive. She had actually cried when she gave me her condolences about my mom, saying, "Your family were all such dear women. They were always so nice to me. I'm so happy they finally found your mother. I graduated a few years after your mother and worked on the school newspaper with her. You can imagine how kids treat the daughter of the mortician, but both your mom and your aunt would always tell people to shut up when they were being mean. It really meant the world to me." This had made me cry too, she really had no idea how information like this was like water to my parched soul. I had nearly forgotten that there were people on this earth besides me who had known them while they were living. I'd decided to have my mother cremated and to have her remains shipped to me. Apparently, you can only ship human remains using USPS Priority Mail Express and they place a Label 139 on the package to indicate its contents.

At first I thought I would bury my mom next to Grandma Goosey and Aunt Becky but I already felt guilty for not getting back to put flowers on their graves very often, so I decided to have her cremated and to spread her ashes in my beautiful forest. I wanted my mom close. Somehow, I didn't think Grandma Goosey or Aunt Becky would mind. If it wasn't so gross, I would exhume them, cremate what was left of them, and spread their ashes on my property too, so all three of them would be here with me. But, let's face it—that is morbidly disgusting, so I banished the thought.

I had a million errands to run and needed to run to shop at the larger actual grocery store (as opposed to the quasi grocery stores in our small town that would work in a pinch but left something to be desired when you really needed to stock up). The larger store was in a town about an hour away. I'd never let Bif come with me on this trip because I wasn't sure the store would allow him in, but thought 'what the hell?' The worst they could do was make me put him back in the car while I shopped and the weather was lovely today, so he would be safe in the car. I didn't feel like being alone after paying for my mother's cremation this morning on top of the knowledge that I was potentially about to be attacked at any moment. Bif would be great company. He almost never pushed me to say more than I wanted. He was lovely that way, really. I smiled at my own silliness and that somehow this gangly border collie had truly become my companion. Bif was, of course, thrilled to accompany me. Everyone loved him, the ladies at the bank would send out dog treats for him just as they would a sucker if Bif had been a human child. He would smile at them, tongue waggling out of his face, and bark a happy thank you every time it happened.

It was a little strange having Rhett follow me all day long as I shopped. I'd sometimes catch a glimpse of him in the store or across the parking lot. He was always within range, keeping an eye on me. Normally, I would have hated it, but Agent McGee had spooked me yesterday and I felt glad that someone was looking out for me. To my knowledge, there had been no sign of the Crawleys in my vicinity. By the time we finally got everything finished, I was beat and so we ran through a drive through for a burger and onion rings and headed home. I know they say you are not supposed to feed dogs human food, but I got Bif his own burger for being such a good boy. We were just finishing our dinner as we drove down the cattle trail/road that led to my house. Yes, it was still a ridiculously rough ride. I really needed to do something about that. I clicked the button on my garage door opener and pulled into the garage and then clicked the button to close it behind me, making sure by keeping an eye on my mirrors that no one entered the garage as the door was closing.

I filled my hands with grocery bags and opened the door to the house and Bif ran in ahead of me. It all happened so fast, I was barely able to react. Bif barked, and I heard a loud thunk and a cry from my pup and terror coursed through my veins. I dropped the bag of bread to the ground and held tight to the handle of the plastic bag filled with canned goods. There are at least three decent sized cans of crushed tomatoes in this bag and I figured if wielded correctly, it could knock someone completely out. I longed for the handgun that was safely stowed in my nightstand as I inched toward the kitchen silently, looking around me cautiously as I went. I couldn't hear a peep out of Bif, which scared me to death. Just before passing through the doorway from the laundry room into the kitchen, I remembered to hit the silent alarm button on my alarm system. I was comforted by the fact that I'd literally seen Rhett following me all day long and knew he couldn't be far behind, and also that Agents McGee and Brothers had both assured me that the FBI would be monitoring the alarm system I'd installed after being kidnapped. I imagined the house being slowly surrounded. "I am not alone. I am not alone. I am not alone," I inwardly chanted to myself to calm my nerves as I slowly stepped into the kitchen.

SASQUATCH SAVES THE DAY

Jeb Crawley was waiting for me around the corner from the door and lunged at me as I crossed the kitchen threshold, but my cat-like reflexes came to life and I swung the bag of cans at his head. Contact! It looked for a moment like Jeb was going to pass out, but as I saw him getting his bearings; I struck again, swinging the heavy grocery bag of cans of crushed tomatoes directly at his head once again. Again, I made contact. This time, I knocked him unconscious. I heaved a sigh of relief and began frantically looking around the room to make sure Abner wasn't hiding somewhere in the kitchen. As I looked for Abner and saw no sign of him, I came around the island to see a pile of fur laying frightfully still on the ground. Oh, Biffy! The side of his head was bloody. I gasped and fell to his side and ran my hands over the thick fur of his warm body, trying to feel for signs of life. His eye was bleeding and looked ruptured. A sob strangled its way loose from my body, just as a thick cord held by two muscular arms came around my neck from behind, and my entire body was lifted off of the floor by my neck. Everything went black for a moment and then all I could think was 'FIGHT'! It was like every fiber of my being was screaming with the need to fight, and so I did.

I swung my knees and legs back and forth and tried to get my hands under the cord that was wrapped so tightly across my windpipe that it felt close to collapsing. I kicked. I wriggled. I fought with all of my might. I knew I was making progress when the two of us lunged backwards against the back door that was leading out to my deck. I had knocked him off balance but still had not been able to get him to release the cord from my neck. Suddenly, I heard a loud crash of glass from behind me and felt a rush of relief as my attacker released my body. As I fell, two gunshots rang out–the sound reverberating through my body–and I landed into a crumpled mass on the kitchen floor. I heard the thud of a body falling hard next to me and I instinctively wriggled away, knowing it was my attacker's body and wanting to put as much space as possible between us as I recovered. The pulsing blackness of my asphyxiation was slowly leaving me and my vision began coming back. It was fuzzy at first, but I opened my eyes to see the blurry but identifiable Agents Barrett and Hart each hold a smoking gun in front of them. I looked to the floor where I had heard my attacker fall and saw the dead body of Abner Crawley, with one gunshot wound to the center of the forehead and one to the heart.

I crawled over to Bif, who whimpered, and relief flooded me to the core that he was alive. Margie knelt down beside me and put a gentle hand on my shoulder and gave me a full, genuine, dimple-laden smile. "The paramedics are on their way. I think you two are going to be okay and you did it, you finally got the Crawleys." I laughed but the strange hoarse sound brought with it immense pain and instead I grabbed my neck and winced, then gave Agent Margie Hart a smile back.

"I don't think I was the one who did anything." I placed my hand on her arm that was patting my shoulder. "Thank you. You saved my life." She smiled and nodded, then gave me a wink.

"Well, us and the big guy." Her head motioned to my back door, and I saw that the glass was broken.

"What happened?" I asked in confusion.

"When Abner and you fell against the door, a giant bigfoot thrust his hands through the glass and grabbed Abner from behind. As soon as you fell, he ran, and we shot." I couldn't believe it. Saved twice by a bigfoot. I wondered if it was Bob again. At the rate we were going, this sanctuary was going to be nothing but payback for my life.

"You didn't shoot him, did you?" I asked in panic.

"Nope." At that, she pulled Abner's body forward so that I could see there were no exit wounds on his back. I'd only heard two gunshots, of that I was sure, so I heaved a sigh of relief.

"What about his hands? I wonder if he needs a doctor." I was worrying about the creature that had saved me yet again.

"They're pretty tough creatures. My money is on him being just fine." Agent Hart patted on the shoulder once more and walked over to where her husband had handcuffed a still unconscious, but apparently alive, Jeb Crawley. I could hear sirens coming down my road and before I knew it, my house was filled with paramedics, law enforcement, and the FBI, in addition to the two other secret government agents from the Agency of Paranormal Affairs who had helped to save my life. Only minutes after the paramedics arrived, Ahmet, who must have heard the sirens, came bursting into the place to check on me. The sheriff's patrol was trying to stop him, but Agent McGee told them to let him in.

"What happened?" Ahmet asked in horror, taking in my quickly bruising neck and tattered appearance. Biff's tail began thumping furiously, and he whimpered and raised his head at the sound of Ahmet's voice and Ahmet instinctively petted the pup's head, but his eyes never left me.

"The Crawley's." I answered. Ahmet's face filled with a torrent of emotions that seemed to span from rage to relief and everything in between. "But we got them, Ahmet. Abner's dead. He's who did this to me. And Jeb has been arrested, but not before I knocked him out with my crushed tomatoes!" I announced triumphantly, as Ahmet shifted from confusion to amusement. The paramedics had me lying down on my overstuffed sectional with Bif on the big ottoman right by my side. We were both bandaged up, and I was already in a bit of an argument with the paramedic in charge because I was refusing to be taken to the hospital. He was in a heated discussion with someone on the phone and the words "refusing treatment" rose from the cacophony of sounds filling my home. Ahmet raised an eyebrow at me and there was the hint of a smile behind his eyes. "Are you being a difficult patient, Ms. Carmichael?" he asked.

"I won't be for you. I just don't want to go back to that blasted hospital–unless, of course, you think I need to." Ahmet began carefully examining my neck and collarbone, and shoulders, occasionally stopping and gently probing a particularly painful spot for a moment. He asked me to move my neck around in the same manner that the paramedic had. "Am I okay?"

"Well, precaution would say you should be x-rayed just to be on the safe side, to make sure nothing is fractured, but a cursory exam tells me you appear to be just badly bruised."

"So you don't think I need to go to the hospital?" I said a little haughtily locking eyes with the paramedic that had walked up behind Ahmet and was listening. Ahmet turned and held out his hand to the paramedic.

"Dr. Ahmet Pamuk," he said with a smile as he shook the young man's hand. "Has she been giving you trouble?" and something about the way he said it eased the paramedic's frustration and he smiled.

"Has she ever," he said jokingly. "But listen, you're a medical doctor, right?" he asked, to be sure he understood. Ahmet nodded. "Well, if you are willing to keep an eye on her through the night, we won't need to make her come in, since I can already see making her do anything is going to be a nightmare." He added wryly. "That way, she can just make a consultation to be checked out by her doctor."

"That sounds good." Ahmet and I said in unison, and we all smiled. Ahmet looked down at Biffy. "What about this guy? Did you do his exam as well?"

"She insisted we check him first," the paramedic's words were laced with sarcasm.

"I see. So what you mean is that she pitched a banshee's fit and would not let you touch her until you patched up the dog first?" Ahmet said knowingly.

"Exactly," smiled the paramedic. "It was nice to finally meet you, Ms. Carmichael. I guess." The paramedic said to me a little wryly, which made me laugh. "I wish it had been under better circumstances. I'd heard you moved here. I'm a big fan." He said this last bit a little embarrassed, and I figured he was probably a little less star-struck by me now that he'd had a meeting with my foul temper.

"It's nice to meet you too," I said, finally looking at the hospital ID on his lanyard and saw his name, "Joe." I smiled at him apologetically. "I'm sorry for being such a pain in the ass." I said, frankly. "Thank you for reading my books." I gave him a genuine smile and could tell that I was forgiven, and he gave me a genuine smile back. I pointed to the bookcase where there were about ten or so signed copies of each of my books on one of the shelves. "Take a signed copy of each as my apology," I instructed him. He stuttered at the thought.

"I couldn't do that."

"Of course you could. I've been wretched. It's the least I can do. In fact, I insist. And I know you don't want to see another one of my 'fits'." I laughed as I said this and so did he. I watched as he enthusiastically took a signed copy of each book from the shelf.

"Hey, you never gave me a signed copy of each of your books!" Ahmet teased.

"They're all yours," I said, closing my eyes and smiling. The shot the paramedic had given me shortly before Ahmet had arrived must be kicking in. I felt so relaxed.

"So, do you think the dog needs to be seen by a vet today?" Somewhere in the back of my mind, I could hear Ahmet asking the paramedic.

"I think he's patched up and stable for now. His eye is going to need some attention, but I've bandaged him up. You should check him to see what you think, but I think he could probably do with some follow-up appointments later this week as well."

When I finally woke up, my house was empty, and the sky was filled with hues of deep peach, pink, and lavender. I could tell through my wall of windows that the sun had already gone behind the mountain range. I could hear someone moving around in my kitchen.

"Ahmet?" I croaked. My voice was rough, and it hurt to speak. Ahmet came into the room with an ice pack and a mug of hot tea for me.

"There you are," he whispered as he placed the ice pack on my sore, swollen neck and sat the tea on the coffee table in front of me. He helped me into a sitting position. "How are you feeling?" I thought about the question. How was I feeling?

"Sore," I answered. "But not too bad, considering." I smiled at him and his eyes softened as he reached out and tucked my hair behind my ear gently. "I must look a mess," I said, suddenly feeling self-conscious.

His hand moved from tucking my hair behind my ear to gently caressing my jawline, so softly I almost thought I was imagining it.

"You look perfect," he said with a smile and stood up and moved to the chair next to me. "Now tell me, if it doesn't hurt your voice too much, how you became the FBI's bait for the Crawleys without telling any of us?"

Apparently, Agents Barrett and Hart had filled him in a bit while I was sleeping and Bert and Matilda, Nona and Vance had come by and confirmed that I had not mentioned this little sting operation to any of them either. (They were also kind enough to put away all the groceries that had been left in my car. Of course, Nona would be the one to have noticed the bags of bread and canned goods and thought to check my car. I keep an ice chest in the back of my vehicle since the drive is so long, so thankfully there were no grocery casualties.) After telling Ahmet the actual details of Agent McGee and Brothers visit yesterday and explaining that the only way to really put the Crawleys away was if I were to go ahead and let them attack me, I stopped talking and took a soothing sip of the hot tea. Ahmet was quiet for a while.

"You should have told me," he said, softly. "I could have been helping to look out for you."

"Yeah," I said just as softly. "But you would have looked out for me too well and they either wouldn't have attacked or, more likely, would have hurt you before attacking me. I just didn't want you to have to worry about me."

"Don't you see, I want to worry about you, Ele. I care about you. I want to be sure you are safe. When you are happy, I feel happy. When you are in danger—" he made almost a low growling sound of frustration. "Well, will you just please stop putting yourself in the way of danger? Please, don't ever do anything like that again without telling me, and let me have your back, okay?" A warmth filled my entire being that was suspiciously close to the feeling of love.

"Okay." I said quietly and placed my hand over his. "Just so you know, I had a feeling it would all go down quickly. That's why I felt comfortable waiting to tell you. That is also why I took Bif with me shopping. I was on pins and needles. I suppose if I had left him here, they might not have had the guts to have broken in and be waiting for me. But more likely, they would have just killed him. I trust that everything unfolded exactly as it needed to." I was quiet for a second. "I wonder if Dorothy knows yet. She was depending a lot on the Crawleys after Sam's death. This is going to be hard on her, especially since her son's not around. Even though the Crawleys were using her, they were all she had." My heart truly went out to Dorothy. She had been willing to sacrifice some of the only support network she had left in order to keep me from being killed.

"She'll be alright. Bert and Matilda were heading over to see her after they left here. They will take care of her. Although, I suspect Bert will invite her back to the Bigfoot Fair Planning committee with you." He smiled as he said it, and I winced. Dorothy had been a gigantic pain in the whole committee's ass and when the Crawleys talked her into going rogue and starting their own bigfoot festival on the same weekend, we had all been relieved to be free of her.

"That's all right." I sighed. "She belongs there. Maybe Matilda will join too and can help rein her in. Apparently, Libby was good at that." Ahmet smiled at me with a mischievous glint in his eye.

"Do you sometimes find it hard to believe that you are here? In Oklahoma working on Bigfoot Fair planning committees and driving down cow trail driveways in a four-wheel-drive utility vehicle? That you've become actual friends with a family of bigfoot and have now tackled the monumental task of creating a safe space for the torrent of displaced bigfoot refugees that we know are bound to be heading our way?" I had that warm, happy feeling in my chest, a tickle that made me feel like I could quite possibly burst into giddy peals of giggling at any minute. My cheeks tingled, teasing me with impending laughter.

"I find it impossible to believe. I wake up every single morning thinking 'what the actual hell?' and then I smile to myself as I start my weird ass day in this paranormal wonderland. They saved me, you know? I don't know if it was Bob or the big guy."

"It was the big guy," Ahmet explained. "Rhet and Margie told us what happened on the down low. I'm not sure they let the FBI in on the little tidbit that a bigfoot was involved in your rescue. Anyway, Nona stayed with you and Vance, Bert and I went out while you were sleeping to check on them. JoJo's parents as well as the relatives that were coming were all at Bob and JoJo's and JoJo's dad–the big guy–" he smiled as he said the nickname I had given the creature because he was the biggest of them all. "The big guy had some cuts on his hands and arms, so I doctored him up as good as new. Or he will be soon. They seem to have extraordinary healing capacity." I sighed, imagining the scene Ahmet had just shared, and smiled at him.

"Sasquatch saves the day!" I laughed as I said it. "Again!" It wasn't the first time, and I suspected it wouldn't be the last. "Sometimes I wonder if when Doug cheated on me and I did that google search for 'luxury cabins in the woods for sale' if I didn't slip into an alternate universe, if quantum entanglement and the multiverse theory aren't very real and this crazy reality we're living in isn't the proof." We simultaneously took a deep sigh, each of us thinking about the reality of our very strange lives. And then my stomach growled. Big surprise.

"Hey, do you like pizza rolls?" I asked, remembering the box I had bought on impulse earlier in the day, but what felt like a decade ago.

"Do you have ranch dressing?" Ahmet asked tentatively.

"You know it." I giggled and got up from my seat. "I'm going to make us some pizza rolls and we can watch more of that show we started the other night. That is, if you're good with staying."

"Lady, you're stuck with me all night. I promised Joe I would watch over you tonight."

The Ella Fitzgerald tune, "Someone To Watch Over Me," started playing in my mind and I gave Ahmet a long stare. Finally, I answered simply.

"I would love that." I ran to the restroom and Ahmet put the pan of pizza rolls in the oven. They're so much better that way than they are in the microwave. We stayed up late watching the British detective show together and when we started having a yawning competition, I asked if he minded sleeping in my room with me—'totally platonically'—I added and could feel my face turning red. I just didn't want to sleep alone. And so we shyly climbed under the covers together. Ahmet opened his arm for me to place my head into the crook using his shoulder for my pillow and we fell asleep this way with Bif snuggled happily on top of the covers between the two of our bodies.

CHAPTER 21

It was a celebration. Bert, Matilda, Vance, Nona, Ahmet, and I all sat around the large conference table at the abstract office. Dobson's signed contract for the coveted land lay before us. Mrs. Huckaby, the closing agent, smiled at us. "I'm not sure I've ever had this many buyers on one contract." We were all smiling as the paperwork passed from one of us to the other until we had all signed on the dotted lines. I owned half and the other half was split evenly between my five friends.

"Well, when the price doubled after I had already made the offer I was comfortable making, some very good friends stepped in and decided to join me in the venture." I looked into the eyes of each of these wonderful humans who were willing to pitch into the cause of a sanctuary for sasquatch and gave them a look of gratitude. "The Sanctuary of the 5S," I said softly to myself. Each of my friends grinned broadly at me, instantly agreeing on what we would call our unofficial sanctuary.

"Excuse me?" Mrs. Huckaby asked, looking confused at the last bit.

"Oh, nothing." I smiled. "Just thinking to myself."

"Oh," she looked puzzled, but moved on. "Well, you are certainly lucky to have such a good group of friends." Mrs. Huckaby took the paperwork from Ahmet who was the last to sign and said, "Alrighty then, if you have the cashier's checks, then I will make copies of this for everyone." She stood up as we each pulled our checks out and handed them to her. She read the numbers on each one, mentally calculating one last time, and then smiled and nodded when the math came out correctly in her head. "Alrighty, one moment then." After she had left the room, Bert spoke.

"The Sanctuary of the 5S," he repeated aloud. "I like it, Ele." He was nodding in appreciation. "I like it a lot."

"It's perfect," said Nona, happily. She'd been headache free for a couple of days now and her doctor said everything looked good with her pregnancy. Her stomach was round and hard under her shirt and she was undeniably pregnant and I had never seen her look more beautiful or the two of them more happy. Vance took her hand on the table and held it.

"Yeah, I like it too." Vance said with a smile. "Bert, would you ever have thought when we made friends with Mac all those years ago that we would someday be helping to start a sanctuary to save the creatures and provide them with a place to live?"

"Never in a million years," Bert laughed, and I saw him squeeze Matilda's hand and give her a wink.

"It took this crazy writer from New York City moving in to give you the idea," laughed Matilda.

"I guess it did," Bert said with satisfaction. "Selling that place to you was one of the best things I ever did, Ele. You know we are all very glad you are here, don't you?" I blushed and shrugged and answered slowly.

"Yeah... I guess I do. I'm pretty glad, myself." Ahmet put his arm on my back and patted it gently a few times, and I watched as Nona and

Matilda exchanged glances. The tingling in my cheeks was back, and I felt like I could burst with happiness.

I watched as Ahmet made his way up the drive on his motorcycle. I'd only called him a few minutes ago; he must have dropped whatever he was doing and come immediately. My mother's ashes had just arrived in the mail and he had agreed to help me spread them when they got here. I was sitting on the porch swing on my front porch, holding the wooden box and weeping once again, when Ahmet walked up onto the porch to sit beside me. Bif's head leaned against the side of my leg and he looked up at me with his good eye, looking like a pirate puppy with his other wounded eye still covered in a patch. Ahmet gently put his arm around me and leaned the side of his head against mine. "You okay?" He asked. I nodded, wiping the tears away with the back of my hand.

"I'm good. Let's put my sweet momma to rest, finally. What do you say?" Ahmet nodded somberly, and I handed him the box. "Let me grab my jacket." When I came back out, I climbed onto the back of Ahmet's motorcycle and we rode to each of the four corners of the Sanctuary and spread a bit of ashes at each spot. Then we drove back to my house and walked the perimeter of my place, leaving a small bit of ashes around the entire perimeter. There was just a little left, and I decided to spread them under the big tree at the spot where I first saw JoJo watching me. It was an odd thing to do, but it felt like I was bringing my mom into every part of my life. Ahmet took my hand as we walked silently back to the house.

Everything really was finally going to be alright. And as if Ahmet could hear my thoughts, he squeezed my hand in agreement.

EPILOGUE

It had been nearly a year since I had found out that Douglas Eubank was cheating on me with his assistant, and Sookie had finally agreed to come and visit. When I told her she could potentially hold a baby bigfoot, and that there were three babies—count them, three—living on the property, she agreed to come to the secret 'Rebranding Bigfoot' Book Release Party that I was hosting at my place for some of my nearest and dearest friends. *Bigfoot Watching Woman Watching Bigfoot* was having a record-breaking first week, and the reviews were delightful. It turned out that more people were open to the idea of a kind and peace-loving sasquatch than we realized. If this kept up, not a soul would ever need to know that this crazy new author, M. Sparks Clark, was really the sensible Ele Carmichael.

Bif was officially the world's best dog and was getting used to the eye patch. The vet told us that there was still a chance that the nerve endings in the eye might heal and he may recover his sight on that side, but the key was to keep the eye covered and let it rest so Bif would continue playing the role of a clumsy pirate as we waited to see. He was still getting used to his lack of depth perception and would often bump into things, but that seemed to be improving by the day. I watched as the ornery cuss kept his good eye on Bert's cocktail sausage with his drooling face. Bert had picked up an hors d'oeuvre in the middle of telling Sookie what appeared to be a very good story and Bif had not been able to control his salivary glands as he watched the bobbing sausage. I decided to have mercy on the poor boy and get him a little bowl of his own cocktail weenies.

Matilda and Dorothy, yes Dorothy, were sitting on the sectional with plates of goodies on their laps, talking animatedly, and Dorothy looked almost happy. She had lost a lot of weight since Sam had died and instead of her usual strong, pushy presence, she seemed almost frail. I was letting her think that the book *Bigfoot Watching Woman Watching Bigfoot* was just my wild imagination, but I did decide to let her in on the secret that I was the author. I doubted that she would ever be part of 5S, but she had done her part to save my life and I would forever be grateful. I think Matilda may have been right. I think it was possible that I intimidated Dorothy, and the more kindness and grace I showed her when her haughty superiority rose up, the less the haughty superiority seemed to rise. It was like she felt less of a need to put on appearances in front of me. She had also brought a well-worn copy of my first Rainey K. Moody book with her to the party and asked me to sign it. I could hardly believe it, and it was impossible to ignore the knowing look Matilda gave me when Dorothy handed me the book. Maybe we would someday find our way to an actual friendship, but I was happy for now to share friendly civility with her.

Vance was standing behind Nona, resting his chin on her shoulder, cheek to cheek, with his long arms wrapped around her and his hands clasped under her baby buddha belly, looking like he was helping support the weight of their child. Nona was laughing as Ahmet was explaining something in vivid detail to them. I walked over to the three of them and as I did, Ahmet put his arm around my shoulder without missing a word of his story. We had gone on our first official date the night before and although it was strange, everything also felt 'as it should be'—for lack of a better way of putting it. I glanced out the large wall of windows and there in the moonlight, at the edge of the tree row where JoJo first revealed herself to me and where I had spread the last bit of my momma's ashes, stood Bob with a son in each arm, and JoJo holding her little girl. I was suddenly flooded with feelings of love and friendship that were not my own, and I quickly sent the feeling back to the two of them. I looked at them and nodded and then let my eyes slowly scan the room, taking in the happy faces, then I closed my eyes and gave a prayer of thanksgiving that I had found a sanctuary of my own and that I was finally home.

About the Author

M. Sparks Clark was first introduced to bigfoot in her very early years of life when she tried desperately to stay up past her bedtime of 8:30 in order to see her father, who was running late after a long day of encyclopedia sales. His reason? He was wrestling bigfoot. He is said to have wrestled bears and mountain lions as well, but nothing quite captured the author's vivid imagination like bigfoot did.

M. Sparks Clark is a pen name Missy Hancock uses for the paranormal adventures she writes. "Sparks" in honor of her late mother whose feistiness lives on in the main character of the Ele Carmichael Novels and "Clark" for the above-mentioned bigfoot wrestler—her dad—who lives in the Kiamichi Mountains of Oklahoma and continues to have occasional encounters with the creatures.

Also By M. Sparks Clark

Bigfoot Watching Woman Watching Bigfoot-An Ele Carmichael Novel (Book 1)
Sasquatch Serial Killer-An Ele Carmichael Novel (Book 2)

Thank you so very much for reading this book. I hope it brought you a little joy and reprieve from everyday life and maybe a laugh or two! If you would like to keep tabs on new releases from M. Sparks Clark (and I so hope you do!), please follow me at msparksclark.com and sign up for free giveaways and my fairly infrequent newsletter. :) You can also follow me on instagram and tiktok: @msparksclarkbooks

www.ingramcontent.com/pod-product-compliance
Lightning Source LLC
LaVergne TN
LVHW041916070526
838199LV00051BA/2637